GHOSTS

ALSO BY DAVID A. ROBERTSON

THE RECKONER TRILOGY

Strangers

Monsters

Ghosts

GRAPHIC NOVELS

Will I See?

Betty: The Helen Betty Osborne Story

7 Generations: A Plains Cree Saga

Tales from Big Spirit series

Sugar Falls

FOR CHILDREN

When We Were Alone

NOVELS

The Evolution of Alice

THE RECKONER BOOK THREE

GHOSTS

DAVID A. ROBERTSON

**HIGHWATER
PRESS**

Canada Council Conseil des Arts
for the Arts du Canada

We acknowledge the support of the Canada Council for the Arts.
Nous remercions le Conseil des arts du Canada de son soutien.

HighWater Press gratefully acknowledges the financial support of the Province of Manitoba through the Department of Sport, Culture and Heritage and the Manitoba Book Publishing Tax Credit, and the Government of Canada through the Canada Book Fund (CBF), for our publishing activities.

HighWater Press is an imprint of Portage & Main Press.
Printed and bound in Canada by Friesens
Design by Relish New Brand Experience
Cover Art by Peter Diamond

Library and Archives Canada Cataloguing in Publication

Robertson, David, 1977-, author
    Ghosts / David A. Robertson.

(The reckoner)
Issued in print and electronic formats.
ISBN 978-1-55379-762-3 (softcover).--ISBN 978-1-55379-763-0 (EPUB).--ISBN 978-1-55379-764-7 (PDF)

    I. Title.

PS8585.O32115G56 2019   jC813'.6   C2018-906644-X

                                            C2018-906643-1

22 21 20 19   1 2 3 4 5

www.highwaterpress.com
Winnipeg, Manitoba
Treaty 1 Territory and homeland of the Métis Nation

FOR ANYONE WHO NEEDS TO SEE THEMSELVES IN A BOOK,
AND ANYONE WHO NEEDS TO SEE SOMEBODY ELSE.

PROLOGUE

"LUCY!"

Reynold fumbled with the door. His hand was so weak and slippery from blood that he couldn't grip the handle, and he ended up having to use both hands to turn it. The latch bolt released, the door swung open, and he stumbled inside, bracing himself against the wall to stay upright. He inched forward, sliding his feet against the floor, sliding his hand against the wall, pressing his other hand against his chest to stem the flow of blood from the bullet wound.

"Lucy!"

Reynold made it to the living room, but then fell forward onto the couch. Footsteps scrambled above, on the second floor. They rushed down the stairs, as Reynold began to see black spots through already blurred vision. His chest was on fire, and each breath was shorter than the last, like his lungs were too full of blood to take in any air.

"What the hell happened to the walls?" Lucy ran into the living room just as he felt consciousness slip away. "Dad!"

"Unnnh."

Reynold tried to sit up, but there was too much pain, and his head collapsed onto the couch's armrest. His eyes blinked open to find Lucy perched on the edge of the coffee table, as far away from him as possible. She watched him with grave concern, and something else. Fear. He patted around at his chest and felt it bandaged.

"Thanks, my girl."

She didn't respond. She had her arms crossed and was furiously chewing at a fingernail.

"Cole Harper shot me in the chest, Lucy. If you're wondering—"

"No." Lucy shook her head vigorously. "No, that's not it. Your goddamn blood is blue!"

"My…" Reynold looked at the bandages, and saw splotches of blue seeping through them. "…blood?"

Lucy covered her face with both hands, and her body shook. Reynold watched her, unsure what to say to his daughter. What could he say? How would she ever understand what he'd become? The hunger. The rage. He said nothing. When she calmed down, she lowered her hands. "And it's cold. Your blood, it's…it's like ice." She stood up and backed away, until her calves hit a dining room chair, and sat down. "Why is it like that? Are you cold? You feel cold to me. You feel cold like your blood. I—"

"Lucy…"

"Are you sick?" she asked. "Tell me!"

Reynold did sit up now, back against the arm of the couch. *Blue, ice-cold blood*, she'd said. But there was something else.

"I'm not sick," he said calmly.

"Then *what*? If I were Cole, I would've shot you, too!"

"I'm hungry."

"You're—" Lucy looked ready to vomit, her face drained of colour. Someone knocked on the front door. She jumped at the sound, almost fell off the chair. She looked at her dad for direction.

You're still my girl, he thought. *Even now.*

The knock came again.

"Answer it," Reynold said.

"But…" she started to say.

"Do it."

She left the room, almost in a trance. Reynold listened. Lucy opened the front door. There was a moment, a split second, of silence.

Then Lucy screamed. She ran back into the living room.

"What…the…fu—" Lucy stumbled back against a bookshelf.

A person in a hazmat suit walked into the living room.

"—what is happening! Who the hell are you?!"

Reynold was unfazed. The man walked around the couch, then dropped a gun onto the coffee table.

"Lucy," Reynold said, "would you excuse us, please?"

Lucy didn't say a word. She walked away, keeping her eyes on the suited figure. Reynold listened for her footsteps up the stairs, down the second-floor hallway, and into her bedroom. A door slammed.

Alone now, Reynold's gaze fell to the gun on the coffee table. He picked it up and rested it on his chest.

A thick silence fell over them as they stared at each other.

"Is it done?" Reynold asked.

"Yeah. It's done."

1

INVOCATION

FIVE EMPTY TIN CANS WERE LINED UP BIGGEST to smallest, easiest to hardest, across two large rocks. Just the way Eva liked them—when she was a kid and now. She pictured Cole standing in front of the rocks, looking at her, making sure that he'd lined them up perfectly. She pictured Cole looking at her the way that he used to look at her, no matter what emotion was running through his body, no matter how panicked he was, no matter how tired, no matter how lost. It made her feel, then and now, that she was the one place of calm for him. Standing twenty feet away from the cans, rolling the sweetgrass ring he had made for her between her fingertips, she could picture him just the way he was the last time she had seen him alive.

"Are you paying attention?" Eva asked.

Cole was standing beside her, watching intently. "Yeah."

"This is called the Fighting Stance." She aimed her dad's gun at the first, largest tin can, and positioned her body just like her dad had taught her.

"That's exactly how I was aiming," Cole said.

"No," she laughed, "it's not."

She took aim. Squeezed her index finger against the trigger. Pop. The can flipped into the air, end over end like a punted football, and landed on the ground.

"Okay, maybe that's not exactly how I was aiming," Cole said.

"Not exactly." Eva aimed at the second can. Breathed out slowly. Squeezed her index finger against the trigger.

"Eva!" Cole shouted from a distance.

Too far away. He was running towards her from the gravel road, from the cemetery. The gate to the cemetery was open. He was running so fast that his body blurred.

"What are you doing?" she asked. "I'm standing here, you don't have to run!"

"Shoot!"

She saw it. The monster chasing him. Towering over him. Emaciated, but powerful. Faster. Its red eyes burning into hers. It gained on Cole with each step.

Eva turned her body and aimed at the monster. She got into the Fighting Stance and squeezed the trigger, but her hands were shaking. The bullet missed. Missed such a big target. Right there in front of her. Right behind Cole. The monster reached out, grabbed Cole, and picked him up.

She took another shot, but only grazed its shoulder.

Cole screamed. "Eva!"

He screamed again, in pain, while the monster tore him apart.

"No!" A coffee mug—half empty, ice cold—plummeted from the nightstand onto the cold floor, erupting into shards of ceramic and black liquid. Eva almost fell off the bed too, but ended up half on and half off, staring at the mess.

"Shit."

The same dream. The same nightmare. And still, she wasn't used to it. Would she ever get used to it? No. She shook her head. She hadn't stopped missing Cole when he moved to Winnipeg. Now, he was gone. Not like in the dream, but no less horrific. Trapped in a fire he set at the X. That's what Mihko had said anyway. That's what Wounded Sky First Nation believed, too, except for a handful of people who knew Cole wasn't the monster Mihko made him out to be, as though the real monster wasn't quite as bad as a seventeen-year-old kid. Of course, nobody had seen the real monster since Cole had died. Nobody knew that the monster was gone—that Reynold was gone—because of

Cole. And Cole had to have been right about Reynold being the monster; they didn't both go missing at the same time coincidentally. Eva might've needed tutoring in math, but that was a simple equation.

"Chief Reynold McCabe." Eva looked away from the broken mug and spilled coffee, and stared at the ceiling. The same people who believed Cole was an arsonist, that he'd died, ironically, in a fire he started? They believed Reynold was still alive and running Wounded Sky from the reserve's own Fort Knox: the McCabe residence. It was all *actual* fake news.

Eva rolled the sweetgrass ring between her fingertips, dizzy with memories. She took a deep breath and got out of bed. She wiped up the coffee and picked every last piece of broken ceramic off the floor. She found herself taking her time with this last task. It reminded her of the night she and Cole had almost kissed. She had picked shards of glass off the floor that night, too. She could easily picture Cole standing in the kitchen while she dumped the broken glass into the garbage, both of them still flustered. She'd told him the kiss would have been a mistake, but now she wished they had made that mistake. Ignored the rock crashing into her living room. She would have placed her hands firmly against his cheeks, and pressed her lips against his. If she had known then what she knew now.

That he'd be dead, and she'd be left waiting for a miracle.

Eva finished picking up the broken pieces of ceramic, tossed them into the garbage. She made herself a fresh cup of strong, black coffee. She sipped at it furiously while trying, over and over, to text Brady, like each time she tried, the text might go through. But she knew it wouldn't. Mihko and the absent Chief McCabe had cut off Wounded Sky's cell service two weeks ago.

She had no idea what was going on with Brady, if he was still okay. And the outside world had no idea what was going on in Wounded Sky First Nation. Cole had told her that according to his friend Joe, the murder spree and the flu epidemic had never made the news, and certainly the monster and the string of fires hadn't either. Not to mention the full-on quarantine. Eva wanted to check on Brady, to make the trek to Elder Mariah's cabin deep in Blackwood Forest, but she couldn't.

Mihko's hired security force, which included some of Reynold's people, had a perimeter around the community, stationed at strategic points within the forest to keep people from coming into Wounded Sky and, more importantly, to keep anyone from leaving. It made the curfew irrelevant.

Where would anybody go?

Eva finished her coffee and left the house. She wanted to try to see her father at the clinic again. Lately, her days had become as familiar to her as the nightmare. She would wake up alone, eat alone, try to visit her father at the clinic and get turned away, check on Cole's grandmother and auntie, and then, when the day was almost over, visit Cole. Visit Cole, and hope that there was nobody there to visit at all. But he was always there, his headstone always defaced, and she was always left with a sunken feeling in her chest. More than once over the last month, she'd reminded herself of what it was to do the same thing over and over again and expect a different result. But still, she was unwavering. And why? Because a little talking coyote had promised her that he'd help her out.

Since then, he'd gone AWOL.

She kept replaying that moment, almost a month ago now, to see if she'd missed something.

"Please come back. I need you back," she said, standing in front of Cole's headstone.

"You know." A coyote appeared out of nowhere by her side. *"I can help you with that."*

"Did you just—"

"Yes, yes, yes." He sounded exasperated, but also amused. *"I just talked, so can we please skip over all the stunned disbelief nonsense? After all, you'll come to the same conclusion: you are not dreaming, I am really here, and, come on, is this the strangest thing that's happened in Wounded Sky over the last few weeks?"*

"It's up there." Eva reached forward to poke the coyote.

"If you're going to touch me to see if I'm a figment of your imagination," the coyote said, *"could you at least scratch behind my ear? That's*

my most favourite spot. My leg starts to kick involuntarily from the sensation. It's just so fun. And pleasurable."

"Never mind." She withdrew her hand.

"Soooooooo…"

Eva stared at the headstone. "Can you really bring him back…?"

"Oh, I can, dear one," the coyote said quickly. "Absotively. Positutely. Hmmm…I'm trying to combine absolutely and positively, but it's not quite working. Also, it's probably redundant."

"The novelty of a talking coyote is quickly wearing off."

"It's just, if you want something from me, well, tit for tat, you know? I scratch your back, you scratch mine. Quid pro quo. A favour for a—"

"Okay! Yes. Just tell me what I have to do." She glanced at Cole's name chiselled into stone, and tried not to read all the vitriol community members had written about him. "Please. I want him back."

"Sigh…puppy love. I've always loved you two. You're so very Jack and Kate. (You watch Lost *right?) People are just dying to see you together, you know?"*

"People are what?"

"Never mind," the coyote said. "But, as for the whole reciprocity talk, let's just say you owe me one. TBD. To Be Determined. Deal?"

"Deal."

Deal. The word echoed in Eva's mind as she walked through the brisk chill of Wounded Sky's autumn morning, the frosted grass crunching underfoot. As the weeks passed, she'd started to believe that even though the coyote had said she wasn't dreaming, she actually had been. So desperately sad about losing Cole, she'd imagined a way that he might come back, just to make her feel better for a little while. The anxiety Cole had told her about, how it ravaged his body with horrible sensations, made her realize just how powerful the mind could be. Why couldn't she have concocted a talking coyote, a trickster spirit? Maybe not the one she'd been taught about in her community, but a trickster spirit nonetheless.

Each night, when she went to the cemetery to visit Cole's grave, she recited the same invocation, hoping to bring the coyote back, so she could be sure that she hadn't been imagining it, so she could believe Cole would return from the dead, that he wasn't gone, that he could finish the job he'd always talked about having here.

Because Creator knew just how bad things had gotten.

"Please be real," she whispered, staring at the headstone, glancing to her side every few moments to see if the spirit being had returned. "Please bring him home, make him live. Please. I'll do anything."

But, tonight, just like every other night, there was no response.

2

LIVE WITH THIS

"EVA!"

Despite the urgency in Michael's voice, Eva did not break stride. She kept walking towards the clinic, and now she couldn't get there fast enough.

"Wait up!"

"I'm busy!" Eva spat back, without turning around. Eyes forward, towards the clinic, which was now visible against the backdrop of Blackwood Forest.

"Can't I just walk with you?" Michael asked.

She could hear him coming closer, jogging towards her, even though she'd picked up the pace. She considered running away, but it seemed too emotional, like she still had feelings for him. So she stopped and let him catch up to her.

"What is it, Mike?"

"I just…" But he couldn't find the words and ended up just looking at the frosted grass, shimmering in the morning sun, as though he'd dropped what he wanted to say somewhere. Like his words were a lost contact lens.

"You haven't talked to me for a month, and now you, what, wait for me to leave the house and run after me? Were you standing outside my place spying on me or something? How creepy is that?"

"I just…"

"*You just?*" Eva crossed her arms. "You came up with this elaborate plan to talk to me, and you've got two words to say?"

"Eva, please."

"Were you hoping that I'd still have glass splinters in my feet, so I'd be easy to catch? Were you waiting for me in the same spot as when you were watching Cole and me?"

"We were dating! Of course, I was jealous. You were…" He stopped and sighed. Closed his eyes and rubbed them furiously. Scolding himself. "I'm sorry, okay? This isn't about that. I can't believe I even did that. I was angry. I…"

"So what's it about then?" She tried to sound less confrontational. He looked meek. Sad. Like he hadn't slept for days. There were bags under his eyes and he was pale and disheveled. Not the Michael she'd known her whole life. "Are you okay?"

He chuckled weakly. "I was about to ask you the same thing."

Eva ran her hands through her hair and tied it back into a ponytail. She didn't want to look as bad as him, even if she felt it, even if it was for different reasons. "I'm fine, Michael," she said. "I'm doing fine."

"I keep thinking…" Michael stared off into the forest for a minute before he cleared his throat, tried to look at her, but didn't really. "Cole died thinking I hated him, that everybody hated him. I keep thinking about how he died like that."

"So are you asking how I am, or how he was?" She glanced at the clinic. Wanted to be there, not here. "It's a little late for that."

"I don't know, Eva. I'm confused. I just…" He shoved his hands in his pockets and a tear slid down his cheek. Eva pretended not to notice. "I wish things were different. I wish things had happened differently. That's all."

"Mike, if you're looking for absolution because of how you treated him, because of throwing a stupid rock through my—"

"No, it's not that. I swear it's not."

"Good, because if this is about some stupid love triangle, I'm going to lose my shit." She straightened, looked him in the eyes, even though he would not look into hers. "If you're looking for absolution, for whatever reason, I don't think it matters anymore. Cole had more important things on his mind. More important than you," she pushed her index finger gently into Michael's chest, then pointed it back at herself, "and more important than me."

"I wish things were different." He met her eyes, tight-lipped, and nodded. He looked even more tired now than he had before.

"Well, they aren't," she said. "There's no such thing as a time machine. There's no DeLorean hidden behind, you know, the 'Wounded Sky' sign ready to take us back a month, so we can save him. There's no bargain to be made with Creator. We're going to have to live with that."

Michael smiled through tight lips. "I don't know if I can." He walked away.

Eva wanted to call him back, to talk to him, to make him feel better. She still cared about him, even if it wasn't like before. They'd been friends since they were kids. She wanted to convince him that throwing a rock through a window meant nothing, that there was so much more going on that he didn't know about. But, in the end, she just watched him until he was out of sight.

"And here I thought that you weren't going to show."

Mark stepped sideways to stand directly in front of the doors to the clinic, as Eva approached the building. Unfazed by his body language, by the gun at his hip, by his cocky and sour demeanour, she stopped just a few feet away from him.

Two could play at this game.

"Morning, Mark."

"Are we going to do the thing where you ask to see your daddy, and I tell you that you can't, and then you get all upset, and then I—"

"I just want to know he's okay. I haven't seen him in a month. I haven't heard from him either." Eva took out her cell phone and waved it in the air. No signal. She wondered if Mark got a signal, if Mihko employees were granted that luxury. The luxury of texting with a loved one—something she'd always taken for granted. "Get him to wave at me from the window, *something*, I don't care. Just let me see his face."

"So we *are* going to do this. Okay. The answer is no."

Eva took one angry step forward. "You asshole!"

A gust of wind pushed across their bodies timed with Eva's aggression. Mark's hat blew off his head and scuttled across the grass into the forest to his left, but he kept his feet firmly in place. And instinctively, slightly rattled, he put his hand on his gun.

"Seriously?" Eva nodded at the gun.

"Just back off, Eva, alright? God, I thought I'd like you better now that City's dead."

"*Cole.* His name was Cole."

"Whatever." Mark eased his hand off the gun, and placed both hands on his hips. Tilted his head to the side. "Look, Eva, if I could let you in, I would." He *tsk*ed. "Thing is, there's some top-secret shit going on inside, and it's my job to keep people out of Mihko's business."

"My dad is *my* business!"

"Your dad wouldn't want you in here! Trust me. It's a safety precaution."

"Oh! And you think *I'm* predictable. You say the same thing every day! Do you enjoy this? What if it was your dad was in there, hey?"

"What am I, supposed to empathize with you now?"

"Wounded Sky is quarantined. People are going missing like every other day. What could possibly be—"

"Yeah, the curfew is a safety precaution, too, genius, speaking of people going missing."

"What could possibly be the safety precaution in keeping people away from the clinic, if all the bad shit is happening out here? Are people sick again? Is my dad sick?"

"And this is where I tell you that it's classified, Eva." He zipped his mouth shut, and doubled down on the gesture just to piss her off, pretending to lock a lock and throw away an invisible key.

"Enjoying yourself, Mark, you dick?"

In response, Mark pointed at his lips, shrugged, and waved goodbye with all the sarcasm he could muster.

Eva shook her head, shot Mark a disgusted look. "You should be ashamed of yourself, doing what you're doing, being where you're from. You're the only Wounded Sky band member who's working for them. This is your home, too."

"And how do you feel, Eva, being friends with that arsonist murderer? Defending him even now, after he died in a fire that *he* started. Arsonist, murderer, *and* idiot. The trifecta."

"I—" she shouted, but stopped. Not worth it. He didn't even deserve her anger. Didn't deserve her disgust. Didn't deserve one more word from her mouth.

She walked away.

"Can we do it again tomorrow?" Mark called after her.

After she'd been walking for a minute, she turned around, to see Mark jogging off into the forest. He must've been sure, she figured, that she was far enough away not to make a dash for the clinic while he left his post. She found the window to her dad's hospital room on the second floor and looked into it, willing him to get up and just pass by, so she could see him for a second. But he didn't. She looked for as long as she could, until anticipation turned to heartache.

The best cure for heartache wasn't more heartache, but Eva had made it a point, after Cole's death, to visit his grandmother and Auntie Joan every day. Having one of Cole's friends around so often, she thought, made his loss hurt a little bit less for them. And it must've hurt even more having to stay here where he had died, and where so many people despised him for what they believed he had done. They'd tried to leave after his funeral, a service attended only by Eva, her dad (the last time she'd seen him), Lauren, and Dr. Captain. They'd tried to leave right after it had ended, right after his body had been lowered into the ground, but they had been stopped at the community perimeter, on the road that led to the ferry.

"Nobody in, nobody out," the Mihko's security guard at the road had told them. "Besides, that little bastard burned down the ferry, too."

Bullshit. It was all bullshit. It was bullshit that, everywhere she went, she had to listen to people talking shit about Cole, ignoring all the good he'd done. It was bullshit that they forgot he had stopped a murderer. It was bullshit that they didn't know he'd given his own blood to stop the illness that killed Chief Crate and the others. It was bullshit that Brady had to leave the community and hide with his kókom and estranged parents. It was bullshit that Cole's grandmother and auntie were forced to stay in a community that hated Cole.

They hardly left their house anymore.

Eva visited them there each day, and once a week, she brought them their rations. Eva had to bring a letter from Cole's grandmother to prove that she wasn't trying to get more food for herself. The truth was, she gave them some of her rations, too.

She didn't want more. She couldn't stomach more.

A hot cup of coffee was waiting for Eva when she arrived at their place. And a plate of food she wouldn't touch, food that she hadn't intended to eat herself when she'd brought it to them last week. When Cole's grandmother saw Eva's reaction to the food—a Klik sandwich and mixed vegetables—a deflated look, like air being let out of a balloon, she said, "Eva, you have to eat, too. You look so thin."

"I eat." She sat down at the table, across from Cole's grandmother and auntie, and picked up the cup of coffee, ignoring the food.

"You don't eat enough," Auntie Joan said.

"I'm never hungry."

"Cole used to say the same thing, back in the city," Cole's grandmother said. "There were times when he said he couldn't eat, that he was never hungry. Sometimes, he got so thin I thought he might waste away into nothing."

"He told me that. But he had anxiety. I don't." She took a long sip of coffee. This was her fuel. Morning, afternoon, night. This was how she tried to avoid sleep, so that she could avoid the nightmare. But it chased her down anyway, just like the monster chased down Cole, while she helplessly tried to kill it.

And failed.

"Do you think depression is that much different from anxiety, Eva?"

"Do you know that you and Elder Mariah could be best friends?"

"Mom has a point," Auntie Joan said, sliding the plate closer to Eva, close enough that the edge of the plate touched her elbow. "Just a few bites. Make us happy."

"No fair." Any mention of any of them being happy felt like cheating. She picked up the sandwich and took a small bite, then put it back down beside the mixed vegetables, which nobody could make her eat for all the happiness in the world. "There, happy?"

But they didn't answer. What was there left to talk about? She'd been here every day, and nothing new had happened, so there was nothing else to say. They'd try to get her to eat, she'd nibble at something they'd made to appease them, and there would be small talk. Most days, Cole wasn't mentioned. Too hard to talk about. Eva was surprised that his grandmother had brought him up this morning. It still felt nice, though, to hear his name, said lovingly. Said sadly. Bringing his name up, to Eva, opened the door for her to ask what she rarely asked of them anymore.

"You should come with me today, to see him."

"I don't…" His grandmother started, but that was as far as she got.

"We don't like seeing…" Auntie Joan cleared her throat, and took her mother's hand, and Eva saw her hand tense as she squeezed the Elder's hand. "…it's too hard still."

"Do you think it's easy for me?" She'd never snapped at them before. She cupped her mouth and apologized, whispering, "Sorry," through her fingers.

"It's okay, dear," Cole's grandmother said.

"We don't like seeing all those things people write about him," Auntie Joan said. "We want to believe, imagine, that people here think of him differently."

"Well, they don't." Eva caught a tear before it fell, rubbed it away. "And I'm the one who wipes those words off his tombstone every day. I'm the one who has to read them."

"You're right." Cole's grandmother reached across the table and touched Eva's arm. "This isn't fair to you."

"It's just," her voice cracked, and the tears weren't easily caught now, they weren't easily rubbed away. She tried, and failed, and stopped trying altogether. She buried her face into her hands. "It's just that maybe if you came to visit him, maybe something would change. Maybe somehow, he would know you came, and something would change."

"What would change, Eva?" Auntie Joan asked. "What do you mean? What do you think is going to change if we go?"

"I don't know." It was so hard to talk through the tears, to push words out when she could hardly catch her breath. "Maybe nothing. Maybe everything."

"When do you go? We'll go," Cole's grandmother said. "We'll meet you there."

"Tonight." She could hardly speak. After a few seconds, after a few breaths, calming herself as best she could, she repeated, "Tonight. I go every night."

The northern lights were bright over Wounded Sky when Eva came to the cemetery's entrance, so brightly lit that it didn't feel like night at all. She stopped where she was, her hand on the gate, which was already partially open. She took time to stare up at the lights, at the swirling ribbons of cool colours, the greens and blues, and wondered if Cole had just decided to stay there, rather than come back. How could she blame him for that? It was true. It wasn't a legend. Cole had shown her that when he'd asked Jayne to burn her name into his arm. It was true that those beautiful colours overhead were spirits dancing. All the kids that had died ten years earlier, all their friends that had died this autumn, were up there.

And Cole.

Down here, straight ahead was just a body. Not really Cole. What she had told Michael this morning, that they just had to live with it, maybe it was okay, maybe it *had* to be okay, that everything happening in the community wasn't Cole's responsibility anymore. It was theirs, the people who had blamed everything on him. It was her responsibility, too. And she needed to stop waiting for a miracle that might never come. The gate creaked as Eva pushed it open, and she took a step inside. But before she could take another, she heard Tristan calling her name, frantically, repeatedly.

"Eva!" Tristan skidded to a stop on the gravel pathway.

"What the hell, Tristan?"

"I saw it."

"You what? You 'saw it'? Saw what?"

He hunched over, hands to knees, trying to catch his breath, and held up one finger.

"You come here shouting my name like you're running a 100-meter dash, and now you want a minute?" She put her hands on his shoulders and made him stand up straight. "What. Is. Going. On."

"I saw that monster, the one that everybody was seeing before."

"The monster?" Eva's mind raced. Nobody had seen the monster since the night Cole had died. He'd killed Reynold, and had died in the process. He died saving Wounded Sky, not setting the X on fire. "No, that can't be right."

"I did. I just saw it. I saw it, then I saw you."

"You couldn't have, Tristan. You didn't." Her hands remained on Tristan's shoulders, and his eyes searched the area, all the trees around them, searching for what he'd just seen. His eyes were a mix of curiosity and fear.

"Tristan!" She slapped him in the face.

"I know what I saw!" He snapped to attention.

"You saw shadows, a bear in the forest, something. You didn't…that monster, Tristan. It's huge. It has red eyes. Is that what you saw?"

If the monster was still alive then Cole had died for nothing.

"No," Tristan said quietly, distantly. "No, no, no. It wasn't that. It was like…" he trailed off.

"Tristan! It was like what?"

"*The Walking Dead.*"

"The what?"

"It was like *that.* Like a zombie. A monster."

"A zombie? Like…a dead person? Walking?"

"Yeah, Eva, that's what I said. Like *The Walking Dead.* You've seen it right? That's what I saw. Wouldn't you call that a goddamn monster?"

He couldn't catch his breath. Eva could see his heart beating through his sweater. Rapid. Hard.

But Eva was calm. Calmer than she'd felt in a month.

She smiled.

"What the hell is wrong with you? I saw a fricking monster, Eva. We need to get out of here. *Now*. Didn't you just hear what I said?"

"Yeah," Eva said. "I heard you."

"And you're just going to stay outside? You're just going to walk into a cemetery when I literally just told you I saw a dead body walking around?"

Eva just nodded.

"Suit yourself, crazy."

Tristan kept running.

Eva stayed where she was, outside the cemetery gates, for a long time. She looked up at the northern lights, suddenly furiously bright, moving fast like a river. Then she looked into the cemetery, and listened to the quiet that only the dead could bring. When she shut the gate, the shrill sound disrupted the quiet.

The time on her phone, the only thing her phone was good for anymore, read 7:50 pm. Cole's grandmother and auntie were supposed to be there in ten minutes. Good. There was still time to go to their house, and convince them not to come.

There was no reason to be at the cemetery.

Cole wasn't there.

3

WALKER

MARK SPOTTED ANOTHER WOUNDED SKY resident heading to the woods, across the field in front of the clinic. It was the third runner this week, but most had tried a little harder not to be seen. With the reserve quarantined, people, on occasion, had made a break for it. It was just, most runners actually ran. They didn't try to escape by walking slowly, and clumsily, in plain view of Mihko's security force. The lights from the clinic were showering over them like a spotlight.

Mark got on his two-way. "Cover me for a sec, okay?"

"What's up?" Another voice asked through Mark's two-way.

"You're not gonna believe this."

"Try me."

"Some idiot's trying to get to the woods, but they're, like, *walking*. Look drunk or something."

"*Oh my God.*" There was laughter on the other end. "Alright, go get 'em. Mihko always needs more lab rats."

"On it." Mark left his post with a spring in his step.

He caught up to the runner, slowed down, then followed behind at a comfortable distance for as long as he could, enjoying the hilariously slow pursuit. Runner. More like walker. This extremely low-speed chase continued until the shadowy, hobbling figure was at the treeline, about to enter Blackwood Forest.

Only then, did Mark say, "Hey, buddy."

The walker tripped over some underbrush, landed in it, stood up, and kept on keeping on.

Mark stifled a laugh. "What're you deaf or something? I told you to stop, bro!"

Undeterred, the walker didn't stop.

"Alright, I'm losing my patience, asshole." Mark drew his gun, caught up to the walker, put a hand on their shoulder, and turned them around.

"Holy shit," Mark whispered. "What the hell are you?"

He pulled out a flashlight and shone it at the thing. What he saw made him stumble backwards, almost tripping over bushes himself. It wasn't human. Skin hung off bone like ratty clothing. The eyes were pale and blank. Thin, cobweb hair. He pushed the gun's barrel right against where the thing's heart should've been. The metal pushed through its rotting flesh. Mark vomited in his mouth.

"Don't you move," Mark's voice quivered. "Not one goddamn inch."

The creature ignored the gun and turned to keep going into the forest as though drawn there. It didn't understand a gun; it hadn't understood Mark's words. There was only one thing it would understand. Mark pressed the trigger down. *Pop.*

Without flinching, the creature reached out and grabbed Mark's arm. His heart pounded.

"Let go of me you freak!"

"What's going on over here?" Someone came running from Blackwood Forest—one of the guards stationed in the woods to keep people from leaving the reserve.

"Help me!"

Mark grunted, trying to free his arm from the thing's grip. How could something so hideous, a corpse, just bones and flesh, be so strong? Mark could not break away. He tried to push his arm back towards it, put the gun close enough that he could clip the creature again. Slow it down. Shock the thing enough that he could free himself, and finish it off.

Pop.

In the spark from the gun's barrel, Mark saw the other guard fall back, clutching his chest.

"Shit!"

Mark grasped the thing's wrist as hard as he could and tried to wrench its hand away from his arm. Mark's fingers dug into its flesh to wrap around bone.

The creature cried out and grabbed the barrel of the gun with its free hand, bending it upwards as though the metal was tinfoil.

The gun dropped to the ground with a hollow thud.

It put both its hands around Mark's neck and lifted him off the ground.

Mark clutched at the creature's wrists, his fingers burying themselves deep within its flesh. The black of night started to encompass everything, blotting out the glow of the northern lights.

"Please," Mark choked out. "Don't."

The creature tilted its head to the side just as Mark's body went limp, and let go. Mark fell to the ground. The creature stood there, facing the field, looking straight ahead, until it turned around to face the black of the forest.

It took a step, then another.

The creature emerged from Blackwood Forest at a large, circular clearing. There, after all of that time moving forward, always forward, it stopped. The field was lush with frosted grass, glittering like diamonds in the rising sun. It stared at the field for a long time, then looked across to the other end of the clearing where, at the edge of the woods, sat a one-room cabin constructed out of nothing more than particle board. Smoke was rising from its metal chimney, into the air, high above the treeline. Near the cabin, clothes hung from yellow twine, tied to a tree at either end. Standing in front of the twine, hanging clothes, was a teenage boy.

The creature reached forward with one arm, as though he could touch the boy, as though he were that close. It crept out of the forest and into the field. It stalked across the field, ever closer to the boy. He was still hanging clothes on the line.

The boy placed one last item of clothing on the yellow twine. A Bon Iver shirt. He picked up the laundry basket and walked to the cabin.

"That's it, right?" The teenager called out.

"Yes, nósisim!" an older woman's voice replied from inside the cabin.

"Ekosi!"

The boy ducked around the corner to the front of the dwelling. The creature followed, but the boy was gone. It stood in front of the cabin door, and was still there when the door swung open. It was face to face with the Elder. She gasped. Her eyes narrowed. She put her hand against the creature's decomposed cheek.

"Cole," she whispered. "You've come a long way."

4

FAR ENOUGH AWAY

"WAKE UP, COLEY."

Cole could hear flames, popping and crackling, but couldn't see anything.

"Elder?"

He had a memory of her, of seeing the Elder out front of the cabin. She'd brought him away from the house and into the woods. She put a tent up that he could stay in. There was a bowl. She'd made a paste out of medicines in it, and covered his body with it. She'd wrapped bandages over every inch of his skin. Over his eyes.

Cole touched his tongue through a slit in the bandages, and more than just his tongue being there, he could feel saliva with his fingertips. Sensations. Taste. Touch. He pushed himself up into a sitting position, and reached forward with both arms, palms facing the fire to catch the warmth. He began to rotate his hands, savouring each moment of heat, and didn't move his hands when the heat began to burn.

He could feel the pain. It was exquisite.

A small hand touched his arm.

"Elder Mariah?"

"No, it's me, silly."

"Jayney?"

"Yeah, who else would it be?"

Cole took a firm hold of Jayne's hand, and smiled underneath the bandages. "It's…so…good…to…see…you…" Cole flicked his tongue around with satisfaction. It was there, all of it. Now, he just needed to learn how to use it again. He spoke deliberately, and Jayne noticed.

"Why're you talkin' so funny?"

Cole shook his head at the reason, the complexity of it, and how he'd ever explain it to Jayne.

"I know you died." Jayne rolled her eyes. "Gosh!"

"My...body...is...healing. No...tongue...not long...ago."

"Gross." Jayne's face scrunched up like she'd just eaten something sour.

"Yeah." Cole felt Jayne move closer to him. She put the non-burning side of her face on his shoulder.

"You were there," she sighed.

He knew what she meant. The northern lights, the waiting room. The space between here, and there. He had been dancing with other spirits, those ribbons of colour. He had fragments of images from that time, from when he was dead. He knew, somehow, that she'd guided him back. And that she belonged there. Choch had pulled her away to help him save Wounded Sky, to use her as leverage to convince Cole to hold up his part of the deal. She would be stuck here until Cole finished his job. What a cruel thing, to have given her a taste, making her bring him back to Earth and into his corpse.

"Yeah...I...was...there."

"I miss it so much and I only got to be there for a second to get you," she said. "Can you tell me about it, Coley?"

"I'll...think...about...it...okay? That's all...I can do. What I can... remember."

"Okay." Her arm wrapped around his waist, and she pressed herself against the side of his body.

Cole started to sweat, but didn't move away. He thought about his time in the northern lights for her, the transition between Earth and the Hunting Grounds. He allowed the fragments to flood into his mind, shards he could remember. The ribbons, like the tiny flames dancing across half of Jayne's body. Each ribbon of colour was a name and a face. Dancing to the rhythm of the drum.

Cole thumped his fist against his chest with the same beat. Jayne let go of him. He heard her stand up, and then he heard her rustling. With his free hand, he pulled down the bandages covering his eyes, and saw her. She was dancing to the beat. Her flame burned brighter than he'd ever seen. He ignored the heat. He continued beating his fist against his chest, and cried. Jayne dancing was the most beautiful thing Cole had ever seen. Her bare feet jerked up, slid back, kicked dirt against the sides of the tent. Her body straightened, then dipped, straightened, then dipped. Her arms were spread out like wings. Her head moved back and forth like a falling autumn leaf.

Cole stopped beating his chest. His hand fell to his side. Jayne stopped dancing. She stood on one side of the fire, which had begun to burn again—Jayne's flames sparking it to life. They stared across the fire at one another. Cole looked deep into her eyes. She into his.

"I'm…going…to get…you home."

"I know you are, silly."

Jayne walked over to the side of the tent, picked up two pieces of wood. They were burning before she even placed them on top of the small flame she'd restarted.

"There," she said. "Now, you won't be cold anymore."

Cole looked back and forth between Jayne and the fire. "You… came here…to…keep me…warm?"

Jayne nodded as though it was obvious. Of course she did. They were friends.

"But…the…boogey…man," Cole said. That's what Jayne had called it before. She'd hid from it. It's why she hadn't been around as much. "You…didn't…come…when…"

"I shoulda been there for you, Coley. I'm so sorry." Her flames dimmed so low that Cole saw tears on the burning side of her face.

He pictured Reynold charging at him after killing Victor in the woods outside the research facility. He'd called for her to help him.

Jayne sobbed. She must've heard his thoughts.

"Jayney…"

"I'm sorry, Coley. I should just stay out of your life!" Her flames burst like an explosion when she shouted.

"No!" Cole said. "I'm...sorry...I just...mean...you...can't go...I...need you."

Cole waited while Jayne calmed herself, and her flames settled. When she'd stopped sobbing, she spoke with little hiccups, the remnants of her sorrow. "You...you forgive me?"

"Of...course," Cole said. "Come here."

Jayne walked through the fire and sat down in front of Cole. He hugged her non-burning side and held her there for as long as he could stand. Maybe a bit longer than he should have. But it was worth it because she smiled again.

"You're...here now. In the...woods."

"Yep. You needed me."

"You...wouldn't go...into...Blackwood before...what changed?"

Jayne looked him straight in the eye with steely resolve. "I decided to be brave."

Cole understood that she wasn't just answering the question. She was telling him something more. In that moment, he made the same decision Jayne had made.

It was time to be brave.

5

EVERY YESTERDAY

AFTER JAYNE LEFT, ELDER MARIAH BROUGHT COLE a simple breakfast. Some fish Brady had caught at the river, just a few hundred yards from the cabin, and preserved berries. She sat with him, and when Cole was hesitant to pick up the fork, she encouraged him. She poked at some berries with the fork and placed the utensil in his hand.

"You should eat a bit," she said.

"I…haven't eaten…anything…" he explained.

"I know, that's exactly why."

Cole made an opening around his mouth, pushing bandages out of the way, and slipped two berries in. They were cool and sweet, and the taste danced across his tongue.

"Well?" she said.

"Good," he said.

Another, fuller, forkful was in his mouth in no time. He watched Elder Mariah while he ate. The last time he'd seen her, when he, Brady, and Eva had rescued her from the clinic, she looked nothing like she did now. At the clinic, she was near death. Shrivelled. Now, she looked vibrant, like life itself was ready to burst out of her.

She'd become healthy, but it wasn't from Cole's blood this time. It wasn't from the cure running through his veins.

"How are you…better?" he asked.

Elder Mariah ran her hand across the ground, and picked up earth as though she were picking more berries for Cole. She held out her hand.

"The land," she answered. "Here, hold out your hand."

Cole did as he was told. With her free hand, she unbandaged his, then turned it, so his palm faced up.

She poured the earth onto his palm.

"Can you feel it?" she asked.

Cole pressed the earth against his palm with his fingertips, eyes closed, and let it slide off his skin, back onto the ground. He nodded. And then he noticed that his scar was gone. He unbandaged his other hand, to find that his scar there was gone, too. He rubbed his fingertips against his palms, eyes closed, and then turned them over, away from sight.

"Will they come back?" Elder Mariah asked.

"I don't know."

When Cole finished his breakfast, the Elder helped him remove the bandages, so she could apply another round of medicine. It was warm in the tent, but goosebumps raced across his exposed skin. They covered his forearms, like the grit on sandpaper. Elder Mariah stared at him.

"What?" he asked.

"I just can't believe it," she said. "The medicine…"

But it wasn't just the medicine, and Cole knew it. One of the gifts that Choch had given him was working overtime. It wasn't healing a broken arm now. It was bringing him back from the dead. The combination of the two—the medicine and his ability—was powerful. Cole wanted a mirror, but also didn't. He kept thinking of the Joker in *Batman*, right after his bandages were removed. Maybe he was that ugly, just not a corpse anymore. It would still be an impressive transformation.

Elder Mariah applied another layer of medicine with care, and bandaged Cole's body again. The paste stung and burned, but it was a good pain. She promised to come back later with supper and see how he was progressing. Before she left, Cole felt a pull, and even though he could hardly remember anything from his trip here, he knew the feeling. The same pull had led him through Blackwood Forest.

He verbalized it. "Brady?"

"Yes," Elder Mariah said. "I'll bring him."

Cole spent the daylight hours alone and, with a mending brain, very little on his mind. This was something his therapist back in Winnipeg had always wanted, and something he could never really achieve. He'd tried, of course, but stopping his thoughts had always felt like using a bandage on a gaping wound.

"How am I supposed to just...stop thinking?" he'd asked her on several occasions.

When he was ten, when he was seventeen.

"It's like anything else," she'd said. "You get better at it with practice."

Living in the moment. No thoughts of yesterday and no thoughts of tomorrow. Just now. She'd called it mindfulness. In his practice sessions, the ones he'd always sucked at, she'd told him to just notice the feelings in his body, not judge them, or analyze them. Just notice them, and say, "I feel this way, and that's alright." Eventually, frustrated, Cole just pretended to do what she'd asked and judged the shit out of his body sensations.

Now, Cole managed to keep his mind clear. He didn't think about anything that had happened yesterday—every yesterday, all the pain and confusion and anger and loss—and didn't think about what would come tomorrow, when he was better, when he would return to Wounded Sky. He felt his body. He homed in on each sensation. The ointment Elder Mariah had applied to his skin. The gentle warmth of the modest fire Cole tended to throughout the day. He was so in tune, he could feel each fibre of muscle mend, each cell of skin heal. Sitting there, mostly unmoving, and just feeling his body for hours, time passed quickly. He would try to remember this, to tell his therapist when he saw her next, because he'd stayed entirely in the moment, hadn't given in to what would have been an unbearable excitement. The anticipation of seeing his friend, actually seeing him face to face, and talking to him for the first time since Brady had taken Elder Mariah and his parents out here. Only when the daylight faded did Cole allow himself one thought: Did Brady know he was alive? Had Elder Mariah told him?

Cole heard the cabin door open, followed by voices: Elder Mariah's and Brady's. He listened to their footsteps, coming from the cabin to his tent. The footsteps stopped outside the tent's flap.

"Nósisim…" Elder Mariah paused, trying to find a way to explain to Brady what he was about to see.

So, he hadn't been told. How would he react?

"What, nókom?" Brady prompted. "Why are you being so weird?"

Evidently, Elder Mariah gave up trying to prepare her grandson adequately. She just said, "Go inside, and we'll talk."

Cole heard the flap start to open, while Brady said, "I'm pretty sure it's not my birthday or anything like that," and in the same sentence, having stepped inside the tent, "holy crap what's this? Who are you?"

Cole kept the bandages over his eyes and didn't respond. He couldn't think of one word to say.

Elder Mariah's softer footsteps entered the tent.

"Why's this guy wearing my clothes? Why's he dressed like a mummy?" Brady asked.

"I've been applying medicines to him," Elder Mariah said. "He was…badly hurt."

"So what, I'm here to learn about what medicines you used? Why couldn't you just tell me that, nókom?"

"Here." Elder Mariah approached Cole, and he felt her unclip the end of the wrapping from the top of his head. She started to unravel the bandages. "Let me show you. Just try to stay calm."

"Okay. You're kind of weirding me out though."

She asked of Cole, "Are you ready?"

Cole didn't say anything. Just nodded, like he still wasn't able to speak. He felt the bandages lift from his body. First, from the top of his head, then from around his forehead. When they were taken away from his eyes, he kept them closed. He kept them closed until he felt the bandages pull away from his mouth, until he heard Brady fall back against the tent, almost knocking over the whole structure.

"No. No way." Brady was breathless.

Cole opened his eyes.

"Hello, my friend."

6

EVERYTHING

MOMENTS AFTER COLE HAD SAID HELLO to Brady, as though he'd been on vacation and not literally dead, Brady woke up. Elder Mariah had propped Brady's head up on her lap, and Cole was sitting across from them, on the other side of the fire, trying not to look too happy, he supposed. To be alive, to see his friend. The 'Hello, my friend,' comment may have been a bit too dramatic, Cole realized. But, in his defence, it just blurted out of his mouth.

Brady lifted his head slightly to make eye contact with Cole, who smiled apologetically. He pulled himself up off Elder Mariah's lap and leaned back on his elbows.

"I'll leave you two alone, so you can catch up," Elder Mariah said and left.

"You're still here," Brady whispered, once they were alone.

"Still here," Cole said.

"How?" he asked. "I mean…*how?*"

"I…" Cole was unsure how to navigate his way through this. He had no clue how he was alive again; though his healing powers had helped him become human again, they surely hadn't brought him back to life. He wasn't immortal. He ended up saying what he really believed, what he thought was probably true. "I'm not done what I came to do."

"Cole," Brady said, "if somebody dies, and they aren't finished something, they don't just…start breathing again. Like, if I don't finish the laundry, and then I die, I'm not going to—"

"I know that this is different than needing to finish laundry," Cole said. "That's one thing I do know."

"Okay, fine," Brady said. "So, you're what, are you a ghost or something?"

"I mean..." Cole looked down at his body, poked at it, an attempt at levity. "...not that I'm aware."

"You're really real," Brady stated. "Like, you're actually alive."

Cole checked his pulse. Strong and steady.

"Look, I know there are things you can't tell me," Brady said, "but you've got to give me something here, okay?"

"You're right, of course you're right. I owe you at least that, it's just..." Cole figured the same rules applied as before: he couldn't tell anybody about Choch or the deal.

"Eva said..." Brady stopped for a second, like putting the sentence together was too hard, or too painful, but then he kept going, gritting his teeth through it. "...that *they* said you got trapped in a fire you started at the X."

"The X?" Cole's jaw dropped. "What are you talking about?"

"It burned down the night you...died."

Cole sighed, deeply. So, they thought he'd died in a fire he'd started. The last in a series of fires that had been pinned on him, thanks to a mysterious assailant that had set him up by doing things like leave his toque at one of the arson scenes. He forced his mind to go back to the moment he died. The person in the hazmat suit had found Cole kneeling over his dad's body, distracted by sorrow and anger. Didn't say a word, just squeezed the trigger. The muzzle flashed. The bullet entered Cole's brain.

"That's a really shitty thing to say. Kids died like that before. Why would they...why couldn't they...that's..." Cole's blood was boiling. "...so effing shitty."

Cole did not *say 'effing,' dear readers. Still doing my job.*

"I know." Brady was reflective. He got up, walked around the fire, and sat next to Cole. "Me and Eva, we never believed that."

He put an arm around Cole's shoulder.

"The last thing I remember," Cole stared into the fire as though it was the muzzle of the gun, "I'd found my dad's body, in the basement of the research facility. And then this…"

"What?" Brady prompted. "This what?"

"This person was there, in a, uh, in a…hazmat suit…" Cole checked to see how Brady was looking at him, at how ridiculous this all sounded. "They just shot me, that's it. I saw the gun fire, and then…" And then what? He saw black for a moment, and in the next moment, was in the waiting room, in the northern lights, dancing with ribbons of colour, to the beat of the drum, with everybody who he'd ever lost, for what at once seemed a moment and an eternity. "I died."

Brady, hanging on Cole's every word, just stared at his friend, waiting for more. When no more words came, he gave Cole a squeeze on the shoulder. "And then you died? That's it?"

"I woke up in my…coffin. I dug my way out. I can't remember much of anything after that, until I was close to here. No brain, you know?" Cole chuckled, but Brady didn't laugh. "I felt this need to come here. I knew the way here, somehow. So, I came here. Came to you."

Brady shook his head.

"How long has it been?" Cole had no concept of time, from when he'd woken up, to when he'd arrived at the cabin. No concept of how long he'd been dead.

"Around a month," Brady said.

"A month," Cole repeated. How much had happened since he'd left? How bad had things got, after he'd failed so spectacularly? He was supposed to save the community, and instead, he'd died. "Well I'm alive now," Cole said, in response to his thoughts.

"I'm glad, my friend."

Brady hugged him and held on for a while.

"Me, too." Cole said.

"You look good, for a dead kid."

"You should've seen me before."

Eventually, they let go of each other, and then stared at one another. To Cole, this felt like the moment where they really said *hi*, where they were really back to old times.

"You know, I don't know how I'm alive, I don't really know why, but I know that I'm not done. I know that I have to go back to Wounded Sky. I know that I have to figure it out."

"You can't go back, Cole. You shouldn't go back. You should get out of here. You should…" Brady took a deep breath, the kind Cole was so familiar with, when he was going through a panic attack. In five seconds, out seven seconds. "…how much more can you go through? And for what?"

"I'm not alive just to run away, Brady."

Brady shook his head. "You don't understand how bad things are, what you'd be going back to. Before cell service cut out two weeks ago, Eva told me everything. I used to run towards home until I got a signal. Eva, she…" Brady stopped himself. "You should run."

This time, Cole was the one who shook his head. "No."

"Cole…"

"Eva told you everything?"

"Yeah," Brady said. "I'm a bit behind now, but yeah."

"Then I want you to tell *me* everything."

Brady suggested they go for walk, get some fresh air. Cole needed it, too. He hadn't been outside since he'd healed, hadn't been able to appreciate the beauty of the land on his journey here. They left the tent and walked deeper into Blackwood, away from Wounded Sky. Brady picked a leaf off a tree, and played with it as they walked.

"The more I think about it, I guess you're right. Of course, you're right. I tried to talk you out of going back, but—"

"I have to."

"—I won't anymore. Eva's still there. Everybody's still there, dealing with everything. All that crap. It kills me, each day I'm not there. It just kills me."

"It *actually* killed me, so…"

"Too soon."

"Yeah, I figured it might be."

Still, they both chuckled. It felt a bit like a deep breath, before things got serious. They walked for a while, until the cabin was far behind them.

"How is it here, with your parents?" Cole asked.

Brady's whole body slouched.

Cole waited.

"I'm trying to think of a good analogy because I don't want to actually address it. It's not as bad as it was at first, but it's still…you know… it's a process."

"Sorry, man," Cole said. "Is that…I mean, is it as awkward as it sounds?"

"It's not *not* awkward," Brady said.

"Double negatives are never really a good sign."

"It's just, you spend your whole life trying to get them to accept you, or at least understand, and they never do. So you leave them, because even if they say they love you, they don't, because they don't love a big part of you."

"But it always hurts."

"Of course, it does, and then, you know, you have to live with them again, after all that time…"

"Supreme awkwardness."

"It's okay. It wasn't, but it is. Living in that place, that super small place, it forces you to talk at least."

"Talking's good," Cole said. "Talking's a start."

"They always liked Ashley…" and if Brady had more to say about it after that, he didn't. "Anyway, let's talk about all the bad crap, shall we? Enough of my crap."

"Let's."

Brady got right into it. "Nobody stepped up after Anna Crate left the race, so Reynold's the Chief now, but he's…how do I say this…

AWOL? Curiously absent from public life after winning the election. Didn't even throw a victory party."

"Has anybody seen him at all?" Cole asked. "Like, since the night I…"

"I don't really know. Eva didn't say."

"Any sightings of Upayokwitigo?"

"No. She would've heard something like that."

So Reynold still might be dead. But then, if he was, he wasn't the reason Cole was brought back to life. What could be worse? What could be left to do? Could Reynold be alive? Cole had all those thoughts, and then he pictured the gun that *he* had been holding. He'd shot Reynold in the chest, right in his heart. Reynold had run off into Blackwood, Cole was sure, mortally wounded. Before Cole had been shot himself, he'd planned to go out into the woods and find Reynold's body. "So Reynold might still be alive."

"Why would he be dead? What's he got to do with Upayokwitigo?" Brady sounded extremely confused. Clearly, Eva had not told Brady anything that Cole had told her.

"Uhhh…nothing. No reason, I guess," Cole said.

"You guess?" Brady frowned, like he'd heard that one before. "You just can't tell me? What bigger secret could there be, than you coming back from the dead? Honestly?"

"That's a good point!" Cole called out, not to Brady, but to Choch.

Thankfully, Brady let it go. "Mihko Laboratories reopened the research facility. Chief and Council said it would be a boost to the economy, but I don't think they've hired any community members, and their presence had almost doubled the last time I heard from Eva. There are more people at the clinic, too, and security all over the place. I mean, *all over the place.*"

"What, like at the mall?"

"All over the place," Brady repeated. "The whole community's on lockdown now, not just the clinic."

"The whole community's on lockdown? What do you mean?"

"Nobody's allowed to leave or come in. That's why the flights stopped coming last month. They're rationing food because of it, the whole nine."

Cole had a vague memory of an encounter in the woods. There had been two guards. A struggle. Gunshots. They'd been trying to keep Cole from leaving. His mind was reeling. He couldn't even think about what he had to do to save the community. "Tell me that's it."

Brady hesitated. "People are missing."

"Like before?" Cole asked, thinking about his murdered friends.

"No, just up and vanishing. Gone."

"Just gone," Cole stated flatly. "Where? I mean, where do you think?"

"The clinic? The research facility?" Brady guessed. "Eva didn't know."

"Shit," Cole breathed.

"So, what's the plan? We'll go back, I'll tell Eva, and we'll, you know…" Brady didn't know where to go from there, just that, it sounded to Cole, he knew they were a team, and they were going to do *something*. "…she'll be so happy, she'll probably faint, but, you know, *then* she'll be happy. Then we'll—"

"We'll tell Eva, of course. But we can't just tell everybody about me," Cole said.

"Why?" Brady asked.

"Because we don't have a plan, short of just going back."

"And we can't tell anybody else because we don't have a plan?"

"Yeah, that's the one thing we do have."

"The one thing we do have," Brady repeated thoughtfully. "Okay, what do you mean?"

"I mean that whatever we decide to do, they won't ever see me coming," Cole said.

"It's historically hard to keep anybody's presence a secret in Wounded Sky."

"It's not when you have a costume."

7

THE RECKONER

WHEN NIGHT FELL, COLE WENT OFF ON his own into Blackwood Forest and found a small clearing by a brook. He sat on a rock by the water. Quiet. Calm. He could see his breath in the cold. Moonlight lit the clearing. He heard footsteps approach, but didn't turn to see who it was. He could guess who it was anyway.

Choch placed a jacket over Cole's shoulders and rested his hands there for a moment. Uncommonly tender.

"Thanks," Cole said.

Choch patted one shoulder, gave both shoulders a squeeze, and sat down beside Cole. The rock was big enough for two.

"My pleasure." The spirit being gave Cole a very long look. An inspection. "Did you do something with your hair?"

Cole smiled. "Still funny, I see."

"If you don't laugh at the world, the world laughs at you."

"I don't even know what that means, and honestly, I don't care."

Choch slapped his knee. He looked around the clearing. "Who killed Cole and replaced him with this guy?" he called out, laughing, hardly able to get the words out.

"I kind of expected to get a lot of death jokes," Cole said. "You should really find some new material."

Choch stared at Cole some more.

"What?" Cole asked.

"I'm just trying to figure out if you're still fun," Choch said.

"I'm sure you'll figure out some way to amuse yourself."

Choch walked to the edge of the brook and just stood there. After a moment, Cole joined him.

"My boy's all grows up." Choch had actual tears in his eyes, and his voice cracked. He repeated himself with a great deal of gesticulation; cupping his mouth, putting a hand against Cole's cheek. "My boy's all grows up."

Cole jerked his face away from Choch's hand. "Who are you now? A waiter? A gym teacher? A stand-up comic?"

"Oh, that's a surprise. It's really fun though and clever. You'll appreciate it, when you see it. You *are* coming back soon, I imagine."

Cole listened to the brook for a moment, then answered. "Yes, in the morning."

"Well, you know, if I may offer some advice or whatever," Choch twisted his toe into the ground sheepishly, "eat a big breakfast. It's the most important meal of the day."

"Thanks."

"So, I guess you've got this all figured out then." Choch clapped his hands and turned away from the brook and Cole. "Not even one million thoughts in your head. I'll just, you know, head on back to my other projects." He whistled as he walked away, not even disappearing. Maybe he intended to get wherever he was going on foot.

"Hey," Cole said.

Choch stopped and turned around eagerly. "Yeah?"

Cole looked down at his palms. Followed the path of each line, lines that Cole hadn't seen for ten years, because of the scars that had taken their place. He ran his index finger along his life line, the one that curled around the base of his thumb. He remembered comparing his with Eva's. Whoever's was longer would live the best. But Cole didn't really believe in any of that; he'd just wanted to touch Eva's hand.

"And what did the scars make you think of?" Choch asked, walking back to Cole. "Did they give you such pleasant memories?"

Cole tried to picture them. Faulty scars. That's what the doctor had called them in the city. Raised. Discoloured. Ugly. But somehow, sometimes, to him, beautiful. "They reminded me of what I'd do for them."

"Technically, *I* did it for them, in a roundabout sort of way. But, to-may-toe, to-mah-toe, I suppose."

Cole remembered pulling the school doors open, and the door handles off in the process. "You were there *after*," Cole said absently. "I opened the doors myself."

"Are you sure? You're not gaslighting me, are you?"

"I remember." Cole looked up at Choch. "I want them back. Can you give them back to me?"

Choch leaned over, so his face was inches away from Cole's palms, looking them over carefully. He lifted his head up. "You sure? They're so nice and pretty and smooth right now."

"Yeah, I'm sure."

Choch nodded, eyebrows raised. "Alright, okay. And you know what? I'll do it for free, because I like you, CB. You're still my boy, grows up and everything."

"No strings?" Cole clarified.

Choch suspended himself in the air, jerking around like a marionette. Then, suddenly, he stopped, and landed on his feet. Smiled. "None. Scout's honour."

Choch pressed his hands on Cole's palms. Steam rose from them, and pain flooded from his hands up his arms and right into his chest. Cole was seven again, standing at the doors to the school, his hands wrapped around the hot metal handles. Moments later, he'd see Eva's shoes underneath a collapsed wall, and Choch would be there. Coyote. Offering him a deal that would change everything, forever. Cole didn't pull his hands away from Choch, despite the pain. Just watched the steam rise like his breath in the cold air. Then, Choch pulled his hands away, and the scars were back. Cole stared at them, before clenching his fists protectively.

"Voila," Choch said. "Now, if you'll excuse me, I need some fresh air."

Choch started whistling again and wandered off into the forest.

It was late when Cole returned to the tent, but he could tell the fire was going before he entered the structure. It glowed a soft orange in the darkness. Brady was waiting for him, tending the fire. A plate of food and a neat pile of folded clothing waited for Cole. He greeted Brady and sat across from him. He didn't waste any time digging into supper.

"Don't eat the plate while you're at it," Brady said.

Cole slowed the pace, but not by much. "It's amazing how hungry you can be after not eating for a month."

"I've read about this thing called 'dry fasting,' where people do exactly that," Brady said.

"*We* fast," Cole pointed out.

"That's true," Brady said, "but not for weeks at a time. I've done it for ceremony, you know?"

"And not because you're dead."

"I don't plan on trying that particular brand of fasting for a long time."

"I wouldn't recommend it. Kind of sucked."

"Do you appreciate it more, though?"

"Eating?"

"No, dummy," Brady laughed. "Being alive."

"Sure," Cole nodded. "I mean, of course I do." But Cole wasn't sure if that was true. Yes, he knew he had a job to do, and was thankful to be back because his friends needed him, even though they didn't know it, or know why. He didn't even know why. When he'd died, though, he'd gone to a good place. He'd felt only joy and peace. Maybe he'd brought some of that back with him, but he still missed it. "It's good to see you again."

"You too," Brady said. "I still feel like I need to rub my eyes each time I see you."

"Likewise," Cole said. "But I'm here."

"Good, because if you'll direct your attention to the clothing and try not to eat it, too…"

"Very funny."

"...I tried to put together what I could, but I couldn't really find a costume, per se. The Halloween bin's back at the house."

Cole couldn't hide his disappointment. He'd pictured himself in something like a Boba Fett costume, or Snake Eyes or something.

"I mean, do you need a disguise or a costume?" Brady asked. "Are you trying to keep everybody believing you're dead, or Superman?"

"I just..." Cole tried to get over the letdown. "It's like what I said. I don't want people to know I'm alive. I want to disguise myself. That's it."

Brady just kept looking at Cole, as though he knew Cole wasn't telling the truth. Of course, Brady knew. He always knew. Him and Eva both.

"I want to wear a cool costume," Cole admitted.

"You'll still look cool," Brady said.

Cole unfolded the clothes one by one. There was a pair of army green cargo pants ("There are so many pockets it's like a utility belt!" Brady encouraged.), a black Pearl Jam t-shirt, a black hooded sweatshirt with an oversized hood, and, finally, a neck warmer with a skull across the front.

"Okay the skull is cool." Cole slipped it on over his head, so it covered everything under his eyes. "It's like an x-ray of my head!"

"I thought you'd like that," Brady said. "And I figured you could just keep wearing the black sneakers, hey?"

Cole started to shed his clothing, in order to put on his makeshift costume.

"Want me to step outside?" Brady asked.

"What? No. Why?" Cole said.

"Sorry. My dad's trying and everything, but we're in this one-room cabin, and even now when he changes, he asks me to go outside no matter how cold it is. We still have some work to do."

"Well, you don't have to step outside for me. You can even check me out."

"You're not my type, loser. Maybe if you had a superhero costume or something..."

"Shut it."

Cole changed into his new clothes. He tried to stand, but was too tall for the tent, so he had to sit down to model the outfit for Brady. "Well, what do you think?" Cole had his hood pulled up and neck warmer in place.

Brady nodded, impressed. "You actually look pretty great. Good costume."

"Thanks," Cole said. "I didn't mean to sound like I didn't appreciate you getting this together for me. It's awesome. Really."

"You wanted to be Boba Fett." Brady smiled wryly.

Cole laughed. "I *did* want to be Boba Fett, but this is better."

Brady got up to go. He stopped at the flap. "So, in the morning? Eat breakfast, head back?"

"In the morning."

"Cool." Brady went outside, but before the flap settled back into place, he popped his head back inside. "Hey, superhero. You got a name? Coley Fett, something like that?"

"There *are* a lot of *Fletts* in Wounded Sky," Cole said. "Close enough?"

Brady feigned a thoughtful expression. "I think I actually have a cousin named Boba Flett…or was that Bubba? Bobby?"

"*Anyway*," Cole said, "I do have a name, and I didn't make it up. *They* gave it to me."

"They? Mihko?"

"Yeah, Mihko," Cole confirmed. "In the folder with the files on all the kids, they'd given me a codename or something. My dad, he…" Cole tried not to picture his dad with Vikki, the woman with whom he had planned to run away. Reynold's girlfriend. Lucy's mom. The plan that had gotten his dad and Vikki killed, "…he was doing his own experiments on me. You know that already, I guess."

"And they worked," Brady said.

"Yeah," Cole said, "but at what cost?"

The fire crackled. On Cole's part, he thought of the moment he'd found the files in Reynold's chest, in the closet in his bedroom. How deep did Reynold's involvement go? Even if he was dead now, Cole needed to figure that out. He knew one thing for sure: all of this was related to the experiments Mihko had run on the kids. Eva. Cole. Jayne. So many of them. Maybe the fire was related.

"So what is it?" Brady asked.

"Huh?"

"The name, space cadet. What is it?"

Cole stared into the fire, rubbing his fingertips against his scars within clenched fists.

"They called me The Reckoner."

8

MAN WITH A PLAN

COLE WOKE BEFORE SUNRISE, WHEN the early morning still felt like night. He'd woken up several times during the night, looking forward to the morning and going back to Wounded Sky. He sat in front of the dwindling fire until it died, leaving only ashes and embers. Then, he put on his costume, and waited.

Brady entered the tent, feeling around in the dark blue glow of the early morning. He found Cole sitting where he had been since waking, legs crossed, hands on his knees, staring at the remains of the fire.

"Oh my gosh, Cole, you scared me."

Brady set down the things that he had brought with him, and tossed a log onto the pit. He blew on it gently until a small flame sparked to life.

"Just sitting here in the dark?" he asked.

"I'm used to the dark."

"Do me a favour." Brady sat down. "Could you save the whole brooding thing for later?"

"Sorry, I was just thinking."

"About?"

"Everything I have to do."

"You mean everything *we* have to do."

"*We* have to do," Cole said. "Sorry."

Brady had brought two backpacks, one for him and one for Cole, and breakfast. Cole demolished the food—a plate of jackfish, hash browns, and berries. When he was finished, he rummaged through the backpack. Extra clothing. Toiletries. Some comics. Snacks for the walk back to the community.

"It's like the packs we brought on top of the school when we were kids."

"Just like old times," Brady said. "I mean, that's really all my stuff, but I didn't want you to feel left out and not have your own."

"Thanks, man." Cole fastened the pack over his shoulders. "I wish we were doing something like that, instead of heading into…"

"Certain death?"

"I was going to say the lion's den. I've kind of already done the dead thing, so…"

"Yeah, but I haven't." Brady put his own pack on. "And I'd prefer not to."

"It wasn't much fun. The actual act of dying."

They left the tent. Predictably, the cold was there to greet them; their breath looked like ghosts. Cole pulled the neck warmer over his mouth and his hood up.

"That *does* look pretty badass," Brady said.

"And, added bonus: it's cold outside."

"What can I say, I thought of everything."

"Even heroes get cold."

"It's efficient. It's warm. It looks cool." Brady raised a finger to coincide with each item on the list.

"You checked all the boxes. I love it."

"No cape though."

"I mean," Cole said, "we both know the pitfalls of capes, according to *The Incredibles*."

"I guess I really did think of everything."

At the cabin, Elder Mariah was waiting for them, bundled up to ward off the chill. She had a smudge bowl, a bundle of medicine, and an eagle feather.

"I know there's no point asking you to stay," she said. "I know that you have to go, but…"

"We'll be careful," Brady assured her.

"I won't let anything happen to him." Cole patted Brady on the shoulder. "He's my special guy."

"Oh my…" Brady rolled his eyes. "Well, at least you're not brooding." He mimicked the patting, but patted Cole on top of his head. "And I won't let anything happen to this nerd."

"Ekosani," Elder Mariah chuckled. "I feel better knowing that you're together. Now…" She placed the bowl on the ground, knelt over it, and lit a match. She held the match to the medicine, until a tiny flame burst to life from it, which she quickly extinguished. She nursed the ember within the bundle, fanning it gently with the eagle feather, and smoke began to billow away from it. Cole accepted the smudge, cupped his hands together, and brought the smoke towards him; ran it through his hair, over his eyes, over his mouth and pressed it against his heart; then pushed it down across the rest of his body. He said a prayer, asking Creator for strength and courage and guidance for the task they had in front of them. Brady did the same, eyes closed the entire time, his lips moving while he recited his own prayer to Creator. When the smudge was finished, Elder Mariah placed the bowl on the ground and embraced both of them.

"Now, whatever you do," she said, "you'll do it in a good way."

"We'll be back," Cole said, "and we'll need your help."

"Ehe," Elder Mariah said. "I'll be waiting for you."

"Kininaskomitin, nókom," Brady said.

"Kininaskomitin, nósisim," Elder Mariah said to Brady, and then to Cole said, "Kininaskomitin, niwákómákan."

"You really think I'm your relative?" Cole asked.

"I don't think you are, I know you are," she said. "I've always thought of you that way."

"Me, too," Cole said. "And I'll take all the family I can get, you know?"

"Yes." She gave him another hug. "I know."

They set out across the field that, just a short time ago, Cole had crossed from the other direction, following an impulse that he wasn't sure that he could describe. He wasn't sure that he could describe the need in going the other way either, back the way he came. Just that it was a different kind of pull. An urgency, in coming here, to heal. An urgency, in leaving, to save others. Cole knew that there were two things he needed to do: stop Mihko and kill Reynold. All of these things coursed through Cole's mind like blood, until they were already almost through the field, and they hadn't yet spoken a word to each other. When he snapped out of it, he saw that Brady had been watching him, with a knowing grin.

"That's how I know that you're all the way better," he said.

"Yeah? Just zoning out like that? Eva would say the same thing, you know."

"You'll have to be better company," Brady said. "This is like an all-day hike, okay my friend? I don't have a podcast to listen to or anything like that."

"All day?" Cole couldn't decide whether this was more, or less, than he'd expected. He had nothing to compare it to.

"Running to get reception and back usually took me a few hours," Brady estimated. "Good exercise and everything. You know, if you're not going to talk, we could just jog now, get there faster."

"If we run, could you play some *Rocky* training montage music?"

"You know what?" Brady punched Cole's arm. "You're out of the family."

They didn't run, and, as much as possible, Cole tried to engage with Brady and not zone out. This wasn't, of course, an unpleasant thing. They hadn't seen each other in over a month, and there was a lot of catching up to do. However, Brady ended up doing most of the talking. At one point, Brady asked Cole, "So what about you?"

"I was dead, remember?" There wasn't much he could tell Brady about his month away from the community.

"Your month away from planet Earth," Brady corrected.

It felt good to be able to laugh about it now; it made Cole feel more alive, to make light of the fact that he'd been dead. Allowed him to escape from the thoughts that would inevitably follow the mention of his death. Like who had killed him and why. A cyclical thought process leading him back to zoned-out ruminations.

"It feels like another world out here, though," Brady pointed out.

"I can see that," Cole said. "It's actually kind of nice walking through Blackwood, now. I can appreciate it. Before it was like, I don't know, *doing*. You know? Like a dog chasing a car. You see the car, you just *do*."

"The dog doesn't stop and smell the sweetgrass."

"Exactly."

"Yeah," Brady took a deep breath in through his nose, "I'm going to miss it out here. Just, the simplicity of it. You're hungry, you go and catch something, or pick something. It's calm. Easy. It made it more tolerable somehow, that all the chaos was back in Wounded Sky. It's not that I didn't care, but…"

"I know what you mean," Cole said. "You couldn't go back. You needed the calm. I could use more of that calm."

"We'll be back, right? When this is over?"

"We'll be back *between* all the chaos."

"Between," Brady repeated. "What's the plan, actually?"

"You said I couldn't think, so I haven't got that far into it."

"Unfair!"

"No really, man, I don't know," Cole said. "I just have a list, I guess, of things that I…*we*…need to do. Get the people out of the clinic, stop Mihko, figure out if Reynold is dead or not, and what he has to do with all of this. It's like this puzzle that I'm trying to fit together."

"Who killed you," Brady added.

"Yeah, that too."

"Listen, if you need to think, I won't run away from you, alright? We've gone pretty far, so it's not like, you know, it'll be *hours* of silence"

"Thanks," Cole said, "but I'm not sure how much thinking will help right now. Let's just get to Wounded Sky and find a place to hole up. Then we can go down the list."

"I can hum the *Rocky* theme song for you," Brady said. "I'd do that for family, you know."

"Oh, so now I'm family again, hey?"

"Yeah, but like, a distant relative. Like a third cousin twice removed," Brady said. "Working your way up, though."

"Well that sucks," Cole said. "Everybody's a cousin up here."

They stopped for lunch when the sun was halfway through its journey across the sky, digging into the snacks Brady had prepared for them. They ate dried meat and berries and read comics together, leaning up against trees, each of them pretending that's what they were there to do, doing their best to revel in the peace before they walked into the turmoil. They traded comics, once they were done reading their own, like they used to do when they were kids. When they were finished eating and reading, they packed up and continued on their journey through the woods.

Hours later, their hike was almost over. The trees thinned out and gave way to the community, but more importantly, a guard was posted on high alert fifty yards into the forest from Wounded Sky. Cole and Brady ducked behind some bushes when they saw the guard, a rifle gripped in his hands, and scanning the area non-stop. They watched him until he looked in their direction, then they hid out of view and tried to see what they could through the foliage. There was no way around him. His head was moving constantly, surveying the entire area. Towards the community, where he was, the undergrowth wasn't thick enough for them to crawl through unseen.

"What do we do?" Brady asked.

"I'm thinking," Cole said. "I remember guards on the way out, around the clinic maybe." They'd circled around to come out of Blackwood closer to the community housing. "I got through them somehow, I just can't…"

"No brain at that point, right?"

"And I think looking like a zombie must've helped," Cole said. "Probably freaked them out or something."

"Was it really that bad?"

"It was bad enough that Elder Mariah didn't want you to see me at first."

"Yeah, that's pretty bad."

"Look," Cole found a small opening through the bush that he could see the guard clearly through. "He's pivoting around with the rifle. Point and shoot. I bet if he sees anything…"

Brady, seeing that the guard was looking away from them, riffed off what Cole had been saying, and tossed a stone. It landed against a tree far from them, sending a loud *thud* echoing through Blackwood.

The guard wheeled around and fired at the tree.

Cole and Brady watched from their hiding spot while the guard stared at the tree for several seconds. Then he went back to scanning the surroundings. Only now with even more intensity.

"Well, that backfired," Brady said.

"Nice try, though," Cole said.

"Tell me you have a better idea."

"I mean, I have *an* idea."

"Is it better than sitting behind a bush until we waste away and die?"

"If it's a terrible idea, we'll die much faster," Cole said. "Does that count?"

"I feel like if we tried to leave at this point, he'd shoot us then, too."

"You're probably right."

"Okay," Brady said, "so let's hear it."

"I'm coming out!" Brady called while giving Cole an unconvinced side-eye. This followed a rather heated exchange of shout-whispering, after Cole had laid out his plan to Brady. But the argument ended after they came to the same conclusion: it was either do it or stay where they were and hope for a miracle.

"Who's there?" the guard asked. He was staring and pointing his rifle in their general direction.

"Don't shoot, and I'll come out, okay?" Brady said. "I don't have… I'm unarmed."

"You come out slow, and you come out with your arms over your head," the guard demanded.

Brady did as directed, stood slowly with his hands up, and stepped around the bush and walked towards the guard.

"Slow like a snail, kid," the guard said. "No sudden movements."

"Buddy, I'm hardly going to move," Brady said.

As soon as Brady had the guard's full attention, Cole rolled across the ground until the guard's view of him was obstructed by a large tree. He pressed his back against the trunk to slide into a standing position, turned around, then climbed up the tree as quietly as possible, while Brady, careful step after careful step, got closer to the guard.

Cole stopped climbing when he was thirty feet off the ground, high enough that his movements wouldn't draw the interest of the guard. Brady was already halfway there. Cole worked to catch up, leaping from tree to tree, until Brady was directly below him.

"What are you doing out here?" the guard asked Brady.

"I was just out looking for medicines," Brady said, his arms stretched high into the air.

"Medicines? Isn't there a pharmacy in town?"

"No, not that kind of medicines—"

The guard didn't let Brady finish. He re-adjusted his aim. "How did you get out here?"

"I walked?"

Cole heard the guard's hammer cock.

"You couldn't have got past me, kid," the guard said. "There's no way past the perimeter."

"I mean, you can't *all* be super-efficient, can you?" Brady asked. "There's always a bad employee. Playing cards, having a smoke break…"

The guard ignored Brady. "Were you here a few nights ago? Was that you, who…" The guard took a forceful step towards Brady.

"Was that me who what?"

"Stop right there. Now!"

Brady stopped, but things were getting too heated. Cole dropped from the limb and landed behind the guard. *He did the superhero landing! I swear!* The guard swivelled around.

"That was me the other night," Cole said.

The guard pointed his muzzle at Cole, but Cole grabbed the rifle and swung the stock across the guard's chin. The guard fell, out cold.

"Cole." Brady looked up to where Cole had jumped from. "Holy moly."

Cole looked up, too. Spotted the limb he'd been squatting on, watching Brady and the guard. "Holy moly."

"And you don't have to heal from that? You didn't break anything?"

Brady and Cole kept looking at the tree, both of them dumbfounded. Cole blindly gave his body a pat down, checking for injuries. "I don't think so."

"So you're indestructible now, or…"

"I landed properly?"

"You landed properly," Brady said. "How does one land properly from that high up?"

"Well, I'm not going to demonstrate it again." Cole handed Brady the rifle. "Here. You know how to use it, right?"

Brady inspected the rifle, rotated it in his hands. "I mean, sure. It works the same as the ones I've used. A little excessive for what that guy was doing."

"Keeping people out, keeping people in," Cole mused. "Yeah, doesn't quite sound like an assault rifle kind of job."

"I think Mihko is just excessive, period."

"And Reynold."

Brady strapped the rifle over his shoulder, and they walked to the perimeter of the community. The sun had begun to fall to the west, and the northern lights, in turn, announced themselves overhead.

"Have you done more thinking, planning, that sort of thing? I did give you lots of quiet time," Brady said.

"As in, how are we going to save the community?" Cole asked.

"I thought we could start with, like you said, where we'll be staying."

Cole hesitated. He had, in fact, thought of a place to stay, but that place was not one that Cole felt Brady would be okay with. The thing was, he had to be. He couldn't see any other option. Maybe, he thought, Brady could think of someplace better.

"I've thought about that," Cole said, "and the only place that works, to me, is Ashley's."

Brady looked surprised, but Cole couldn't tell if that surprise was also anger.

"We can't go to my parents' place. We can't go to your place or Eva's. I just…"

"No," Brady said, "you're right. That's…that's where we have to go."

"You sure?" Cole asked. "I feel like I suck at making plans."

"I'm sure. It's okay. Maybe it'll be nice to be there, too. Be around his stuff. Sometimes, it's good to think about…I don't know. It's like Eva keeping that ring you made for her, right?"

"Except I'm not dead. Not really."

"You are to her."

Brady couldn't hide a look of sadness on his face. Would being at Ashley's make that sadness any better? Did the ring make Eva feel better about missing Cole? Had she thrown it away?

"I'm sorry," Cole said.

"I know."

9

TO THE BATCAVE!

COLE AND BRADY MADE THEIR WAY under the cover of the treeline to Ashley's trailer, extra cautious, expecting to see community members, as well as Mihko employees, walking around town. But Wounded Sky was a ghost town. A few guards intermittently patrolled the area, looking for what, Cole and Brady didn't know. Brady thought that, if what Eva had told him was any indication, they had their eyes out for residents trying to escape. The guards in the forest were the last line of defence.

"Maybe that's why people are going missing," Cole guessed at one point, as they hid out of sight while a guard passed. "They try to leave, get caught, and then—"

"Yeah." Brady didn't let Cole finish the thought.

From where they were hiding, Cole could see the remains of The Fish, and, for the first time, the X. Where Mihko had placed his body to burn the night he'd been murdered. The remains of both structures looked untouched since the fires. The Fish still had a partial wall up, the rest charred and skeletal. Some tables and chairs amid the debris. The X was worse. It looked like a giant fire pit. Ashes the colour of television static. Collapsed and broken wooden beams the colour of charcoal.

"We should keep moving." Brady gave Cole a nudge to kick-start him. Cole felt it, but didn't move. "You okay?"

Cole wanted to change the subject, badly. Keep moving, like Brady had said. He hadn't died there, maybe his body hadn't really been burned there, but it could have been. Somebody had to have con-firmed he'd burned to death, and thinking about that, about his body being incinerated, was too much. Thinking about fire. It didn't matter that he would've been dead already. Staring at the X felt like the mak-ings of a panic attack. It wasn't yet, but he didn't want to tempt fate.

"So," Cole said, "no cell service even this close to the centre of town?"

Brady checked. "Nothing. It's like it just got shut down entirely."

"It probably did."

"It's not about keeping us safe, this stupid quarantine."

"No," Cole said. "It's about keeping everything a secret. What they're doing to us."

"Do you think anybody would even care, if they knew?"

Cole thought about how there was no news after the murders. Thought about what the reaction would've been if there had been. "I think some people would. I'd like to think that anyway."

"But when help comes, it comes in the form of Mihko."

"True. It's about keeping everything secret, keeping us from getting help, assuming anybody would come."

"It's a moot point, anyway."

"Just would've been nice to let Eva know that we were coming," Cole said. "Give her a heads-up."

They returned to the edge of Blackwood and started walking again.

"So how do we contact her? Let her know...you're alive?" Brady asked. "Any telepathic superpower?"

"Not that I'm aware of." Choch and Jayne could hear his thoughts, but that didn't count. "Really, it's probably better to tell her in person. If breaking up with someone over text is bad, how's telling them you're alive? What emoji would you use?"

"Good point," Brady said.

"We'll have to wait until dark and go see her."

It was funny, Cole thought, that he'd not felt anxious about much since waking up in a coffin, even when waking up in the coffin. Not about facing the guards. Not about how he looked like a zombie. Of course, it was hard to feel anxious when you had no brain, he supposed. But he wasn't even anxious about coming back to a community that hated him. Not even after hearing Reynold may still be alive. Hardly thought about it when staring out over the remains of the X. But thinking about Eva, thinking about telling her that he was alive, thinking of seeing her again, even thinking about the ring, made his heart race.

"I miss her."

"I know you do." There was a pause, like Brady wasn't sure if he should say anything. "She misses you, too."

"Yeah?"

"Cole, she thinks you're dead. Of course she misses you. You're one of her oldest friends."

"She doesn't think that…"

"No, for the millionth time, she doesn't think you died the way they said."

"Somebody shot me."

"I know, you've told me that already." There was no annoyance in Brady's voice, not until he added, "And I've asked you, since we're repeating old conversations, why you went off on your own. Again."

"I didn't want—"

"I know you didn't want her to get hurt, but maybe this wouldn't have happened, if—"

"I know," Cole said. "I know. I just…I wasn't thinking straight. Everything was so bad. Everybody hated me. I found out that my dad had been killed, and because he was cheating on my mom… I—I—"

Brady hugged him.

"I'm sorry," he said. "I didn't mean to guilt you. I know what you were going through. I know it, but I can't imagine it."

Cole muffled his face into Brady's shoulder and wondered what Brady would think if he knew all of it. All the Reynold stuff, and the monster stuff along with it.

They stayed in their embrace. "I just mean that when things are that bad, we need to be closer, not farther away. We'll always be with you, okay?"

"Okay."

"And not only because it's pretty cool having a superhero as a best friend."

"I'm not a superhero." Cole scoffed at the thought.

"Not sure how you define hero, or super, but I'd say you're pretty damn close, Mr. Reckoner."

"*The* Reckoner."

"He says defensively for *not* a superhero."

They paused in the field near Ashley's trailer, the place where Cole, Brady, and Eva had spent so much time as kids and where Cole had reconciled with Eva before going to the facility with Victor. Cole saw cans on the ground around the large rocks, riddled with bullet holes.

He lined them up perfectly.

"You good?" Brady asked.

Cole adjusted one can, so all the labels were facing out, across the field. "Yeah, I'm good. Let's go."

They navigated the last bit of forested area, between the field and Ashley's trailer. The broken-down Ford Mustang, overgrown with long grass and weeds in the gravel driveway, the trailer with its new window, and new doorknob. The former broken from a gunshot that killed Ashley in front of Cole, the latter from Cole's grip when he, Eva, and Brady had come to investigate Ashley's murder. Nobody was there, and it looked like nobody had been there since Cole had come to gather Ashley's hockey equipment as protection against Reynold.

"Well," Brady walked up the stairs to the front door, "here's your Batcave."

Cole, several steps behind, shook his head with a smile. "Right." He stopped beside the car. He looked it over, in its sad state of disrepair. There was something reassuring about it being the way it had always been since they were children, how it held good memories. Just like the field. Even the memory of Wayne finding them in the field and giving them shit was a good one, the kind of trouble kids got into. Just normal kids. Kids who'd yet to experience the horror of losing their classmates, teachers, parents.

"Think we could fix this up, get it running?"

Brady was standing in front of the door, hand on the handle. "Why?"

"Just, I don't know. Wouldn't it be nice? Drive it around, like we pretended to do. Remember?"

"Yeah, I remember. We used to take turns at the wheel, make believe we were cruising around Wounded Sky—"

"And farther."

Brady joined Cole in front of the Mustang. "Well, maybe we should, you know?"

Cole tried to brush it off. "Yeah, with all the other stuff we have to do?"

"Come on. We can't save the community every second of every day." Brady gave the car a kick, testing its sturdiness. "There has to be some time for automotive repairs."

"Really?" Cole put his foot on the bumper and leaned against his knee.

"Then you could cruise out of here, but on your own terms."

Cole liked the sound of that. Leaving, coming back. On his own terms. Then, the bumper broke off, and he fell against the hood. Brady helped him to his feet.

"A lot of work to do, though."

"Maybe not if we do it together."

Cole gave a pat to the hood, then dusted off his clothes, only slightly embarrassed. "You're going to get sick of me, if we do everything together."

"It's like I told you." Brady pulled Cole towards the trailer. "As long as you're not relying on me to do your laundry and make you meals and cheer you up and—"

"Okay, I get it." Cole gave Brady a playful shove. "It's not like that anymore, anyway," he said, turning serious. "I'm focused. I know what I have to do."

"You don't even have a plan!"

"I don't have a plan, but I know the goal."

Brady sized him up. "You do seem different. It's in your eyes."

Cole put his hand around the doorknob. Unlocked. No door-knob-crushing needed here. He turned the knob and pushed open the door. They stepped inside. It smelled dusty and stale. And whenever Cole came here, it felt too quiet. Not eerily quiet, just that it needed to have Ashley in it.

"How's the pill thing going? Okay? Has that changed?" Brady sat down on the futon and pulled out a comic. Flipped through it, but didn't really read it.

"I don't think the anxiety died with me." Cole sat down beside Brady. "But I don't think I'll need those pills again, either. I don't know if I've really thought about them since…"

"Why not?" Brady exchanged one comic with another on the coffee table.

Cole took the one Brady had discarded. "It's just, I'm thinking differently I guess. Like, it'll always be there, but I'm not going to let it control me. *I'm* going to control things. I'm driving…"

"*Cruising.*"

"Yeah," Cole said. "I can't get away from it, but it'll be in the passenger seat." He flipped through the comic book Brady had put down, *The Fury of Firestorm* #1. Stopped at a scene where a Native American man, John Ravenhair, broke into a museum and stole a buffalo headpiece and a staff. John Ravenhair became a villain known as Black Bison. "Look at this," Cole showed Brady the scene. "He declares vengeance on people who stole his heritage."

"Oh, right," Brady said, "and he re-animates stuffed animals and is able to command them."

"See, speaking of superheroes—"

"Or villains."

"—right. Let's make sure that I don't, well—ignoring the argument about me actually being a superhero—let's make sure I don't, you know, start throwing dream catcher ninja stars…"

"Or use your talking stick to get people to tell the truth."

"Or summon Thunderbird with my medicine pouch." Cole tossed the comic book onto the coffee table. "Collector's item, though."

"A real relic from the past, right?"

"I do need one thing. I mean, as a non-stereotypical Indigenous superhero…"

"Not named Black Bison or Chief Running Cloud or Shaman or…"

"Right."

"And that would be?" Brady put down the comic he'd been looking through, *Elf Quest*, on top of *The Fury of Firestorm*. He gave Cole his full attention.

"It's time to put a team together."

10

THE BLOODHOUND GANG

"OKAY, WHO IS GOING TO BE ON THIS TEAM?" BRADY ASKED.

The team needed to be small, but effective. Everybody needed a purpose and needed to be trustworthy. It was going to be a short list, Cole admitted to himself. How many people in the community were actually on his side? He probably could count them on one hand. Still, he thought it would help if he wrote down names. Ashley's school supplies were on his desk, untouched since his death. A cup full of pencils and pens, a binder, a couple of textbooks.

"Is it okay if I borrow some paper and something to write with?" Cole wasn't willing to just start using Ashley's things without asking, especially after losing his hockey equipment at the facility the night he, Cole, had been killed.

"Yeah," Brady said, "of course. Thanks for asking."

"Sure."

Cole got a pencil from the cup and a clean sheet of paper from Ashley's binder, then rejoined Brady on the futon. He spread the paper out on the coffee table and wrote TEAM at the top. He drew a line under the word, made a column on the left side, and wrote the number '1'. He wrote *Eva* beside that number.

"Obviously," Cole said.

"We could just stop at her," Brady said. "We've come this far together."

"We have," Cole said, "but for what we have to do, we're going to need allies."

"Like?"

Cole thought for a second, and then wrote: *2. Dr. Captain.* "People are still at the clinic, and we're going to break them out. She'll need to be out there to help your kókom."

"Especially if some of those missing people are actually there, too."

"Right." Cole breathed. In for five. Out for seven. "What would they be doing with them there, though? What's Mr. Kirkness still doing there? Why can't anybody go in? Come out?"

"I don't even want to think about it," Brady said. "I just picture my kókom the way she was…"

"I know." Cole gave Brady a pat on the knee. "But she got better, right? And we'll need to get the others better, too."

"Right. Who's next?"

Cole wrote *Lauren* next, beside number 3. As soon as he did, as soon as he'd finished writing the letter *n*, Jayne appeared and started to jump all around the place, burning hot. Excited. She chanted, "Lauren's on the teeee-eem, Lauren's on the teeee-eem!" over and over.

Brady went to the window and opened it. On the way back to the futon, he remarked, "It's so hot all of a sudden. Do you feel hot all of a sudden? I think I'm having hot flashes."

Cole stifled a laugh.

"You're too young, and possibly the wrong gender, to have those." Cole shot Jayne a look to calm down, so she wouldn't burn so hot. "I'm feeling hot, too. So don't worry."

"Phew."

"Aren't I the one who worries about things?"

"Maybe you're rubbing off on me." Brady winked at Cole. "So why Lauren?"

"That's my sister! Yay!"

"Because she likes me." Cole was trying his best to ignore Jayne. "And she's one of the only people who doesn't think I murdered people, burned buildings down, all of that. *And* she's a cop."

"Alright, fair enough. Lauren it is." Brady checked over the names.

"She's on the team?" Jayne looked at Cole hopefully.

Cole nodded, and Jayne burst into flames again.

"This is getting to be a pretty big team, my friend." Brady pulled his shirt away from his sweaty body. "I thought you wanted to keep the fact that you're not dead a secret and everything."

Cole wiped sweat away from his brow. It was dripping into his eyes, and they stung. "It *is* hot in here."

Brady had taken a comic book and was fanning himself. When he wasn't looking, Cole made a shooing motion to Jayne. Jayne stomped her foot and crossed her arms.

"I'm just happy, you know that?"

Cole mouthed *please* to Jayne, and showed her the sweat on his forearms.

"Sorry!" Jayne's fire doused within seconds and returned to a low burn.

"Okay, now it's *cool.* Are you sure I'm not—"

"Yes, I'm sure." Cole looked at Jayne and sternly jerked his head at the door and repeated this twice before she shouted, "Fine!" and disappeared into a cloud of black smoke.

Cole wiped at his face again. "Who else…"

Brady took the pencil from Cole, wrote the number 4, and another name: *Tristan.*

"Are you kidding me?" Cole took the pencil from Brady.

"Do I look like I'm kidding?"

"Actually yes, you kind of do."

"Okay maybe I was at first, but come on, you can see the benefits, right?"

"The team is supposed to save the community, not beat the shit out of me."

"He only wanted to do that because he thought you killed Maggie," Brady said.

"And what do people think about me at this very moment?" Cole asked.

"Point taken, but he's actually kind of reasonable."

"Actually, kind of..." Cole pulled up his hood and aggressively wiped the sweat away from his face.

"If we need muscle, he's pretty darn strong."

"I'm the muscle, Brady! Hello?"

"Can you ever have too much muscle?" Brady got up and opened the front door and the window all the way. The room became cold fast, but neither of them complained.

"No, okay? No." Cole erased Tristan's name so hard that it ripped the paper. Under the ripped area of paper, he wrote *Pam*. "Now, if you think that Tristan would be a better teammate than Pam, I'm all ears."

"Oh." Brady took the pencil from Cole's hand, gently this time, and placed it on the table. "She can't..."

"You actually don't think he'd be a better teammate than Pam?"

Brady fidgeted, like he was sitting on something sharp. "It's not that."

"What's up with you?" Cole asked, but thought he knew. He'd lamented the problem of liking two girls the night he went for dinner with Pam, ignoring the fact that Brady lost his boyfriend. Cole had acted selfish, and Brady rightfully called him on it. To make matters worse, he'd not told Eva about the dinner with Pam. Brady clearly didn't want that drama around.

"Look," Cole said, "I know Eva's with Michael, and I'm not going to make it a thing, okay?"

"Eva's *not* with Michael."

"What really?" Cole sounded too excited. Cleared his throat. "Really?" More calm. Better. Also too late.

"Really. So over."

"Okay, well," Cole tried to gather himself, "Pam and I aren't a thing. We're just friends. And she's just really good with computers, and there's this, like, keypad in the basement of the facility that I think she'd be good for. Plus, if we have to, you know, hack our way into places, and—"

"She's missing, Cole."

"She's what?"

"She's one of the people who's gone missing."

"And you didn't think to…" Cole got up to pace back and forth, from one end of Ashley's trailer to the other. He stopped in the middle of the trailer, and squatted, facing Brady. His face was pleading. "Why didn't you tell me?"

"I didn't know how," Brady said. "Sorry, I know I tell you to be honest. I'm a hypocrite."

"Okay." Cole stood up and started pacing again, thinking about something else now, another piece of the puzzle: how to find her. "Okay, okay…she's got to be at the clinic, right?"

"Where else would they go? I mean, it's a wild guess, but really, where?"

"The RCMP detachment?" Cole took a shot in the dark. A hopeful shot. At least there, Pam would be safe. "Got caught after curfew, locked up for it…"

"No, too many people have gone missing," Brady said, "and there's like, *one* cell there. Plus Lauren wouldn't go for that. Ever."

"Yeah, you're right," Cole agreed. "Alright, how many people have gone missing?"

"Eva thought, like, around eight or something?"

"*Eight?*"

"I think there's thirteen people at the clinic still."

"They *have* to be there, then. There or the facility. That's the only places they could be. Eight people? The community hall?"

"No, you can't go in there, but you can *see* in there."

"If she's at the clinic, I can do something about it," Cole said. "We already broke in, right? I'll just have to do it again. We broke into the clinic. I broke into the facility."

Cole went for the door.

"I thought we were putting this team together to break people out of there."

"We are," Cole said. "I just…I have to know if that's where Pam is too. If she's not, we'll have two places we need to go."

"I'll come with." Brady got up, went to the door.

Cole shook his head.

"Are you serious? Cole, I literally told you that we have to do this stuff together."

"Just wait for me, alright? We don't know what security's going to be like, and I can get in on my own way easier."

"So I'll just slow you down."

"If I go first like this, alone, the team will know how to get in when we all go. *Together*. Please, Brady."

11

RECON

THE EARLY EVENING WAS DARK enough to hide him, so Cole took the most direct route to the clinic. His neck warmer was pulled over his mouth and his hood was up. Even concerned for Pam, Cole allowed himself to appreciate being here, especially now, when the night gave the impression that the community wasn't in chaos. Whether most of Wounded Sky still hated him or not, he did not hate them.

"Are you sure you just aren't glad to be alive?" Choch asked, now walking beside Cole.

"Maybe," Cole said. "But, you know, it's still home here, whatever's happened."

"It has rather grown on me, too," said Choch. "I'll give it that. I suppose you don't really appreciate the charm of Wounded Sky, unless you live in Wounded Sky."

"I suppose not."

"And I will say," Choch said, "you just never know what people think of you, either. It's been a month, CB."

"Brady says there's always a bunch of graffiti on my headstone."

"That Eva has cleaned off..." Choch cleared his throat. "Repeatedly."

"It doesn't matter. When I'm done, people will know the truth. I just have to stay focused."

Choch slapped him on the back. "I've missed our walks, you know? I mean, they're not entirely the same, but I've missed them still."

"Whatever did you do with yourself while I was gone, and you had nobody to annoy?"

"Oh, I kept busy. Old projects, new projects." Choch removed his hand from Cole's back. "There's only one CB, however. I'll tell you that."

"What other projects do you have? Are you just out annoying people while getting them to save the world?"

"Hey, Charlie!" A couple walking opposite them, back towards the centre of the community, stopped and waved at Choch.

Choch peered out into the dark, then snapped his fingers. "That you, Bill?"

"Darn straight that's me!"

"Bill Robinson, whaddya know!" Choch dragged Cole over to the couple. Cole followed reluctantly, but kept his head down. Choch shook hands with Bill, and tipped his fedora at the woman Bill was with. "Franny."

"What brings you out this late? You're going to hit the curfew, aren't you?" Bill asked.

Choch gave Cole a playful squeeze on the arm. "I'm just showing my nephew here the community."

"How'd he get here?" Bill asked.

"Oh, that's right. Silly me." Choch waved his hand in front of Franny and Bill's faces while saying, "Justin's always lived here. He's just ugly and likes to cover his face."

"Hey," Cole said. "Is that necessary?"

"Well you *were* ugly, so…"

"What brings you and Justin out this late? You're going to hit the curfew, aren't you?" Bill asked, having been reset a few seconds by Choch.

"Oh, Justin only likes to come out at night because…" Choch nodded at Cole with a twisted face, indicating his pretend ugliness, Cole supposed. "You know."

Franny touched him on the arm. "If it's any consolation, I think you're a fine-looking young man."

"That's because she's married to me, right Charlie?" Bill guffawed.

Choch joined in. "Hey-oooooo!" Choch said through the laughter. "You *are* one ugly sunnuvabitch, Bill Robinson!"

"Lucky Franny don't see good, eh?" Bill said.

"Now, Bill, it's the inside that counts." Choch's laughter died down and he wiped tears from his eyes. "But all the same, maybe Justin can let you know where he got that neck warmer! Pro tip!"

"Can we…" Cole motioned to the clinic.

"Settle down, Justin, settle down." Choch collected himself. "Well, we best be off, curfew and all." He shook Bill's hand again, and this time, kissed Franny's hand. "You're a saint, dear."

"We'll be by the mall tomorrow to pick up some things. See you there, Charlie?" Bill asked.

"Don't you come around causing trouble now, Bill." Choch pointed a finger gun at Bill.

Bill mockingly grabbed his heart, as though he'd been shot.

Choch and Cole, Franny and Bill, went their separate ways. Choch shook his head with a smile. "That Bill…"

"Charlie," Cole stated. "Charlie Chochinov."

"Charlie Chochinov," Choch repeated proudly, straightening his fedora. The fedora didn't match the rest of the spirit being's outfit: jeans, an orange windbreaker, bright white sneakers.

"Charlie Chochinov dresses like a middle-aged guy whose best years were in college," Cole said.

"Well, Justin Johnson's ugly." Choch pointed duck lips to the air.

"JJ's a cool name, C-H C-H is not."

"JJ *is* a cool name," Choch lamented.

"So, what do you do? Bag groceries? Work at the post office?" Cole wondered.

"Mall cop." Choch's eyes brightened.

"That's actually…" Cole glanced at Choch. "I should've guessed that."

"Since the dawn of time," Choch said. "I mean, you clearly aren't going back to school, and there's no Fish to work at, so I had to work somewhere."

"Yes, because you need the income."

"Ear to the ground, CB. Ear to the ground."

"You wear aviator sunglasses don't you?"

"Wouldn't you?"

"Probably," Cole conceded.

"They'd be a great finishing touch for the little costume you've pulled together, wouldn't they? Neck warmers with skeleton faces on them, all that jazz."

"I have to cover up the ugly, don't I?"

The clinic loomed in the distance. Cole could already see a guard at the front door, just as there was before, and one at the side of the building. He hoped that, just like the last time he'd been there, a guard would not be inside. He thought of ways he could get in without being seen, still wanting the element of surprise.

"You know, I usually don't do this, but I could give you a better costume, if you wanted." Choch pulled at the sleeve of Cole's hoodie. "I mean, Spider-Man, Superman, Firestorm, they all have those amazing little costumes. Bright, you know? They scream: superhero."

"No thanks," Cole said. "I'm not going to announce my presence by wearing bright tights."

"Alright, *suit* yourself," Choch said with a smirk, delighted with himself. Cole ignored the pun. The spirit being continued. "I guess this does help you get around in the dark, but what about a name like Sneaky Man?"

"Oh, God…"

"Or Dark Man!" Choch snapped fingers. "Yeah! The Reckoner is… such a mouthful."

"*Dark Man* was an awesome movie by Sam Raimi."

"Oh, right. Copyright infringement and whatnot."

"I'm good, Choch. Really. Costume, name."

They only made it another three steps before Choch asked, "So aren't you gonna ask me why I'm here? Get mad at me? Tell me to GTFO, as you once put it?"

"Nope," Cole said. "I figure you're keeping tabs. 'Ear to the ground,' right?"

"You know what, CB? I didn't miss you at all!" Choch then disappeared.

"God, if I only knew how to deal with you earlier," Cole said to the absent spirit being.

Cole crouched where he, Eva, and Brady had hid the night they broke into the clinic to save Elder Mariah. That night, they'd tried to reason with Mark to let them in. Cole had ended up summoning Jayne to start a fire, which distracted Mark long enough for them to sneak past him. That strategy wasn't in the playbook tonight. A guard was still stationed at the front door—maybe Mark, Cole wasn't sure—but the garbage can hadn't been replaced. Nothing to set on fire. And if it was Mark, he'd know the gig anyway. He could walk up to Mark and knock him out—just as he'd done upon leaving the clinic with Elder Mariah. Cole would get in, and Mark, or whoever was at the door, wouldn't know it was Cole. His identity would be protected, but Mihko would know somebody had broken in.

"So what, then?" Cole whispered to himself, scanning the clinic, front to back, bottom to top, thinking of something, anything.

He just wanted to find Pam.

He kept looking at the roof of the clinic, two storeys up. Was it any higher than the electric fence he'd jumped over at the facility, when he'd encountered Reynold?

"Maybe a bit," Cole whispered again. "Twenty feet, give or take?" He measured this in basketball hoops. He figured two hoops, stacked one on top of the other, looked about right.

Are you talking to me or…? Choch asked in Cole's head.

No, I just assume you're listening anyway.

Because I could come back, if you—

Nope, I'm good, thanks.

Cole figured he could make the jump. He had cleared the fence at the facility with room to spare. If he could get a running start, no problem. But the only way to do that would be to run straight through the open, across the field. If he did that, he'd be seen. The clinic didn't have a back door. There might not be a guard, but there was no space for him to build enough momentum to jump onto the roof. Same went for the side door. Cole was agile, but not that agile.

Typical Blackwood trees surrounded the clinic: tall, thick, strong. They covered the clinic almost protectively with branches that hung conveniently over the roof, as though to say: *Come on Cole, try it.*

"Breaking door handles and climbing trees," Cole said. "Why'd I think anything different?"

Cole made his way to the back of the clinic under the cover of Blackwood Forest. As he'd hoped, there were no guards there. He hid behind a tree for a few minutes, waiting to see if a guard was patrolling the exterior of the building. When nobody came around, he stepped out into the open. He supposed there'd be no reason to have a guard patrol the back of the clinic. Mihko might have had an idea what Cole could do—they'd covered up Cole's failed break-in at the facility the night he'd encountered the creature—but to them and everybody else, Cole Harper was dead.

Cole found a particularly thick tree with branches stretching over the roof. He scaled it and walked the branch like a tightrope until it was safe to drop down onto the roof. He landed and rolled, like he'd seen in countless movies. It kind of worked. He waited to make sure that nobody had heard him, frozen as though by one of Choch's tricks.

"Now what?" Cole did a quick survey of the roof. It was flat, with some ventilation sticking out in one spot. No easy access inside the clinic. No door that conveniently led up to the roof from the second floor. "For once, I wish Choch was right about this being a story," Cole said *to himself.* He walked over to the side of the clinic with no door and no guard. The windows to the second-floor rooms were reachable, but getting into them wasn't going to be easy. Cole pictured himself falling to the ground and having to retreat to Ashley's trailer on a broken leg. He could handle a broken leg. He'd be able to walk on it by the morning. His arm had healed fast when Tristan had broken it, and he was healing even faster now. But what if somebody heard? How would he outrun guards on one leg? He didn't heal *that* fast.

Pam is worth the risk, he thought. He held tightly to the edge of the building and lowered himself down the side. The tip of his toes brushed a window ledge. He took a deep breath and let go. His feet landed on the ledge, but one foot slipped and he lost his balance. At the last minute, three fingers caught on the ledge. Cole swung his other hand up beside it, secured his grip, and pulled himself up and to his feet.

The room was dark, but somebody was inside. Lying on the bed, motionless. Sleeping. How sick were they? Was Pam sick? What if that was Pam? Cole slid open the window, and climbed inside the room. Whoever it was, they were attached to a monitor and an IV drip.

"Hey," Cole whispered.

No movement. He walked to the bed and found a man there. Unconscious. Pale. Gaunt.

"Hey," Cole whispered again and nudged the man's shoulder. "Wait a minute." He leaned in closer, and, as his eyes adjusted to the dark, he recognized who it was. "Mr. Kirkness."

Cole shook his head. "What did they do to you?"

Scott, the murderer, had shot Wayne in the stomach, but last time Cole saw Wayne, he was doing better. Healing. Looking good. Now, he was unresponsive.

Cole tried to wake him. Repeated his name, but not so loud as to bring anyone into the room. Cole shook Wayne gently, but not so hard as to break him. He looked like he could crumble into dust and blow away. As Cole's eyes adjusted to the dark room, he could see Wayne more clearly. He found it hard to separate how Wayne looked now from how Elder Mariah had looked when they'd rescued her from this very place. The only difference, maybe, was that she'd gotten sick from the virus and had been admitted. Wayne had been here for another reason entirely, so how did he get sick? From others here? Was it airborne?

"Everything's a fog," Brady had said to Cole, when Cole asked what Elder Mariah knew about her sickness, about getting better, then bad once more. "She remembers when you cured her, but then over the next while, she got weaker and weaker, and then...nothing. It's all a blank."

Elder Maria had only known that she needed to get out of Wounded Sky, and Brady and his parents needed to come with her. She wouldn't say how she knew, and maybe she really didn't know.

Cole put his hand on top of Wayne's head, leaned in, and whispered, "I'll come back for you, I promise."

A promise to Wayne. A promise to Eva.

Every patient Cole found was in a state similar to Wayne. Sick, hooked up to tubes and heart monitors, wasting away in a hospital bed. It was unnatural.

He needed Dr. Captain.

The first floor was more of the same, although there, Cole entered rooms not just to check on patients, but also to hide from two nurses and a doctor, as well as a security guard. In the room he was in now, there was yet another sick patient. He checked to see if this patient was as sick as the others (he was). Cole heard the doorknob start to turn. He raced to the door and clamped his hand around the knob to keep it from turning.

"What the…" The nurse tried again, but couldn't budge the handle. "Somebody lock this thing?"

The nurse muttered about finding a key, and Cole listened while their footsteps receded down the hallway. When he couldn't hear them anymore, he opened the door, and walked to the next door just as a guard turned the corner.

Cole lunged for the door, opened it, and got inside as fast as possible. He put his back against the door and listened for the footsteps. They approached, stopped outside of the door, paused there for an agonizingly long time, and then kept moving.

Only then did Cole look around the room. In the moonlight streaming in through the window, he could see the patient.

Pam.

Cole rushed over to find her unconscious. Drained of life. He put his hand on her cheek to feel her cold, clammy skin. Checked for a pulse because he didn't believe what the heart monitor told him: she was alive.

"Pam," he said, "Pam," hoping that somehow, she'd wake up. She didn't.

He forgot about listening for guards, forgot about everything but Pam. He pulled up a chair and sat at her bedside, held her hand. He stayed there longer than he should have, praying for her to wake up, to be healthy. He knew he should have protected her from this, but didn't because he'd let his guard down a month ago. He'd found his dad's body and didn't see the person dressed in the hazmat suit until it was too late. He didn't act, just felt the bullet enter his forehead.

"Think," Cole said to himself.

He wanted to take her with him, now. He went to the window and looked out. The guard at the front door was to the left. They'd see Cole leave with her in his arms if he tried to get her out the window. The guard or one of the Mihko staff in the clinic would see them in the hallways, and even if by some miracle they didn't, she was too frail to leave the way he'd come. There was no way. He took her chart from the foot of her bed. He would give it to Dr. Captain.

"I'll come back for you," he said. He would come back for everybody.

He tucked the chart under his shirt and snuck back up to the roof. There, he pulled out the chart and read what he could under the moonlight, under the northern lights he'd called home for a short time. But not much of it made any sense to him, other than the fact that it had been filled out by Dr. Ament—her signature was on the chart—and there was information about Pam. Her name, height, weight, age, parents, cultural background. Cree. A box at the bottom of the paper had a note on it, filled out by Dr. Ament. The same handwriting as her signature. Pam's date of transfer. To where? Cole had one guess. The research facility.

He read the date over and over, before looking up to the northern lights, and whispered, "Two days."

He had to move fast.

12

VISITATIONS

DR. CAPTAIN'S PLACE WAS BETWEEN THE clinic and Ashley's trailer. Cole had stayed in the Blackwood Forest since jumping off the roof of the clinic, managing to make a clean getaway. The only evidence of his visit was Pam's missing chart. The medical information was now stuffed underneath Cole's hoodie, ready to be handed over to Dr. Captain to decipher. He left the woods and found the path that led to Dr. Captain's place. Cole felt bad that he'd been gone so long. Brady was probably worried about him, but with only two days left until Pam would be "transferred," and with Wayne looking so sick, he needed to be efficient.

Another set of footsteps joined Cole on the path to Dr. Captain's place, echoing in his mind. He looked to the left, to picture sneakers step-in-step with his. The last time he had seen Alex, they'd been walking from the cemetery, hand-in-hand. He'd found her there, standing in front of the rounded white headstones in neat little rows. Teachers, classmates. His mom. Her dad. She told him she went there often, on walks. She felt guilty because she didn't want her dad to go to the school that night. She wanted him to stay home with her. Told him that she didn't want him to come back. Ever. Then he didn't, dying along with everybody else in the fire. Cole wondered if the guilt she'd felt then, as a child just wanting her dad to stay home with her, was something like the guilt he felt. After their walk, after bringing her right to her front door, after she'd kissed him on the cheek goodnight, she had been killed by Scott. Why? Cole still didn't know, other than she'd been in the files, too. And Scott wasn't around to ask anymore; at least, he hadn't been in any of the rooms Cole had checked.

He liked imagining her footsteps, pretending she was there with him. He looked up from her sneakers to her. She seemed so real that he thought Choch was playing a trick on him. He could even see her breath in the air, like puffs of cigarette smoke. She glanced at him, and they made eye contact.

"I'm so sorry."

"Stop being a whiney bitch."

Alex, being Alex.

She took his hand, and he could feel her fingers tangled up with his. When they'd walked together before, it was her hand in his. Stop being a whiney bitch. Cole stifled a laugh. Imagining her here, now, made him realize just how much like Pam she was.

"Is that why you're here now?" he asked.

"Come on, dude," she said. "You're feeling guilty enough as it is. What do I look like?"

"No, not like that. I mean…"

"Pam's right, though," she said. "It's incredibly, freakishly easy to mess with you."

Cole listened to their footsteps, soles against gravel.

"She's dying," he said.

"I know."

"Am I dreaming you're here to, I don't know, motivate me or something?"

"I *am* dreamy," she said, "but I'm guessing that's not why. Motivate you how, exactly?"

"To save Pam because I couldn't save you?"

"Harper, that's still whining," she said. "I thought you were all superhero mode now, kicking names and taking ass."

They stopped at Dr. Captain's door, right where they had stopped a month and a bit ago. He had let her go inside, and he left, and soon after she got shot. The saliva from her lips had still been wet on his cheek.

"Stop it!" she laughed, and two-hand pushed him in the chest. "Jeee-zus."

Cole stepped back, and then steadied himself. "You're not really here. You're…" he looked skyward, at the northern lights. "…up there, where I was. I remember you…" Cole closed his eyes and pictured it up there, closed his eyes tight, trying to recall everything he could. There were ribbons of light. Dancing.

"I don't dance," she said.

"That has to be why you're here. I'm trying to motivate myself. Right?"

"You tell me."

"That's why you're here."

She let go of his hand, and they stood there, face to face, looking at each other warmly.

"It's not so bad, you know," she said. "I'm with my dad again. There's music. I like music. I love a good beat. Dancing," she shrugged, "I'll get used to it."

"I don't remember much about it. I try to remember more, but I can't," he said. "It's like this…dream."

"Well, don't rush back, okay? You've got work to do." She pushed some hair behind her ear. She looked up, like she needed to get back. Like she was really here, but belonged somewhere else.

"Did we dance up there?" he asked. "When I was there? Am I crazy to think that?"

"Please, Harper." Alex rolled her eyes. "I don't kiss and tell."

"Who's out here?" The front door swung open. Michael was there and Alex was gone. Cole scrambled to lift the neck warmer over his mouth.

Cole's heart raced. He wondered if Michael had seen him. He wondered if Michael was one of the many who hated him now because of the lies that had been spread. Or if Michael hated him because it actually *was* Michael who threw the rock through Eva's window, interrupting Cole's near-kiss with her.

He wanted to run.

"Nobody." *Brilliant answer, Cole. Nobody. Well done*, he cursed himself.

Michael looked confused. "Who are you?" He peered through the dark.

Cole stepped out of the light that had been cast from inside the house, through the doorframe. He tried to pull his neck warmer up higher. What had Choch called him? Who had Choch created for that couple they'd encountered? Franny and Bill. "Justin?"

"You don't sound too sure about that."

"Yeah, I am."

"Justin Johnson." Michael looked surprised that the name had come from his mouth.

"JJ." Cole tried to sound more confident with the lie.

Michael hesitated for moment, and then his eyes lit up, like he'd just had an epiphany. "Are you sick or something?"

"Uhh, yeah."

Michael checked his phone for the time. "How sick are you, that you'd risk being out after curfew?"

"Got some kind of a flu. Puking all night." Cole kept trying to make his voice deeper, so that Michael wouldn't recognize it as his.

"Mom doesn't see people this late, JJ. Everybody knows that. A, it's curfew, and B, you're going to tip off Mihko that she's doing this, and then where will people go? We're trying to help." Michael went to shut the door. "Come back tomorrow."

Cole put his scarred palm against it. Michael looked startled. "What are you doing?" He tried to push the door closed, but Cole wouldn't let him.

"There's no time." Cole almost lowered his neck warmer, to show Michael who he really was, but didn't. "Please."

"You're not going to die overnight."

"People did a month ago, Mike."

"That flu's gone. You know that. Just…"

"Please."

Michael looked Cole—JJ—over carefully, like he was a doctor too, and could assess the urgency. But then he relented. Another sigh. "Just hang on a sec, okay?" He left the door open and disappeared down a hallway.

Cole listened.

"Mom," Michael said. "JJ's here to see you. Says he's got the flu or something."

"JJ?" Dr. Captain sounded confused.

"Justin? From school. Justin Johnson?"

"I don't know any JJ."

Cole heard Dr. Captain's footsteps. She walked across a room, then down the hallway and to the front door. Whatever reality Choch had pushed into Michael's mind, he hadn't done the same for Dr. Captain. She tilted her head as though to get a look at Cole from a different angle. But what could she see? His hood was up, neck warmer on, eyes probably covered in shadows.

"I'm sorry." She wrapped her robe around her body from the cold coming into the house. "Justin?"

"JJ," Cole stated, only because Michael was standing behind her, watching protectively. Cole understood that. He'd lost his sister, right in this house. All he had left was his mom.

Dr. Captain's eyebrows furrowed. "JJ," she repeated to herself.

"*JJ*. You feeling okay, Mom?" Michael stepped closer to Cole and Dr. Captain. "He's been in school with us since we were kids."

Cole faked a heavy cough to sell the fact that he was sick, just to get himself inside the door. "Honestly, this won't take long, Dr. Captain. I just need something to help me sleep maybe."

"Store's all wiped out, right?" Michael said.

"Yeah, man," Cole said. "Like, just try to find Advil, or NyQuil never mind."

"Justin," Dr. Captain said more confidently, as though trying to convince herself. She stepped to the side, leaving the doorway clear for Cole to enter the house. "Come in."

"Thanks." Another cough, and then Cole entered the house, trying not to think about where Alex had been shot. *Don't be a whiney bitch*, he imagined her telling him. He followed Dr. Captain, but paused, and turned to Michael.

"It's good to see you, Mike."

Confusion rested across Michael's face as though Choch had taken back the 'JJ' plant from his mind.

"Yeah, you, too." The three words were said deliberately.

Cole and Dr. Captain ended up in Dr. Captain's makeshift "office," which Cole quickly recognized as Alex's bedroom. Pieces of furniture were missing, like Alex's bed, her dresser. But posters of her favourite bands and favourite movies remained, along with an old record player with a collection of records, some matching the posters. Arctic Monkeys. Bob Dylan. Simon & Garfunkel. Temple of the Dog. Traveling Wilburys. Books that she'd read. *Nine Stories. In Our Time. Tom's Midnight Garden. Olive Kitteridge.* These things were the stuff of Alex, the stuff that Dr. Captain wouldn't, couldn't, remove.

It was at once the coolest, and saddest, doctor's office Cole had ever been in. A far cry from the office he had visited regularly in the city: his therapist's. Her office had cream walls, a big corner desk unit, small circular table in the middle, two chairs on either side of the table, and an air conditioner that always drowned out her voice. Especially when he didn't want to hear what she had to say. Dr. Captain had replaced the bed and dresser with a poker table and two chairs. She sat on one, Cole sat on the other.

"So, *JJ*," she said, "what can I do for you?"

Cole had the files under his hoodie, but didn't want to take them out yet. He'd left the clinic to see her, and had pictured himself handing them over to her, but hadn't considered until now the whole telling-Dr.-Captain-you're-not-dead thing. So he didn't respond.

"I know my son never went to school with a Justin, and I don't know why he's convinced of it, unless…"

Cole waited for her to continue.

"If you're nervous about coming here, if it's something serious my son's helping you out with, it's confidential," she said. "I know this isn't an actual hospital, but I'm still a doctor. It's private."

"Doctor-patient confidentiality." Cole was still lowering his voice to disguise it. Sounded like he had a cold. Appropriate.

"That's right," she said. "So if it's, you know, *sex*-related, if it's that you're feeling depressed, if it's that you hurt your thumb in shop class, it's okay. You don't have to hide your face here, alright?"

"Alright." Cole wanted her to see Pam's file, to tell him if she was going to be okay or how urgently Pam and the others needed to be out of there, not transferred to wherever Mihko planned to take her. It couldn't be anywhere good. "Just, don't scream." He pulled down his neck warmer slowly, as though this might lessen the shock.

She gasped and almost fell off her chair when she saw his face. She cupped her mouth and shook her head back and forth repeatedly.

"Hi, Dr. Captain."

"Cole." She was barely audible. A whisper of a whisper. She was crying, too. She took her hand away from her mouth. "How…"

"Long story?" He grimaced. While he knew in coming here he'd have to *show* her that he was alive, he hadn't gotten to the part where he told her *how* he was alive. He was drawing a blank.

After uttering those two very unconfident words to Dr. Captain, he didn't follow up until Dr. Captain, staring at him like she was seeing a ghost, repeated, "How?"

"I guess, if you're wondering *how* I came back to life," this was Cole, winging it, "I would say to you, in response," *think Cole, think you stupid idiot,* "that I was never actually really dead in the first place?" *Perfect, end it like you're asking a question. Slow clap.*

"But you *were* dead," Dr. Captain said. "You died in the fire. I saw the autopsy report Mihko did."

"But did you see a body?" *Please don't say that you saw a body.*

"Well, no, but…"

"Dr. Captain," Cole started, newly confident because she'd not seen his body, which meant that anything could be true. He went over a million movie plots. "There's a lot I can't tell you, but I guess, if Mihko would go to that much trouble to make it look like I died, you know it's bad."

"But why fake your death?"

"There's stuff that's happening over there that they don't want anybody to know about, and there are some things I found out, the night I…" Cole caught himself from saying *the night I died*. "They caught me in the facility, held me hostage. I've been locked up for a month. I broke out a few days ago. I've been laying low," he pulled at his neck warmer to demonstrate how he'd managed to lay low, "until now."

"Okay." Dr. Captain was taking some deep breaths that Cole could totally relate to. "Okay, you weren't dead. This isn't crazy…so…what kind of stuff did you find out?"

"I was hoping you'd ask." Cole took Pam's chart out of his hoodie and handed it to Dr. Captain.

Cole watched her eyes as she glanced back and forth from the chart to him. Eventually, her eyes stayed on the chart. When she finished, she placed the chart on her lap and turned to Cole.

"And this is Pam's?"

"Yeah, I just went to the clinic and took it."

"You just…walked into the clinic and took it?"

"I didn't exactly walk."

Dr. Captain shook her head. "What *can* you tell me?"

Cole reached over, lifted Pam's chart, and held it like it was fragile. "Just this. I just thought you'd know what this is."

Dr. Captain gave him a good, long look, then took the chart back. Read it over one more time. "Is she alive?"

"She's alive," Cole said. "Barely. I mean, I'm not a doctor, but…"

"With these vitals, I'm surprised," she said, "and relieved. Where are they taking her? It says here that she's getting transferred."

"I don't know. The facility, if I had to bet."

"These…" Dr. Captain's whole face looked troubled, confused. "There's some sort of a strain here. A virus or something."

"A virus?" The entire first week after Cole returned to Wounded Sky flashed in his mind. Seeing Chief Crate collapse in the X, Elder Mariah looking like death in her clinic bed, the number of Wounded Sky residents that had died or had become gravely ill. "What kind of virus?" Cole was afraid to ask. "Anything like—"

"I can't say," Dr. Captain must've known what he was about to ask, "but I know what would help."

"The files."

"If I could just see them, it'd give me a better idea of what to do. I could see if there's any relation between the sickness last month and now. A chance to do *something*."

"And if I got you the files, you could help people get better?"

"People?"

"There are like, at least nine people in the clinic, sick just like Pam. Maybe more. I didn't get to a couple of rooms, but..." Cole knew he'd not accounted for everybody who'd gone missing. There were more to find. "It's not just Pam."

Dr. Captain went over to a small desk—Alex's—and put the chart into one of the drawers and closed it.

"The answer is yes." She put her hand over her forehead for a moment, closed her eyes, like she had a migraine. "If I had the files, I think I could help them get better. Me and Elder Mariah."

"I'll get them."

13

US

COLE STOPPED ON THE PATH THAT LED to Ashley's trailer, at a fork in the road, where the other direction passed through metal gates to Wounded Sky Cemetery. Inside the cemetery were the graves of his classmates, his mom, his teachers, his dad, and his own. He thought about going there. His last visit seemed so long ago. He had very little memory of leaving the cemetery as a walking corpse. The last time he had visited he'd used a rock to erase the word *Father* from his dad's headstone. That night Cole also found Vikki's headstone, with whom his dad had had an affair. Vikki, who'd been murdered with his dad by Reynold McCabe. He stared down the pathway into the cemetery, until a small hand took his.

"Hey Jayney."

"Want me to come with ya?" Jayne squeezed Cole's hand reassuringly.

"Actually yeah, I do."

"Alright, let's go then."

She sparked brighter and escorted Cole down the path, through the gate, and into the cemetery.

"Where we goin'?"

Cole knew that she would see her friends, not just the headstones. She came here all the time and was just as excited each time. He wondered how that worked, which friends she saw, which ones were still here, and which ones were not.

"Oh, they come and go, if they want to," she said. "I'm just stuck here that's all."

It was far more pleasant to have Jayne read his thoughts than Choch.

"I don't tease you; that's why, silly."

"You never have."

First, they visited the graves of their lost friends and teachers. The neat, quiet rows of white headstones belying the horror they'd experienced in their deaths. Cole prayed quietly at his mom's grave while Jayne waited. Her fire was dim. Of course, Jayne's grave was there, too. And even though she saw her friends, they'd died how they'd died, and the memory of that probably never went away, not even in the afterlife. After Cole had prayed, he put his hand on the cold stone and kissed it.

"Miss you, Mom."

"I see her sometimes, you know that?" Jayne whispered.

"You really do?"

"Yeah, but she doesn't come down too much."

"Why not?"

"Last time I seen her down, she was dancing 'round your grave."

Cole pictured her dancing, a ribbon of light swirling around his final resting place, which wasn't his final resting place. He knew that's how it was because he'd been one of those ribbons. "Why would she dance around my grave?"

"I guess because there's all that mean stuff, and she wanted there to be happy stuff. You were there, too."

Cole felt a tear form and smiled. "I don't remember that."

"I remember cuz I was so happy to see ya!"

"I bet I was happy to see you, too, Jayney."

He wished he could remember that one thing, out of anything. The time he'd danced with his mom.

They visited his dad's grave next. The word *Father* hadn't been repaired. Still chipped away thanks to Cole's actions. He didn't regret it, even now. He was still mad at his dad for what he'd done, but nobody deserved to die for their indiscretions. Cole tried to pray for his dad, as he'd prayed for the others. But he didn't know what to pray. Words escaped him. He looked at the ground to gather something, some thoughts, some words. That's when he noticed the one thing that was different.

"The dirt's been disturbed." Cole grabbed a handful of earth.

"Yeah, silly," Jayne said. "He's here now, you know."

"He's here…" Cole let the dirt fall back into place, leaned forward onto both palms, and dug his fingers into the ground. "Nótáwíy." Then he prayed and didn't stop until Jayne tapped his shoulder.

"Coley?"

Cole wiped tears away from his cheeks. "Yeah?" He pulled himself to his feet. "I'm good."

"You're sad a lot when you come here," and Jayne was sad in response. She was dim enough that the night actually seemed like the night.

"Tears can be from different things. It's okay." Cole stared at where the word *Father* was supposed to be. He looked at the disturbed ground. The place his dad's body, his actual body, now occupied.

Cole laughed.

"What's so funny? You were just cryin' for all those different reasons."

"It's just…" Cole shook it off. "…now he's here, and my body's gone. You know? How does that work?"

"I dunno."

"You know, if somehow getting shot in the head helped get my dad back here, from there, I think it was worth it."

"You're so weird, Coley."

"Come on." Cole took Jayne's hand and led her to the one spot he'd avoided so far. He wanted to just walk on by, head back to Ashley's trailer, where undoubtedly Brady was anxiously waiting for him. Now, there he was, strolling through the whole place. But at the last place, Cole's grave, somebody was there already.

Eva.

She couldn't see him in the dark, and she couldn't see Jayne's light, but Cole saw her clear as day. Seeing her took his breath away, like his lungs were still decomposed, like he was leaving his grave for the first time.

Nobody would've guessed that he'd risen from the dead. Cole had expected Choch to have covered up his resurrection, like the spirit being had covered up Cole's jailbreak. But seeing it was different. Though he didn't remember, he must've left a big hole where he'd dug his way out from six feet under. Now, there was a neatly filled-in area the size of a coffin. Eva stood at the end of it.

Cole approached slowly, so as not to alarm her. And right in front of her, so she knew somebody was there, even if she couldn't see who. When he was ten feet from his grave, Eva asked, "Who's there?"

There was no sadness in her voice, though she was standing at his grave and presumably had been before he'd arrived, standing for who knew how long. Why didn't she sound sad? Was she mad at him, for going to the facility without her, and had that anger overtaken the mourning?

"Nobody," he said in a low voice. *People, he is literally trying to sound like Christian Bale as Batman, I swear.* He stood at her side, looking at his headstone as she looked at him, sizing up his dark figure.

Jayne tugged at his hand. "Want me to go?"

Sure, Cole thought. *I'll catch up with you later.*

She lifted his hand up, gave it a quick, burning kiss, then skipped off, back to the part of the cemetery where their friends were buried.

"Nobody?" Eva asked. They were alone, and without Jayne's light, she was just a silhouette. Two shadows, standing side by side, staring at an empty grave. By then, she'd looked away from him, back at his grave. Not knowing that the stranger a foot away from her was Cole. "You sure look like somebody, unless I'm going crazy."

He wasn't sure when, or how, to tell her. He'd thought about it a lot today, but had yet to come up with the best way. He'd stumbled upon her entirely unprepared. "I just knew him."

"You're not from Mihko, are you?" she asked. "Because I know it's past curfew, but a girl's gotta do what a girl's gotta do."

If she was worried about getting caught, she didn't act it. Although this wasn't entirely out of character for Eva. Cole had always known her to be defiant, a no-shit taker. "No, I'm not from Mihko."

"Well, everybody knows everybody here, and what do you have, a cold or something?"

"No, it's just…" Cole cleared his throat and tried to speak with a deep voice, but not gravelly. "…frog's in there. Allergies."

"You sound ridiculous." She looked at him again, for a long time. He wondered if her eyes were adjusting to the dark, if she could see anything in him that looked familiar. His neck warmer was still over his face. "So you're not from Mihko, you have allergies…I give up. Unless you wanted to play twenty-one questions or something. Are we doing that?"

"Justin?" Cole said hesitantly, wondering how far Choch's influence went. Just to Michael and Franny and Bill?

"Nope," Eva said almost playfully, like there was already a game taking place, just one that Cole wasn't privy to. "There's no Justin in Wounded Sky."

"I'm just visiting for—"

"*Nobody's* visiting Wounded Sky," Eva said matter-of-factly. "Nobody in, nobody out," she said as though quoting somebody else, somebody from Mihko. Maybe that Xavier person, the head Mihko guy that had spoken at the assembly the school put on for Cole before everything went to shit. Or during the shit. During seemed more accurate.

"I don't know what to say." He caught himself letting his voice go normal. Maybe it had to be that easy.

Just tell her.

"I have an idea." She turned to face him head-on. Her arms were crossed impatiently. "Wanna hear it?"

"Uhhh, sure?"

"Okay, so repeat after me."

"Okay."

"Sorry it took so long…"

"Sorry…it…took so long?"

"…I know you've been waiting forever…"

"…ummmm…what are you talking about?"

"It's getting late, allergy-throat-guy. Let's go. No questions."

"Okay, okay…I know you've been waiting forever."

"…but now I'm back, so let's finish this shit and save the community."

"What?"

"Say it."

"I don't know what to say, I…"

"You know *exactly* what to say because I just told you what to say."

Cole's body felt ready to explode. His heart was jack hammering. He was crying. His hands and knees were shaking. All of the things he felt when he had a panic attack were hitting him hard. He stumbled, she caught him. He tried to reach for a pocket, forgetting that he didn't have a pill container. She grabbed his arm to stop him.

"No," she said softly. "Say it."

"I'm back," he said, but barely, because he couldn't really talk. He was sobbing and shaking and a mess, and she was completely put together, cool. "I'm back."

"Yeah, you are." She lunged forward and hugged him, and he felt crushed in her embrace, and for so many reasons he never wanted her to let him go. Because he loved her. Because he needed the support right now. Because it made him feel the most alive he'd ever felt. "But it took you long enough."

"I still don't know what to say," Cole said, his cheek pressed against the top of her head. "I don't have any words."

He was still shaking. She held him tighter.

She shifted her head, so she could look at his grave.

"I've been here every night since you died."

"I…" he wanted to say how he didn't die, to feed the same line to her that he'd fed to Dr. Captain. But she didn't deserve it, and she knew so much already.

So he didn't.

He looked at his grave too. How neatly it had been set normal. And then, how the headstone itself was unsullied. No graffiti. Beside the headstone, there was a bucket. Inside the bucket was a sponge.

"You looked after me, even when I was dead."

"Somebody had to."

Eva backed away, slid her hands down his arms, and held his hands, his shaking hands, and rubbed her thumbs along his scars.

"Do you need your pills?" she asked.

"I don't even have them. I forgot about that," he said. "And…I want to feel this."

Without planning the movement, they turned to the headstone, Cole's headstone, but she kept a firm hold on his hand. Over time, Cole's body began to settle, just with her touch, and a bit of breathing work.

"You owe me, you know," she said.

"I know," he said. "I'm sorry that I was gone so long. I just…woke up when I woke up."

"No, I mean for filling in the mess you left behind," she laughed. "I had never dug, or un-dug, a grave before."

"*You* did this?" Not Choch. Eva. He looked at the grave all over again. She hadn't just shovelled dirt back into the hole, she'd made sure it had been done perfectly, like he was down there still, like he deserved that sort of care. "Ekosani."

"I didn't want anybody getting any ideas. Figured if they killed you, it would be good for us if they thought you were still dead, right?"

"Us," he repeated. Out of all that, that's all he heard. *Us.*

She just nodded, tugged at his hand, and they walked through the cemetery to the gate. They stopped where the path forked off in two directions. One of them went to Ashley's trailer, the other to where, eventually, Cole knew they would need to go: the clinic, the facility. *Us.* Him. Eva. Brady. And, as though Eva knew what Cole was thinking, she repeated that same word again. As though that was the only word she had said. The only word that mattered.

"*Us.*"

That word carried weight. That word said so much more than just what Cole had thought it had said. Not that they were in this together, but they should have always been in this together.

But they were now. He was back.

"Let's do this."

14

UNSAID

"CAN I JUST POINT OUT," Eva said, "that for the very dramatic 'Let's do this' comment, I can't help but notice that we're not actually going to Ashley's trailer at the moment."

It was a valid and obvious observation. Cole had been very gung-ho earlier, and, standing together at that fork in the path, he'd told Eva where Brady was. A short walk from the cemetery. Maybe a minute, two at the most. In addition, he'd told Eva how long Brady would have been waiting for him to come back at this point, and without cell service, Brady was completely in the dark.

"I have two perfectly good answers for that," Cole said, but then didn't answer because, suddenly, he felt like he was seven again, and they'd just found out that they liked each other. It had changed their relationship. It was new, and then it was a point of stress, and then it was weird and exciting and confusing, and now it was new again. How could it not feel that way, after coming back to life?

"You know, when you die," Cole said, not actually providing either of the answers he'd mentioned. "I haven't actually thought about this yet, but when you die, and then come back to life, you realize some of the things that you took for granted, or the things that you never did or said that you wish…" He trailed off because he felt stupid.

"That you wish…" Eva prompted him to continue, but it was too late. Cole didn't know how to say what he needed to and figuring it out would have taken all night.

"Never mind," Cole said. "What I was saying was, first, I'm not sure when I'll get a chance to see my grandmother and auntie again, so I wanted to see them. Not *see* them see them, but just, I guess, even just see them through the window. Something."

"I did notice that we were headed in that direction."

"With what we're going to do, if anything happens to me *again*, I want to see them," he said. "Even if they can't see me."

"You don't have to explain yourself to me," she said. "It's not that far."

They were still holding hands, walking out in the open, as though emboldened by each other. Mihko be damned. She swung his hand by swinging hers for a few steps.

"I'm not sure I'll be able to come back to life a second time, that's all. You know, if—"

"Cole." She stopped, and it made him stop. She made him face her by pulling at his arm. She didn't let go of his hand, but put her other hand against his cheek, and then slapped it lightly, and, afterwards, had a difficult time hiding a smile.

"What?" He smiled at her smile.

She got serious quick. "I'm not going to let anything happen to you."

"Shouldn't I be the one saying that to you?"

She shook her head. "I already know you won't."

There was a moment, then. A second. Less. Cole used to play this game with his watch, which also had a stopwatch. He'd try to see how fast he could stop the timer after starting it. The fastest he'd been able to do it was in .07 seconds. Start, stop. That's how fast this moment felt, a moment where, standing together, alone underneath the clear sky, it felt as though they might kiss. But the moment passed because Eva started walking and dragged him along with her.

"This is a two-way street, Cole." She looked back at him, and he caught up to her. "Somebody has to look out for you, too, you know."

"I know," he said.

"Now," she said after they started, once more, walking side by side, "you said you had *two* perfectly good answers. What's the second answer?"

That I wanted to hold your hand for longer, he thought to himself. *For as long as possible.* He imagined saying it to her. Imagined another moment where, after saying it, they stopped and stood together, just like they had been moments earlier, and didn't say anything, but rather leaned in and kissed. And only after kissing would he tell her what he'd been trying to say earlier, only now, he'd say it perfectly. Romance-movie perfect. *When I opened my eyes, after being dead, I thought about all the things I didn't do, when I was alive. The things you think about, when you're on your death bed, like that girl you let slip away. I guess what I'm trying to say is, when I opened my eyes, the only thing I wanted to see was you.*

"Cole."

"Huh?"

"Where were you just now? You totally zoned out."

"Oh, sorry. Just…" No. Now it would just be weird. The moment hadn't circled back around and reintroduced itself. "I started thinking about, like, Mihko stuff. Community-saving activities. That's, you know, *so* important right now. Sorry, didn't mean to strand you in reality."

"That's okay." She didn't sound convinced and was giving him side-eye. "*Anyway,* the second answer?"

"Right, yeah," he said. "I just…" *Say it, CB! Moments never pass! You make the moment! I'm sitting here eating popcorn at the edge of my seat!* "…why weren't you surprised to see me, back at the cemetery?"

"That's why we aren't going to Ashley's trailer right now? I'm confused."

"I wanted more time to ask you, that's why." He chuckled awkwardly. "Ashley's trailer is so close, I guess. And some of this, Brady probably shouldn't know, you know?"

I just rolled my eyes at you, CB. Just saying.

"So, to recap," Eva said, "you wanted more time to ask me why I wasn't surprised when I found out you'd come back from the dead."

"Yes, that's exactly it."

"Okay, so, I can't tell you how much I've wanted to say this," she said. "Not more than seeing you again, but it's up there. Here goes: I can't tell you that."

"What?"

"Sound familiar? You said it to me and Brady just about every five seconds."

"Yeah, but—" Cole stopped, and because they were still holding hands, Eva stopped right after him with a wicked smile. It was just as well. They were close to his old place, now. They couldn't have gone too much closer, without risking his relatives seeing him. "I literally couldn't tell you guys or else…" *Careful now, CB. Foot off the gas. You're going 160 in a 100.* "…something bad would've happened. For real."

"Okay, well," she took both of his hands, and looked him dead in the eyes. "If I tell you," she said methodically, "something bad will happen. *For real.*"

"Touché."

"All I can tell you is that I knew you were coming back to life, I just didn't know when. So when I saw you, and you were trying to act all secret identity, I was relieved, but I also thought I may as well have some fun, because at that point, you were back. So why not?"

"You knew it was me the whole time?"

She let go of his hands. He wanted to reach out and hold her hand again, but also didn't want to seem desperate. Then, she pushed him. Two hands to the chest.

"Come on!" she said. "Do you know how Clark Kent looks exactly like Superman, and so when people can't make the connection, it's *super* unbelievable?"

Cole pulled the neck warmer over his mouth and just shrugged.

"I've known you your whole life, Cole. A neck warmer isn't going to change that. Yes, I knew it was you the whole time."

"Hmmph."

"Look," she took his hand again, and that was all that mattered. She could've said anything. "If it makes you feel any better, just because

I knew you were coming back, doesn't mean I didn't miss you like crazy, okay?"

Nope. It actually did matter what she said. His heart started racing again. He could feel a vein pulsing in his neck. But he took a deep breath in through his nose and out through his mouth. Tried to do so without her noticing, even though their eyes were locked. If she noticed, she didn't point it out.

"I missed you, too," he said.

"Can you miss people when you're dead? What was it like? Being dead?"

"Oh, I can't tell you that."

"Asshole!" Eva laughed and slapped his chest again, then turned away from him, to his parents' house. "As far as I'm concerned, they can have you."

Cole looked there now, too. And in the kitchen window, he could see his grandmother sitting at the table, and Auntie Joan walking over to her with two cups in her hands. Auntie Joan sat down and handed his grandmother a cup. They were talking. What were they talking about? Cole strained his ears to hear, but they were too far away. He couldn't even hear muffled voices. But, he guessed, he didn't need to hear them. It was good enough just to see them, and to know they were okay. Brady had had to take Elder Mariah away from the community to protect her, but with Cole dead, Auntie Joan and his grandmother were safe.

It needed to stay that way.

"They can't know I'm alive," he said. "I hate that they can't know. I hate that they have to keep that pain when they don't have to. I'm right here."

Eva let go of his hand to put her arm around his waist, her head against his shoulder. "I've seen them every day since you died."

"Really?"

"Yeah," she said. "I didn't want them to be alone."

"Thank you."

"They're okay, you know?" she assured him. "They hurt, of course, but they're strong, too. They can hang on a few more days. They can hang on until this is all done, and then they can see you again."

"You're right."

"Of course, I'm right," she said. "Now, are you really ready to do this?"

"Yeah," he said. "I'm ready."

Brady had a spring jacket wrapped tightly around his body and was doing laps around the Mustang when Eva and Cole got to Ashley's property.

"Oh, thank goodness," he said in one expelled breath. He ran up to the pair and gave Cole a bear hug. "I thought something had gone wrong, and you couldn't even let me know!"

"I'm okay, man," Cole said, smothered in the embrace. "I'm alright." He patted Brady's back.

"Hey." Eva peeled Brady off Cole. "I'm feeling a bit like Chewbacca at the end of *The Force Awakens* here, B."

"I was getting there!" Promptly, Eva received a hug of equal force. "How've you been? I was so worried when I couldn't get texts from you."

"Thaaat's better," she said.

Brady let go of Eva and turned back to Cole.

"I mean," he shook his head and yes, even shook his finger, "just because you didn't have cell service…"

"Or a cell at all."

"*Or* a cell at all." He was revving his engine now. "Scratch that. Because there's no cell service, you should've just come back quick and given me an update. You run really fast, right? I was waiting for you *all night.*"

"You're right." Cole put both his hands out, displaying his scars to Brady. "You're totally right. Just, one thing happened after another, and…well, I thought about you. I knew you'd be worried."

"And yet." Brady let Cole fill in the blanks.

"And yet," Cole repeated quietly.

"Don't ever do that to me again, okay!" Brady put his hands on Cole's shoulders and took a deep breath, closed his eyes, opened them. "*Please*. I've already lost you once, literally. I am not prepared to lose you again. Got it?"

"I got it, really. One hundred percent." Cole put his hands on Brady's forearms.

"Ahem." Eva walked up to their arms, ducked down, and emerged between them, so she was standing directly between Brady and Cole. "We good?"

They let go of each other.

"Yeah, we're good," Brady said. "I'm just glad you're okay, both of you."

"I'm sorry," Cole said.

"It's okay."

"Are we going to hug again?" Eva looked back and forth between Cole and Brady and didn't like the look in their eyes. She was trapped in the middle.

"Eva sandwich!" Brady laughed.

They collapsed into each other, and it morphed into a three-way hug. They all laughed; a one-month journey of hell had brought them to this moment. When the dust had cleared, when they'd let go of each other, prying themselves away, they sat together on the futon in Ashley's trailer where it was warm, and they could be inside. Cole watched while Brady and Eva got reacquainted, Brady telling Eva about his time away from the community, and Eva filling Brady in with all the news of the two weeks he'd missed.

"Does somebody want to explain the outfit, now?" Eva asked, one arm around Cole, the other waving in front of him like his clothing was a gameshow prize.

"Oh, he's a superhero now," Brady said. "That's something *you* missed."

"I see." Eva stood up and took a good, long look at Cole. "I like it. It's understated. Subtle. No bright colours, no cape. That's been done to death."

"Can I just say," Cole interrupted, "the Star Wars reference, the superhero costume talk...I didn't think I could like you more than I already did."

"Thank you." She bowed. "Now, I was saying: the colour scheme is great. The neck warmer is super cool..."

"Right?"

"Right," she chuckled. "It's all working." She nodded with her upper lip tucked underneath her lower lip. "Now, most importantly, do you have a superhero name?"

"He does," Brady said.

"Skull Face? Cargo Pants Guy? The Black Hood? Zombie Boy?"

"You know about..." Brady got off topic for a second.

"Yes, I know about the whole coming-back-to-life thing," Eva said. "Now, I was in the middle of guessing superhero names. It's actually fun."

"The Reckoner," Cole said rather self-consciously. He felt stupid saying it, but also wanted her to like it.

"I was *guessing*, Cole."

"Sorry."

"Not bad, though," she said. "I mean, Cargo Pants Guy must've been a close second, right?"

"That was almost the one."

"I wish I would've thought of that," Brady said.

Eva plunked back down on the futon and put her arms around the boys. "So, what've you two been up to since coming back?"

"Well, as you might've guessed, I've been sitting around here wait-ing like *an ass*," Brady said.

"You forgave me, remember?" Cole said.

"And you?" Eva asked Cole.

The night came flooding back, and, in particular, the fact that he'd seen Wayne. He'd been so selfishly excited to see Eva, he'd forgotten about what had happened between leaving Brady and seeing her. How to tell her? It felt harder than when he didn't know how to tell her that he was alive. The difference was that she knew he was alive all along. She didn't know, as far as he was aware, that Wayne was so sick.

"Cole." Eva waved a hand in front of his face. "You're doing it again."

"Sorry," he said, not making eye contact with her. Instead, he looked at the floor, at one spot on the floor, where whoever had cleaned the trailer missed a single spot of blood.

It was orange now.

"Did you see something?" Eva put her hand under his chin and lifted his head. "Cole."

This wasn't a moment he could let pass by. "I saw your dad."

"What?" Eva sat down on the coffee table. They were eye to eye. "Tell me everything."

"He..." Cole started shaking again. "He was sick, Eva. I'm sorry. He was...like Elder Mariah was. Everybody there was."

"Pam?" Brady said.

Cole nodded. "There were, like, at least nine people there. They were all sick like before. I didn't get to a few rooms, either. Guys..." He looked at both his friends. "...I think Mihko is making them sick. And some of them are being moved from the clinic. Probably all of them, eventually."

"Where?" Eva asked.

"I took Pam's chart," Cole said. "It didn't say where, just that she was moving in two days. But, I don't know if there's anywhere else they'd get moved to, but—"

"The facility," Eva said.

"Yeah," Cole breathed.

"Two days," Brady said. "We've got to move if we're going to do something."

"We're doing something," Eva said.

"We'll get them out tomorrow," Cole said. "We've got to get our team together; we've got to plan it out. If they're moving Pam in two days, it has to be tomorrow."

Eva stood up again and went to the window. She stared out of it and turned around as though somebody had said her name. Fast. Her eyes were wide. Intense. "We have to go tonight."

"Eva," Cole said, "we can't just—"

"Cole, my dad's sick. If he's as sick as Elder Mariah, then who knows…" She covered her face, breathed, uncovered it. "…who knows if he'll be around tomorrow. It has to be tonight."

There was no please. There didn't need to be. There was no please, and there was no argument.

"You're right," Cole said.

"Yeah." She sat down on the coffee table again. "I'm always right. Now, what do we do?"

"Ummm," Cole scrambled to think. Rubbed his temples. Tried to process everything. Come up with something. "Okay. You guys have to go get the team."

"What is this team you keep mentioning?" Eva asked.

"If we're going to do this, especially tonight, we're going to need help," Cole said. "And since we can't text anybody, we're going to have to go out and get them."

"Lauren and Dr. Captain," Brady said to Eva.

"You guys round up those two," Cole said.

"What about you?" Eva asked.

"I'm going to have to get those files, once and for all."

"Cole…" Eva got quiet. "…that's at Reynold's house."

She knew all about Reynold. What he'd done to Cole's dad, to Vikki. She knew Cole had gone off that night to kill Reynold, and for all anybody knew, for all Cole knew, he hadn't been successful. Reynold might very well be alive.

And if he was, he'd be at his house.

"There's security all over his place," Eva warned. "You'll have to get through *them* to get inside. And what if…what if he's there, too."

"What's going on?" Brady asked. "So what if he's alive? Cole's got superpowers. Literally."

Oh, go ahead and tell him about Reynold. You're a team after all.

"No," Cole said, "the guards aren't the thing. Reynold is. He's Upayokwitigo."

"WHAT?" Brady leapt to his feet and looked squarely at Cole. "*Reynold?*"

"I went out that night to face him. I knew I had to face him," Cole said. "I thought I'd killed him, but you're all saying that he might still be alive. So…" Cole got up now, and walked slowly to the door, put his hand on the doorknob. "…I'll have to go and find out."

"And if he's alive??" Eva asked.

Brady went to the corner of the trailer, picked up the rifle, and handed it to Cole. Said it all with a look.

Cole took the rifle, but placed it on the ground. Shook his head. "I don't need it."

"Cole," Eva rushed to the front door. "You're not Batman. There are guards. There's Reynold. You'll need all the help you can get."

She picked up the rifle and handed it to him, but he wouldn't take it.

"Don't be an idiot!" Brady said.

"One rifle against how many guards? How many guards are there? Have you seen?" Cole asked Eva.

"Lots," Eva said.

"Then that," Cole pointed at the rifle, "will only slow me down. If Reynold's alive, a gun didn't kill him anyway."

Cole opened the door, stepped outside. Before he could walk down the stairs, Eva gave him a hug.

"Be careful," she said.

"I'll be back."

15

WHO MADE WHO

REYNOLD MCCABE'S HOUSE *was* a fortress, just as Eva had warned. The last time Cole had been there, he'd managed to get through two or three guards and into the house by arranging a movie date with Lucy. Easy. Yes, they had been ready to shoot him, but after Lucy confirmed that he was supposed to be there, there was no problem. Good thing, too, because now he knew exactly where he needed to go to find the files for Dr. Captain.

But there was no easy way, now.

Cole could see the house from the path he'd forged through Blackwood Forest. It looked like nobody was allowed in the McCabe residence, for any reason—because he was alive, or because he was dead. Either explanation seemed plausible. There were guards at each door and several around the perimeter, all armed with rifles and handguns. He could see two trucks, as well, housing guards in their cargo beds. There was one certainty: Cole's secret was about to come to an end. There'd be no tree climbing. Too many guards to get around, and Cole was sure there'd be some in the forest behind the house.

"I have a suggestion," Choch said.

"And what would that be?" Cole asked.

"You could just turn around and do the break-in thing at the clinic and leave this whole McCabe business alone."

"I can't do that."

"Elder Mariah *did* make you well all on her own, without the help of any silly medical files, you know."

"I have super healing."

"Fair point, CB. But don't underestimate the power of traditional medicine. If she got well without the benefit of those files, why couldn't everybody else? Potential plot-hole alert!"

"It's not just about that. Having those files may help us figure out more than just how to treat people. It'll help us figure out what's actually happening here. Isn't that part of my job?"

Choch shrugged, then groaned. "*Fine*, but keep this in mind: you ain't coming back to life again, partner. Cat Man is *not* your superhero name."

"What's the difference? Do you just decide when I'm resurrected and when I'm not?"

Choch breathed in through his teeth. "Not exactly."

"Not exactly," Cole re-stated. "Could you elaborate a little bit?"

"It's like, okay, if this were a Disney movie. *Aladdin*, let's say. One doesn't just arbitrarily get three wishes, they have to rub the lamp first." Choch paused, perhaps waiting for Cole to react. "Get the analogy?"

"Somebody…wished…for me to be alive again?"

"Maaaaybe," Choch said. "Let me just say, that my favourite game show is *Let's Make a Deal* and leave it at that."

"*Is* that a game show?"

Choch rolled his eyes. "Honestly, you watch too many crime shows. Expand your horizons. Netflix has everything."

"Eva." It all made sense. That's why she expected him to come back to life. Why she couldn't tell him. Just like he couldn't tell her. He spun around and grabbed Choch by the collar. Lifted him in the air. "You better not have made a deal with her."

Choch pointed at his throat and pretended to choke.

Cole dropped the spirit being on his feet.

"I can neither confirm nor deny that assertion." Choch straightened out his mall cop uniform. "But to answer your question, I don't cheat. You died. That was it, until…"

"Eva wished me back to life."

Choch shrugged.

"I'm warning you."

"CB." Choch put his arm around Cole's shoulders. "This is going to be a distraction for you, isn't it?"

"Can you blame me?"

"No, and I suppose I can't really blame she-who-shall-not-be-named, either. I mean they. Not she. Whoops. They didn't break the rules."

"What rules did you give her?" Cole hissed.

"You know, I promised myself I wouldn't do this, and it does seem narratively convenient, but I need you to stay focused."

Choch raised his hand, locked and loaded to snap. "We're in the endgame now."

"No wait, don't—"

Snap.

Cole looked at Choch for the first time since the spirit being had arrived. He was in his mall cop outfit. He'd added flare to it. Buttons that read "Native Pride" and "Don't Worry Be Happy" and "All You Need is Love," and some had superhero emblems on them. Batman. Superman. Cole looked them over, but decided not to mention them to Choch, who, he figured, wore them specifically for Cole to mention.

"Pretty cool though, right?" Choch asked.

And thinking about them had been enough.

"Sure." Cole considered that he'd actually rather like to have the Batman button.

Choch took it off his uniform and clipped it onto Cole's hoodie.

"There you are. A superhero button on a superhero. *Meta.* You know, maybe one day there'll be The Reckoner buttons. After all, with merchandising rights, television rights…oh! Who do you think would play me?"

"I'm not doing this." Cole clenched his jaws, trying not to let the spirit being bother him. Cole had been doing such a good job. Head down, staying focused.

"Personally, I want to say Steve Buscemi, perhaps, but then you'd get, you know, the Indigenous community up in arms, a white actor playing an Indigenous character. But, and this is the thing, I can look like whomever I want to. If you wanted to get a choice actor into a movie, just to sell it, I'd be the character to do that, amIright? I mean, I could look like Tom Cruise right now if I wanted to." And for effect, Choch turned into Tom Cruise for a moment, then back into mall cop Choch.

"In what world does Steve Buscemi sell a movie? And Tom Cruise right now unless it's a *Mission: Impossible* movie."

"*Boardwalk Empire*? *Edge of Tomorrow*? Hello? Am I speaking your language?"

"No, Choch, you are not speaking my language."

"See?" Choch slapped Cole on the shoulder. "This is *us* right now. You and me. Me pissing you off, you getting pissed off, me enjoying myself altogether too much, you wanting answers, which keeps me around…le sigh."

"Don't say 'le sigh,' please."

Choch actually sighed instead.

"The question is, who would play Cole Harper, huh? I mean, undoubtedly people will be wondering that. Whenever I read a book, I—"

"It doesn't matter!" Cole shouted, but caught himself. He looked around to see if any of the guards had been alerted to his presence. He repeated in a whisper: "It doesn't matter. Shut it. When this is over, I won't even have these powers anyway."

"Well, if you're lucky, maybe I'll let you keep them," Choch said. "I mean, don't get me wrong, CB, you've bumbled your way through some of this, but all in all, hey, listen: isn't it about time the world got an actual hero?"

"There are lots of heroes out there that don't have superpowers. People like—"

"Whoa whoa whoa," Choch said. "We go for subtle social commentary around here, okay? Yes, we all love Emma Gonzalez, but let's stick to supernatural mystery. Deal?"

Cole closed his eyes and took a deep breath. "Who says I'll even want these powers anymore, if you even let me keep them?" he asked evenly, attempting to recapture some focus. "Do I get a choice? Shouldn't I get a choice?"

"Who says I gave them to you in the first place," Choch mumbled like a pouting toddler.

"What did you say?"

Choch had mumbled so inaudibly that even Cole's keen hearing didn't pick it up, or he didn't want to believe what Choch had said.

Choch frantically looked at everything but Cole, like there was a fly buzzing around that he wanted to swat. He settled on looking up at the northern lights and refused to look down while Cole waited for a response.

"Choch!" Cole shout-whispered.

"Yes?" Choch feigned ignorance.

"What. Did. You. Just. Say?"

"Le…" Choch stopped himself. "You know, the easiest thing here would be for me to just rewind the clock and not even slip up like that. *Not that I'd ever do that to* you, *CB.*" Choch winked at nothing in particular. "The boss is going to be *so* mad at me…"

"Don't you do that to me," Cole said. "Just tell me. You owe me at least that, and I've been through enough that I can take whatever crap you're about to throw at me."

"Okay, well…" Choch said reluctantly. "Speaking of *owing* people things. Think back to the day we met."

Cole went back to that moment, ten years ago. He—

"No, no, no," Choch said. "Don't *actually* think back to the day. Talk it through. Pretty please. God knows, we don't need more expository writing."

"Yeah, I was just…" Cole closed his eyes to be there, to remember everything "…I was at Silk River, making that sweetgrass ring for Eva. I saw the sky light up. It looked like the sunset or something. I ran as fast as I could, and…when I got there, the school was on fire. It was just…" Cole started to feel his body shake, and his pulse quicken.

"Go on, boy."

Cole looked down at his palms, at the scars he'd asked Choch to give back. "I opened the doors, went inside, looking for them, following the screams…the screams…"

Choch put a hand on Cole's arm, which was trembling. "I can calm you."

"No," Cole said quickly. "*Never* calm this. I can do it. I'm okay." In for five seconds, out for seven. "I…I found them, in the gym. I saw Eva's shoes, under the wall. It had collapsed on her, on Brady, on…" Cole pictured Jayne's joyous face, half burning. "…and then you were there."

Choch snapped his fingers. "That's right. And *then* I was there."

"And now we're here," Cole said, "and why are we talking about it? Why would you make me talk about it? It's always there, even when I don't think it is. Every moment, like a picture. Things fade when you get older, but not that. Never that."

"And yet…"

"What? Stop this bullshit. What?"

"Tell me something, CB." Choch scooted over to Cole, right close, thigh to thigh. Gave his trembling leg a quick pat. "How fast did you get to the school, when you ran there?"

"What? I don't know, I ran. I got there as fast as I could. The school was burning, my friends were in there."

"How would Robertson put this…" Choch thumbed his chin like a wise old man. "…was the grass violently whipping against your shins? The surrounding trees blurred like smeared paint? The—"

"I—I don't remember."

"Okay, well let's try this: when you got to the school, however fast you ran there, how did you open the front doors?"

"I…opened them." Cole showed Choch his palms, as though the spirit being didn't know about the scars. "I put my hands around the handles and pulled. I opened them." Cole's anxiety was quickly changing into something else, something he'd never felt before. He'd scanned his body for years, for the symptoms of his trauma, but he'd never felt this.

Disillusion. Disbelief.

"This is getting heavy, right?" Choch laughed hysterically. He'd undoubtedly shielded the guards from hearing at least him. "Sorry, go on. But talk, remember?"

"I don't understand why you're asking me all of this."

"You wanted to know, CB. I just want you to figure it out for yourself because, you know, I do feel bad about it. Don't get me wrong, it needed to happen, but still, sometimes even tricksters feel remorse. Somewhat."

"Why are you asking about running? About opening doors to a burning building?"

"If you were any later than you were, your friends would've died. Your dear Eva, Brady. If you weren't able to open those doors…"

"They were open…they…"

"*Now,* you can think."

Cole was seven. Running up the steps to the school. The flames erupting from it, painting the world red. He saw his little hands wrap around the handles. He felt the metal burning his skin. He felt the strain of his effort, trying to open the doors, get to his friends, follow the screams. He saw…chains, strung from one door handle to the next. Thick, black metal chains. Locking the doors shut. Locking the kids, his friends, teachers, his mom, inside.

Chains.

"No…" Cole whispered. "It can't be…"

He pulled harder. His muscles burned like the fire raging inside the school. Steam rose from his hands. The chains broke. The doors burst open. The links clattered down the concrete steps.

"How can that be? I…I couldn't lift that wall…you *gave* me that strength. You…"

"Can I tell you what amounts to a parable?"

Cole didn't answer. His mind was flailing. All he could manage was a nod, like he'd been startled awake.

"Great." Choch got into storytelling mode. "There was a boy, or girl, whatever. Let's say a girl. There was a girl, and her father was teaching her how to golf. On the third hole of a golf course, there was a large body of water in front of them. Now, across the water, was a junior tee. That's where the kids could hit from, so they wouldn't lose their ball. So, the father hits his ball. It sails through the air and lands safely on the other side of the water. He's ready to drive the cart over the bridge and go to the junior tee, when he sees his daughter teeing up her ball on the adult tee.

"He runs up to her as though her life's at stake. He says, 'My girl! You can't hit the ball from here! You'll lose it!' But his daughter begs him to let her try, so he relents. He says to his daughter, 'Fine, hit the ball, but you'll see that you can't do it.'

"Well, the girl, she takes a mighty lash at the ball, but it lands in the water. She picks up her tee, and walks to the cart, head down, shoulders slumped. Looking utterly defeated, you see. The father, well, he sees what he's done. He sees what has happened. So, he calls out to her. He says, 'My girl, get back over there. I *know* you can do it. Hit that ball over the water, and we'll go for ice cream afterwards.' The girl's body language changes. She runs back over to the tee, sets her ball up, and takes another swing. This time, the ball lands over the water. It lands *past* her father's ball!"

Cole stared at Choch.

"Do you see what I mean?"

"I…I already had these powers?"

"I mean, in fairness," Choch said, "you had *most* of your powers. I did give you the whole healing thing. Too late to address the palm scars, mind you. But not too late to help you heal from savage knife attacks! Hello!"

"You…" Cole felt a rage burning in his chest, like all the pain from the night, all the fire, was now inside him. He forgot where he was, forgot about being quiet. "You tricked me! I didn't need you! I never did!" Cole jumped to his feet, lunged at Choch, and wrapped his hands around the spirit being's neck. "All those years of pain!!"

"CB…" Choch choked out with Cole's considerable strength, his *own* strength, focused entirely on Choch's neck. "…CB…you needed me to…tell you…you could hit the ball…"

"The therapy! The anxiety! Everything!"

"...and...who...would've...died...if you hadn't...come back...for the...ice cream..."

"You did this! You!!"

"...think...about...it..."

As Choch's eyes began to roll back into his head, Cole loosened his grip. Choch gasped for air. Cole fell to his knees, arms resting over his legs, palms pointing upwards. He stared at the scars.

"Look at me," Cole whispered, tears streaming down his cheeks. "Look at what I am. This broken piece of nothing."

"No, Cole."

Choch crouched down beside Cole, rubbing his neck with one hand, the other on Cole's back.

"You are everything you should be, and everything people need you to be. Look at all the things you've been through, and all the things you've done. Powers or not, you *are* a superhero, son. You are The Reckoner. I just...gave you a nudge."

Cole looked up at Choch. "I never asked for any of this."

"Heroes never ask to be heroes. They just act, when they're needed. When they know something's wrong, and that it needs to be righted. You ran to the school, you broke open those doors, you saved your friends, you came back here and saved countless lives."

"You brought me back to life," Cole whispered. "For more of this torture."

"Yes, yes, I did. *Just me.*"

Cole shook his head. "I don't know what to do now. I don't know what this means." He looked over his whole body. The power and the brokenness.

"There's no deal," Choch said. "You can go. You know that, now. No tricks. There never was a deal."

"The deal..." Cole breathed.

"Whoever plays me in our movie, however, should automatically get an Academy Award," Choch said. "Remember when I warned you not to tell Eva about any of this, and you found that loophole, and I got soooo mad. *Acting.*"

Cole straightened up. "I can't leave. Not now. This *is* my job."

Choch clapped slowly. "See? Heroes. They're not born. They're made. Or wait…is it…"

"Let's get one thing straight." Cole moved closer to the spirit being, index finger pointed at him.

"Don't you finger point me!" Choch gasped.

"*You* didn't make me."

Choch's face scrunched up to one side. "I mean, if it weren't for me, I'm not quite sure you would have lifted that wall, which means that your friends might've died, which means you wouldn't have moved away, which means—well, I mean, even if all that still happened without me, who got you back here?"

"You tricked me," Cole said. "*Again.*"

"And you are my gullible little…sorry…big guy," Choch said. "In my defence, whether I have fun or not, I've always had the best interest of this beautiful place at—"

At that moment, Cole heard the whiz of a bullet cutting through the air and watched as it stopped right in front of Choch's face. The spirit being went cross-eyed looking at it, plucked it out of the air with two fingers, and dropped it.

"You really just did *The Matrix* after somebody tried to kill me."

"Awesome, right?" Choch looked completely pleased with himself. "Can you say, just this once, 'He is The One?' Pretty please?"

"No," Cole said. "Stop it."

"I almost got killed, too, you know. I *always* freaking die. That was way too close. I should just…" Choch patted around on the ground until he found the bullet, then picked it up and flicked it at the guards. It shot out of his hand as though the spirit being had used a gun and hit one of the trucks.

"What the hell, Choch!" Cole got down onto his stomach and stared out at Reynold's house from cover.

"Come out with your hands up, now!" A guard called out.

"Le sigh," Choch said. "I guess it's time to be a hero."

16

LSD

ANOTHER BULLET WHIZZED BY COLE'S HEAD. He looked back to see if Choch had stopped it because firing back wasn't that bad an idea right now. Why hadn't he taken the damn rifle from Brady? He hadn't thought of firing shots from the forest, where he had cover.

"But you're a lousy shot, anyway," Choch said. "Remember?"

"Except for when I'm like two inches away from the target," Cole admitted and saw that the spirit being hadn't caught the last bullet that was fired.

"Oh, you weren't a big fan of the whole bullet-catching thing. You know me, I aim to please."

"That's a warning shot!" A guard called out from the direction of Reynold's house. "You won't get many more of those!"

Maybe his cover wasn't that great after all. Cole shimmied behind a tree and slowly rose to his feet, making sure to keep the tree between himself and the guards.

"I hate to do this," Choch gave Cole an exaggerated grimace, "but I kind of have an appointment."

Cole peeked at the guards and another shot ricocheted off the bark right by his face. "Well, you're not going to help, anyway."

"Just remember," Choch said as he faded away, "you can only die twice." When his body was completely gone, he added, "Wait, was that a James Bond movie? Hashtag copyright."

"Move! Now!" The guard demanded.

"We'll give you to the count of three!" Another called out.

Cole could hear at least two guards begin to make their way over to him, step after step. He could hear the hammers cock on their guns.

"Three…"

Cole's muscles tensed.

"Two…"

Cole stepped away from the tree and lowered his body to the ground. His palms were pressed hard against the dirt, one knee to his chest, the other leg stretched out, foot firm against a tree root. As though he were about to start a 100-metre dash.

"One!"

Cole erupted from the ground and charged the security force. They let loose on Cole, firing their guns. Cole jerked from side to side while still in motion, narrowly avoiding the shots. He felt one skim his left arm, but ignored the slight pain. He laid his shoulder into one of them, who flew through the air and smashed into a truck. The guard's gun popped skyward. Cole turned to the other guard, caught the gun, and fired before they could get another shot off. The guard looked down at the wound in the middle of his chest, then his knees buckled, and he crumpled to the ground.

Cole heard other members of Mihko's security shouting. Calling everybody to the front of the house. All hands on deck. They assembled by the truck that the other guard had hit; he was now on the ground unconscious. Cole counted seven, not counting the one he'd knocked out and the other he'd shot. They were face to face, mere metres separating them. Guards on one side, Cole on the other. Cole brought his hood up over his head, keeping the gun in his hand.

"Who are you?" one of them asked, his rifle aimed at Cole.

Cole couldn't help but notice the shakiness in his voice.

"We'll…" another started, looked around at the others as though for approval, then continued. "…nobody else has to get hurt, kid."

"I was just about to tell you the same thing," Cole called back, deepening his voice. "All I want is to get inside. Everybody can leave. Just let me through."

"Nobody gets inside!" another said. "Nobody sees Chief McCabe!"

"You must *really* want to die!" said still another.

"Drop the gun!"

Cole lowered the gun, but kept it in his hand. Cocked the hammer.

"I said drop it!"

How fast could he move? With one person shooting, a bullet had grazed him, but every other one had missed. Narrowly. Now, there were several guards, all with their weapons aimed in his direction. How many could he take out before they started shooting? And that was if he'd even hit anybody else—he'd shot the one guard while they were both standing still. Eva had taught him how to shoot before he'd gone off and gotten killed at the facility, but now, he'd have to shoot while running.

All bets were off.

Cole moved to the left and raised his gun. He sprinted forward, shooting at the guards in the same motion. Trying to keep them off-balance. And it worked—for a moment. With the speed Cole had summoned, a moment was long enough for him to cut the distance between him and the security force in half. By that time, he'd emptied the clip and knocked down two more. Then, while Cole kept running at them full bore, they returned fire. He wasn't The Flash. He dodged some bullets, some simply missed him, but others hit him. He tried not to break speed. Not when he felt a shot enter his thigh, not when he felt another hit his shoulder.

When Cole got to the truck, it was five against one. They came at him, all at once. Swinging wildly. Shooting. Cole swung back. Knocked one guard out with a fist to the chin, and that one took another down with him. Cole managed to grab one of their guns. Another bullet grazed his neck. They were much better at connecting with their fists though. Those came hard and often.

Cole stuck the muzzle of his gun into a guard's stomach and pulled the trigger. By then, the guard knocked down by his partner had recovered and came charging back. Three on one. Cole turtled and allowed the guards to wail down on his body while he picked up another gun, dropped by the man he'd just shot. He channelled all the adrenaline coursing through his veins and violently straightened his body, knocking all three guards off-balance. In the split second it took them to gather themselves, Cole kicked the guard in front of him in the balls, crossed his arms and shot the two others at once. When the one he'd kicked came up for air, Cole shot him in the chest.

All three fell to the ground at the same time.

Nobody stood up again.

Cole surveyed the scene, from where he'd fought the first two guards, to the area around the truck. Nine of Mihko's security force were wounded, unconscious, or dead. He didn't give himself time to think about what he'd done. He took a step towards Reynold's house, when one of them weakly reached out and grabbed his ankle. Cole looked down at him, aimed his gun directly at his head. A flashback. *A gun inches away from his face. A barrel sparking fire. A bullet hurtling at his forehead. Blackness.* Cole shook his head, closed his eyes for a moment. He kicked the guard off his leg and tossed both of his guns away.

"You should be gone by the time I get back," he said.

At the door, Cole was ready to kick it down when it swung open, revealing a shocked Lucy.

"Who the hell are you?" She looked around Cole, at the carnage he'd left behind, then back at him. His hood was up and his neck warmer was raised over his mouth. He needed the files, and he wasn't going to hurt Lucy.

Cole lowered the neck warmer and the hood. "Lucy."

"Holy shit." She shook her head, closed her eyes. "No, no, no. Nope." She kept them closed for another moment. Opened them again.

"It's me," Cole said, "but I was never dead." There was no deal anymore, but that didn't mean everybody needed to know he'd come back from the dead. He needed an un-freaked out Lucy.

"You were never dead?"

"Mihko faked my death, kept me locked up in the basement of the facility," Cole said. "I was getting too close to the truth."

"Okay," Lucy appeared to be calming down, her voice steadying, "and what truth is that?"

"That everything that's happened in Wounded Sky since I got back, and even before then, even ten years ago, is because of *them*. The sickness, the murders…Lucy, they were killing us to cover up what they'd done."

"Mihko," Lucy repeated thoughtfully, and maybe, Cole thought, unconvinced. She zoned out, and Cole could relate to that.

"Lucy." Cole grabbed her shoulders, gave her a light shake.

She snapped out of it, looked past Cole to the guards again. "And you did that."

"Yes." Cole remembered that he'd been shot multiple times. The pain came like a hot knife being twisted into his flesh. He tried to forget the pain, to tell himself that, by morning, the wounds would be healed. The one gift Choch had actually given him.

Lucy looked down, where blood was pooling on the floor, around Cole's shoes. "You're bleeding."

"I'm fine," Cole reassured her, but was feeling a bit faint. "Lucy, I need those files, the ones in the chest. Okay? I'm going to go get those files."

"No," Lucy said. "You can't go up there."

He moved her to the side. "I'm going up there. I have to."

"You don't get it, Cole. You *can't*."

But Cole was already walking away from her, to the stairs to the second floor. "I don't have a choice."

"The fire, the guards, they're nothing…" she whispered. To herself? Her breathing was louder than the words she'd just spoken.

Cole stopped. "Nothing? What do you mean 'they're nothing'?"

"It's not just Mihko," she said even quieter, so quiet that only Cole could've really heard her. "He's worse."

He's worse. Reynold. The monster. Upayokwitigo. He was alive. Fine, okay. So be it. Cole had beat Reynold before, he could beat him now. He had to. "I'm not afraid."

Cole kept moving.

"You should be," he heard Lucy say.

Cole walked down the hallway, into Reynold's room, and went straight for the closet. He pulled the blanket off the chest and ripped off the lock. He opened the chest and rummaged through it until he found the file folder with the information on the experiments Mihko conducted on him and his friends. He stuffed the folder into his hoodie pocket, and turned to leave.

The panic Cole thought he'd pushed away came crashing back. His heart kicked into a fast, hammering beat, zero to sixty. His knees felt like they'd crumbled into one million pieces. His body vibrated, and his skin turned cold. He couldn't breathe.

"*You.*"

It was Reynold McCabe. It wasn't Reynold McCabe. Cole searched, in that forever moment, for anything human in what stood before him. He found nothing.

"*You,*" it said again.

Upayokwitigo stood so tall, it needed to crouch in Reynold's bedroom. Its hunched-over posture made the ice giant even more frightening. It was massive, but at the same time, skin and bones. Starving. Its ribs were like icicles, sticking out sharply through its pale blue skin. Deep red eyes. Sharp, decaying teeth. Lank hair falling over its shoulders.

"*You!*" it hissed.

Reynold. Hungry for power. So hungry, the hunger had turned into something else. Had turned him into something else. This monster in front of him. This wasn't what Cole had encountered in Blackwood Forest, outside of the clinic. That was something newly hatched, still growing. Caught in an insatiable hunger. Feeding, but never feeling full. Needing more and more.

Move, Cole demanded of himself. *Move now.* But his legs wouldn't work. He'd had nightmares like this, where the terror was so great that he desperately wanted to wake up and ended up stuck. Conscious, but paralyzed in terror.

Lucy had been right.

It stepped forward, and the room shook. Cole heard footsteps running up the stairs.

"Cole!"

No. What would it do with Lucy here? Did it even know Lucy anymore? Did it even know anything or anyone?

"*You!*"

It knew him. It knew Cole. Just like Cole knew himself, now. Knew himself and his anxiety. There were two monsters with him right now, and he had to beat both.

It took another step.

"Cole!"

Now. Cole drew in a breath and charged at the creature. Leaped in the air and connected with it, throwing both of his arms around its body. Cole felt the creature's sharp bones cut his skin. The thing staggered back, then tried to pry Cole off. Cole dug his fingers in hard. So hard he felt its skin break. It screamed. Cole let go with one hand and wailed on the thing with kidney shots. One after the other while it tried to rip Cole away.

"Cole!"

"Get away!" Cole shouted back at Lucy.

"*DIE!*" it cried at Cole.

Cole forced himself to hang on, to not let go, to not let the thing pull him off. He gripped harder, until he had his hand wrapped around one of its ribs. The monster punched down on Cole's back with both hands. Cole couldn't breathe. He was getting weaker and losing his grip. It clutched his shoulders with both hands and with one violent motion pulled Cole off and threw him across the room.

He hurtled towards the wall.

"Unnnh!"

Lucy grunted as his body slammed into hers. Her body crushed under his weight, and they both went through the wall, into the next room.

Drywall dust and bits of broken wall fell over their bodies. Cole rolled off Lucy, got to his knees, and looked her over. She just looked asleep except for a stream of blood coming from the corner of her mouth.

Cole wiped it away.

"Lucy?"

She didn't answer.

"Lucy!"

She didn't stir.

With a trembling hand, he pressed two fingers against her neck. Prayed to feel something, anything. But there was no pulse, and Cole knew Lucy wasn't there anymore. She was above, in the other place. A ribbon of light dancing in a sea of diamond stars. But now, in this moment, there was no comfort in that thought. Cole buried his face in his hands. Another life. How many more did there have to be?

There was crunching behind him. He gathered himself, turned away from Lucy, to Upayokwitigo. He who lives alone. Alone. Without its daughter. Lucy.

"What did you do!?" Cole cried out to it in anger.

It turned its red eyes away from Cole, to the ground, to Lucy. For the first time, Cole saw something human in the thing. Human for the briefest moment. Then the monster reared its ugly head at Cole with all of its terrible hatred and hunger.

"*You! You took her from me!*" It screamed so loud that Cole had to cover his ears.

It tore the wall apart and burst into the room. Cole backed away, stepping over Lucy's body. Putting her between them. When it saw her again, it picked Lucy up and roared. The entire house shook.

Cole shouldered his way through the door and ran down the hallway to the first floor. He heard thunder behind him. Closing in on him. He didn't bother opening the door, instead running right through it. Behind him, the monster roared down the stairs. By the time Cole had sprinted past the guards, he could hear it at his heels. He could feel the vibrations of its heavy, awful steps. He wouldn't get to Ashley's trailer. It was too fast. As fast as him. And he was getting weaker, more faint, by the second. He looked ahead anyway, as though he could see the trailer now, but instead, he saw Choch, standing firmly on the pathway. He looked like Cole had never really seen him before: intense, powerful.

"Get into the woods. I got this!" Choch lowered his aviator sunglasses.

Cole did as he was instructed, veered to the right, and beelined into Blackwood. He dove into the forest and, behind the cover of a tree, turned to look at the monster. He turned in time to see Choch flex his entire body and transform into a half-man, half-coyote beast.

Choch roared as Upayokwitigo charged him. They collided.

Choch threw the monster over his shoulder like it was a paper airplane, and it tumbled across the ground. It rolled, braced its feet against the ground, and came right back at Choch. They collided again, and this time, Choch bit into the monster's shoulder, and it let out a scream. The monster staggered backwards, holding its shoulder. Choch spat out a piece of its flesh.

Cole backed away from the tree, deeper into the forest, never taking his eyes off the battle.

The monster readied itself to charge at the spirit being again, and it did. Everything happened in slow motion.

Choch didn't brace himself for the impact. Rather, he turned to Cole, now safely in the forest. When Choch and Cole met eyes, Choch softened his stance. Relaxed. The monster thrust its hand into the spirit being's chest and pulled out Choch's heart. Orange and dripping blood.

"NO!" Cole screamed.

Choch looked down at his chest and fell straight backwards.

The monster dropped Choch's heart on the ground and turned to the woods. Peered through the trees. Snarling.

Cole took one last look at Choch's body and sprinted away, deeper and deeper into Blackwood.

Cole only stopped when he was sure that he was far enough, sure that the monster hadn't followed him. He was in a misty clearing near Silk River. A large rock sat on the riverbank, a chair for resting and taking in the beauty. Cole might've appreciated his surroundings if he wasn't so overwhelmed. He stumbled forward to sit on the rock. Tried to catch his breath. Tried to calm his pulse. Tried to stay on the rock and not let himself pass out. Five seconds in, seven seconds out. Breathe. But it wasn't just the anxiety, not this time.

He was still bleeding. His shirt, hoodie, pants were soaked with blood.

Snap.

Something was approaching. Cole stood up and managed to stay on his feet.

Snap.

Another twig broke underfoot. Somebody, not something.

"Who's there?"

Cole could see a figure in the mist, coming towards him. He readied himself for another fight. Clenched his shaking fists. One hard breath out. Blood rushing through his body, blood rushing out of his body.

Choch emerged from the mist, clutching his chest. His hand fell away to reveal a large hole where his heart should have been.

"Holy shit," Cole said. "There's a fucking hole in your chest!"

"Why does this always happen to me?" Choch fell forward. Cole caught him, and they both ended up on the ground, the spirit being lying in Cole's arms.

"Hold me," Choch whispered. "It's getting cold."

"I'm right here." Cole clutched Choch's hand.

"You're not mad at me, right?"

"No, I'm not mad at you anymore."

"But you were?"

"Don't talk, alright? Don't you talk." Cole tried to cover the hole in Choch's chest with what remained of his mall cop uniform.

"Wa…watch…" Choch's lips were shaking. His hand felt ice cold.

"Watch what? What are you trying to say?" Cole put his hand on Choch's forehead.

"Watch this," Choch rasped, "and…tell me…where…it's from…"

The spirit being's eyes rolled back and his head fell to one side, lifeless.

"Where *what's* from, Choch?" Cole asked, a tear leaving his eye despite all the frustration the spirit being had given him over the last decade. Where would Cole be now, if Choch hadn't intervened? Where would Wounded Sky be if Cole hadn't been tricked into coming home?

Cole felt Choch's hand evaporate, and the rest of his body faded into nothing, leaving behind the spirit being's tattered clothes.

"Oh," Cole whispered, "of course."

A Jedi death.

17

MIRACLE

EVERYWHERE COLE LOOKED, IT WAS BLACK. The stars, moon, and northern lights were obscured by Blackwood's thick trees. When Cole stumbled out of the forest it was black there, too. He had one hand pressed against the bullet wound on his shoulder and the other on his thigh. He'd lost a lot of blood, and was bleeding faster than he could heal. He was losing consciousness. Being out in the open, being out where the sky was bright and wide, made that impossible to ignore. He had one focus as he staggered through a ditch and climbed to the path: get to Ashley's trailer.

Cole pushed himself as hard as he could to just make it to the steps of the trailer. He moved slower with every step. His toes dragged against the gravel path. He lost his footing every other step, fell repeatedly. Each time he fell, he was sure that it would be the last time, that he wouldn't be able to get back up. He was sure, even as he got to his feet and willed his body to keep going. He was sure that soon, he'd be back up in the northern lights, back dancing with all the people who'd died, all the people he'd let down. This time, he wouldn't come back. And as the spots in his vision began to converge, he started to picture, against the forming canvas of black, all the faces that would soon join him in that dance because he'd come here to do a job, deal or not, and hadn't finished it.

"Hey!"

Cole took his hand away from the wound on his shoulder just long enough to pull the neck warmer over his face. Funny, he thought, that he did that, because when he died on the path, his face would be seen anyway. When Cole heard the voice, approaching slowly from somewhere behind, he didn't stop.

The singular focus of getting to Ashley's trailer remained.

"Hey, are you deaf or something?"

The footsteps, as cautious as they were, closed the gap, and Cole knew that somebody was walking beside him. But he didn't look. Couldn't look. His hand was on his shoulder, stemming the flow of blood, as though one drip of it kept inside his body would give him enough strength to get him where he needed to be.

"You're the thing I saw, aren't you? Except you're not a thing, you're just some weird bastard. You scared the shit out of me, you know that?"

Cole's foot hit the back of his heel, and he toppled forward onto the ground. He lay there, listening to the footsteps stop beside him, and tried, once more, to get to his feet. He got halfway there, but started to pass out and fall again. This time, however, whoever was there, caught him. They put their hands under his armpits and pulled Cole to his feet. Cole stood there, unable to take another step, unable to slide one foot forward across the gravel. He stood there and gently swayed back and forth, like a blade of grass in the breeze.

"What the hell are you on?"

Face to face now, Cole saw that it was Tristan. Tristan, however, didn't know that it was Cole. He reached forward, cautiously, and pulled the neck warmer down to expose Cole's face.

"Harper?" Tristan sounded breathless. "You're dead."

"Have…have to…get…to…Ashley's…"

Cole felt a cold cloth against his forehead. Then, an acute soreness in his shoulder and his thigh. He was lying down. There was a pillow underneath his head. He could see a faint red through his eyelids. A light was on, wherever he was. Somebody was sitting with him. He could feel the weight at his side, on the soft surface he was lying on. The cold cloth was lifted off his forehead and replaced.

"Cole?"

Eva. Cole's eyes blinked open, and he saw her. She wasn't alone. They were in Ashley's trailer. Dr. Captain was sitting on the coffee table, and the files that Cole had had in his hoodie were with her. Tristan was sitting on the floor, across the room, stewing. He looked like he wanted to hurt somebody. His arms were crossed, fists white-knuckled. Lauren was standing by the door, leaning against the wall, in full uniform. Brady was sitting at the foot of the futon, looking at Cole with concern and relief. And Michael was standing behind Brady, at the corner of the trailer. There were bags under his eyes. His hair was unkempt, and he looked pale. Hands thrust into his pockets. Cole knew how it looked when somebody's nerves were fried. Michael's nerves were fried.

"You're back," Eva said.

"Yeah." Cole strained to sit up, but ended up only going halfway, propping himself up on his elbows. The cold cloth rolled off his face and flopped against his chest. Eva took it, folded it up, and placed it on the coffee table beside the files.

"Cole, lie down," Eva said. "Come on."

"I'm okay," Cole said. "Thanks." And then he looked at Tristan. "Thank you."

Tristan nodded. "They better be right about you."

Cole had to assume that Tristan was filled in on what had happened and what needed to happen now. He scanned the room, every face. "We need to get those people out of the clinic, and then I'll have to deal with Reynold, too."

"How'd that go for you just now?" Brady asked.

Cole ignored the comment because there was nothing he could say in response. On the one hand, Brady was right, it had not gone well. But he'd got the files, and now Dr. Captain had them. Mission accomplished. All it cost was Lucy and Choch, and Cole did his best not to think about them. The spirit being's death hurt more than he ever thought possible, but there was no time to dwell on it. "What time is it? How long have I been...?" Cole started to panic. Was it too late? Was Pam already transferred? Was Wayne dead?

"Just an hour or so," Eva said. "It's not too late."

"Just an hour or so…" Dr. Captain leaned forward, pulled the shirt away from the wound on his shoulder. Cole noticed then, that he'd been taken out of his bloody clothing and had new clothes on his body. Brady's, of course. The ones that he'd packed. Cole looked at the wound. It wasn't a wound anymore. It was closed up. Fast, even for him. Discoloured, blistered. Not a scar. Not natural. Dr. Captain continued, as she felt around the wound "…this has been cauterized. I don't understand. I saw the wounds when you came in." She shook her head, and then said under her breath, "*I saw them.*"

"Jayney." Cole hadn't meant to say her name out loud. It just came out. He knew it had been her. There was no other way for that to have happened to his injuries. The same thing must've happened to his leg. Jayne. Jayne happened.

"What did you say?" Lauren pushed herself off the wall.

Cole didn't answer. He was too busy swearing at himself in his mind, for being so stupid. Still out of it, from the bullets, from the blood loss. That's what he had to boil it down to.

"You said my sister's name." Lauren was right beside him now. "Why?"

"I…" Cole considered pretending to faint. It'd be believable. He'd been shot four times. And, while his eyes were closed, he'd figure out how to answer. But then he'd leave Lauren waiting for an answer about her sister, and Jayne would know what he'd done. He thought fast. "I was just having a dream about her. It seemed so real." Cole rubbed his face as though he needed to wake up. A bit of acting that Eva might've caught, but not Lauren. "I'm sorry, Lauren. I didn't mean to upset you."

Lauren might've caught it, too. Not just the face rubbing, but the whole thing. She looked at him sideways, her eyes narrowed. But she moved on, and Cole didn't know what to make of that. "Jerry radioed in earlier. Said something bad went down at the McCabe residence." She looked at his bullet wounds deliberately, so he could see that she was. "I'm guessing, according to what Brady said just now, you had something to do with that?"

"I needed to get the files," Cole said. There was no getting around it. "I didn't want anybody to get hurt. They shot first. They would've killed me."

"Obviously," Tristan said. "You looked like a slice of Swiss cheese."

Cole's heart felt like it jumped into his throat. "Do people know I'm back?"

Lauren shrugged. "They wouldn't let Jerry close to the house. He just saw a bunch of bodies in the front yard. Mihko told Jerry they'd handle it, and Jerry's a lazy ass and agreed."

"Or he's doing what Reynold told him to do," Cole said.

"He could be," Lauren said. "Either way, nobody knows what went down over there. Mihko's keeping it close to the chest, as usual."

"I was just defending myself," Cole said. He would've found another way, he would've tried to.

"*Bodies*," Tristan said. "You took out armed guards? Just you? Even if they shot you, Harper, that's…" Tristan shook his head. "…I knew something was different about you, that night I saw you at the Fish."

"You tried to hit me," Cole reasoned. "It was a reflex."

"That was one hell of a reflex."

"Yeah, well, those reflexes weren't that great tonight."

"How did you…" Michael walked from the corner of the room, to the middle of it, behind his mother. Standing, Cole noticed, almost exactly where Ashley had been standing. But he didn't finish his sentence, just kept looking at Cole. He'd been looking at Cole, since he woke up.

"Michael?" Eva said.

"When Tristan carried you inside, you looked close to death," Michael said. "Now, you're not."

"That's what I was getting at before," Dr. Captain said. "This isn't medically possible."

"How did you survive?" Michael asked.

Cole looked at Eva, then Brady, for some help. But they looked just as confused as he was. There was no good answer. There was no good lie.

Because 'I can't tell you' had been all used up, and wouldn't fly, Cole chose to act amazed himself. "I don't know. Last thing I remember was Tristan, and then I passed out. I thought I was dying."

"You don't just come back like that," Michael said. "You can't."

"But he did," Brady said defensively. "He's right here, Mike. Maybe it was a miracle."

"I don't believe in miracles," Dr. Captain said, "but I also saw Cole an hour ago, and now, and I don't think we're going to get a better explanation."

"I didn't mean to sound like I wanted to argue or something," Michael said to Brady. "I just…" he looked at Cole again. "…I'm glad you're back, Cole. If it was a miracle or not. Maybe, I don't know, maybe it was."

"You survived *that*." Dr. Captain reached for the files and scanned through them. Something, Cole figured, she must've already done when he was unconscious. "And you survived this." Cole saw that she stopped at his file. She read it over and then looked up at him. "Your dad gave you some kind of regimen. I mean, all the kids got something. I don't even know what some of these doses they gave any of you are. But Cole, you got both."

"What does that mean?" Cole asked. "Tell me it was worth it, getting those files." He pictured Lucy. Was it worth her life? She'd be alive, if he hadn't gone there tonight. Another thing he'd have to live with. "Please."

"It was," Dr. Captain assured him. "It looks to me like they were developing a biological weapon. A super flu. And if it got into the wrong hands, whoever wanted to use it, they wanted to make sure they had a cure."

Cole felt a chill through his body. The cure was rushing through his veins. "My dad wouldn't be a part of something like that. He wouldn't use me like that." His dad cheated on his mom, yes. But the love his dad had had for him, that wasn't fake. Cole continued out loud. "He was doing those tests on me because he was trying to find a cure on his own. Maybe he knew what they were doing, maybe he'd found out, and was like, I don't know, getting the cure before they did?"

"And then he died," Lauren said.

"Right," Cole said. "Right. He died."

Had he died because of Vikki? Or if Reynold was behind everything, he *and* Mihko, couldn't he have killed Cole's dad because he was secretly trying to find a cure? And it just so happened that he was able to get rid of the man who was going to run away with his girlfriend? Cole went over all of this like he'd do when prompted by Choch, but then it felt like it all fell apart. As the spirit being would've said: a plot hole. "But why destroy all their work like that, by killing my dad in the facility and shutting it down? It doesn't make sense." Maybe it really was jealousy that had led Reynold to kill his dad and nothing more.

"Maybe they weren't sure what your dad knew," Lauren said. "They were playing it safe, locking the whole place down."

"And ten years later…"

"You came back," Eva said.

"Alex, Ashley…you," Brady said, "just to wipe it all away?"

"And with you dead, the cure would die with you," Dr. Captain said.

"They're doing it again," Cole said. "That's why people are sick. They're trying to make another weapon, and I won't be able to cure them."

"They've had a month to…mutate it…change it," Dr. Captain said. "Elder Mariah got better, but if all those people at the clinic are sick…"

"It can't be too late." Choch had said he had time. He was a trickster, not a liar. Not when it mattered, anyway.

"They're guinea pigs," Brady said. "Mihko's experimenting on us like we don't even matter. Like we're not even human."

"We matter," Cole said. "Alex, Ashley, Maggie…they mattered."

Tristan nodded, got up, and looked like he was about to head out onto the ice for a big hockey game. "You're goddamn right they did."

"Pam," Cole said.

"My dad," Eva said.

"All of them. We're going to save them, and we're going to do it tonight."

"We knock those guards the hell out and get those people somewhere safe," Tristan said.

"Now?" Michael said. "Don't we need to plan? We can't just run in there."

"I have a plan," Cole said. "And after what happened at Reynold's place, we don't have until tomorrow. Are you in?" He locked eyes with Lauren, Dr. Captain, Tristan, Michael, Eva, Brady.

He didn't need to hear a response. He saw it in their faces.

18

ASHES

THEY SPLIT UP. COLE, TRISTAN, MICHAEL, BRADY, AND LAUREN headed
to the clinic, while Dr. Captain and Eva set out to find two boats they
could use to transport the rescued patients from the clinic to Elder
Mariah's cabin. It had taken some heated arguing to get Eva to agree.
After hearing her part in the plan, while Cole still had more to go over
with the others, Eva had stormed out of the trailer, slamming the door
behind her. He followed her outside to find her leaning against the
Mustang, arms crossed, her breath smoky in the chilly autumn air.

*"That may as well be steam coming from your ears," Cole said, lean-
ing against the car beside her.*

*"You can't keep me from going with you," she said. "Look at what
happened tonight when you went off without me again. You said you
weren't going to do that, right? And then what did you do?"*

"We needed to get the others to the trailer. You know that."

*"We could have done it all together. I mean, I know I need a math
tutor, but that hour you were unconscious? That was some free time,
Cole." She paused. She'd had her back to him, but now she turned to face
him. "You could have died."*

"And you would have died, Eva."

"You don't know that!"

*"Eva…" Cole's voice softened, trying to reason with her. "…I can do
things you can't."*

Michael, who had followed Cole, walked over to face them both.

"I think Cole's right," he said.

"This doesn't involve you, Mike," Eva said. "Not anymore."

"This isn't about that," Michael said. "I still care about you, and I…"

Cole decided to just stand there and stay out of it.

Eva kept her arms crossed, waiting. "You what?"

"I can't lose anybody else."

That had sealed it.

Eva and Dr. Captain went to find the boats, and Cole left with the larger group to the clinic. Cole, having reclaimed his hoodie and neck warmer from a pile of bloody clothing in the corner of Ashley's trailer, led the group along the outskirts of Blackwood. As the clinic neared, Michael joined Cole at the front to walk with him.

"How did you escape? What happened?"

"They, uhh," Cole thought up some details, "caught me snooping around the facility, trying to find out more about what was happening, what they were doing. There's this, like, room in the basement they kept me in. Glass walls. Like, unbreakable walls."

"So what did you do?"

"Faked passing out," Cole said. "When they came in to check on me, I just bolted. Ran to Elder Mariah's cabin until I figured out what to do."

"Just bolted?" Michael asked. "That's it? They didn't…hurt you? Anything like that?"

Cole sighed. "What are you doing here, Mike?" He'd not been on their list of team members because Cole didn't think Michael, upon finding out he was alive, would want anything to do with the team.

"Brady came to get Mom, and I've been trying to look out for her," Michael said.

"Can't lose anybody else." Cole acknowledged what Michael had said earlier.

"She's all I have now," Michael said. "I told Brady we're a package deal, so…I don't know, I hope that's okay."

"I should've asked you from the start, I guess."

"I don't blame you, that you didn't."

"Well, thanks for coming anyway, man." Cole patted Michael's shoulder. "We could use all the help we can get."

"You're welcome."

"Honestly, I didn't think you'd want to, after—"

"I was a jerk before," Michael said quickly. "You didn't deserve that. How I was treating you."

Cole shrugged. "I was, too. But none of that matters anymore. What happened before doesn't matter. Just now, that's it. Okay?"

Michael nodded, paused, then said, "I'm sorry, though. I'm really sorry."

"It's okay," Cole said. "Sticks and stones, right?"

"Yeah, sticks and stones."

"Hey," Tristan called from behind them, "we're here. You guys wanna bro hug and get it over with, so we can do this thing?"

They found a spot in the forest where they could stay hidden and assess the situation. It wasn't good. With the incident at McCabe's house, security at the clinic had been beefed up. Tripled. And the guards, just like at Reynold's, had guns and rifles. Lauren had one gun, and Brady had the rifle. They were seriously outgunned.

"I'll take them out," Cole said. He wanted their help; the bullet wounds that hadn't yet fully healed screamed for some assistance. But he didn't want to be responsible for another death. "I need you guys to help get the patients."

"No fucking way," Tristan said. "I'm not here just to push wheel-chairs out of that place."

"I know, Tristan, but if we all go and get slaughtered, then who's going to save the people in the clinic?"

"I'm going," Tristan said.

"No, you're not," Cole said.

"What? Because I can't heal like Deadpool?"

"Yeah, that's actually exactly why. The patients are the mission here. This isn't some revenge thing. It can't be." "Just listen to him, Tristan,"

Brady said. "He knows what he's talking about."

"*I* can't lose somebody else," Cole whispered, trying to hold it together.

"You care about me?" Tristan asked, chuckling. "I tried to beat the shit out of you, more than once."

"You were upset about Maggie," Cole said. "I know what that feels like."

"Because I thought you had killed Maggie. Now that I know who did, I'm sorry Harper, this *is* about revenge for me. Shouldn't it be for all of you?"

"Seriously, get your act together. Like, now." Lauren gave Tristan a long, hard look. She put on her cop face. "You're staying. Got it? I'll go with Cole."

No argument there. She had a gun, and she had the cop face. Cole waited for one of them to say something again, but for the time being, they were all quiet. "Okay, Lauren and I will take those guards out. Once we're in, follow behind us."

"Here." Brady handed Cole the rifle. "Don't say no this time."

In hindsight, Cole admitted, a rifle would've been helpful at Reynold's. He took the weapon from Brady.

Lauren cocked the hammer on her gun.

"I can help! Remember I did before?" Jayne appeared beside Cole, crouching in the bush, looking out at the clinic, burning hot and bright.

Cole nodded at her, and it was more than him just accepting her help; it was him thanking her for cauterizing his wounds.

"You're welcome, Coley!"

"So what's the play?" Lauren asked Cole.

Lauren and Cole (and an excited Jayne) looked over the scene. Two guards roamed the perimeter, two guards at the side door, two guards at the front door.

"I'll take out the four guards at the doors," Cole said. "You take care of the two walking around."

"You know how to use that thing?"

"Point and shoot," Cole assured them. "You go through the bush. I'll come at them from the front. They'll be distracted."

"What do we do if you get shot?" Tristan asked.

"*And* you can't heal from it," Michael added.

"If anything happens to me," Cole said to them, "you do what you're supposed to do."

"We will," Brady said.

Cole took a deep breath and covered his face with the neck warmer. "Let's go," he said to Lauren. "Fast and hard."

Lauren ran off into the bush, and Cole dug his heels in, ready to run at them as fast as he could, so fast that they'd hardly have a chance to shoot at him. Jayne was at his side. Her fire made it seem like daytime.

"What do you want me to do, Coley?" She was digging in as well.

Cole looked at the guards, awash in her personal sunset. He had seen that same light ten years ago. The image of the elementary school burning down flashed in his mind. Mihko was behind that, too. Cole knew it. They had to be. He'd heard the screams of his classmates. Trapped inside. The chains on the door handles. They'd been locked inside. Why? To cover up everything that Mihko had done? Cole felt that same fire in his chest. He looked at Jayne, resolute.

Burn.

Jayne didn't question Cole. She just gave one quick nod, and her face scrunched up. "Okay, Coley." She disappeared in a puff of smoke, and the night went black.

As soon as Jayne was gone, Cole was too. He pushed off the ground and propelled his body forward. He'd almost reached the guards when they noticed him. It was too late for them. They got shots off, but missed. Cole was moving too fast. He went for the guards at the side door. As he ran full-speed into one of them, the night lit up once more. He heard the guards at the front door shrieking. The guard Cole body checked collided with the clinic wall. A shot rang out somewhere behind the building. Lauren. Cole turned around to face the other guard, rifle raised, and found the muzzle of the guard's gun staring right back at him.

"Drop it," the guard said.

"Alright." Cole lowered the rifle and raised both hands.

The guard approached Cole until he was only a few feet away, his gun never wavering, aimed directly at Cole's heart.

"I'm going to enjoy this," the guard said.

Cole threw his palm over the muzzle as it went off. He felt the bullet cut through his hand, and pulled the gun out of the guard's grip. He threw an uppercut. The guard flew back several feet and collided with a tree. Out cold.

"Enjoy your nap, shithead."

Cole turned in time to see guards, in flames, running away from the clinic. Arms flailing. Crying out in agony. Moments later, Jayne was at Cole's side. Hand on his shoulder, watching him clutch the hand that had been shot. Blood was pouring onto his lap from the bullet wound. She tried to cauterize the wound, but couldn't.

She had no flames.

"I'm sorry, Coley." Tears were falling from both her eyes.

"It's okay."

"I never wanted to hurt anybody like that." Her voice was shaking.

"I know," he said, "I know. I'm sorry. I shouldn't have asked you to do that."

"Did I do bad?"

"No," Cole said, but what else could he add? That she'd done good? Had he done good earlier, at Reynold's? Had the men he'd shot survived? He couldn't see how. Lauren had said that Jerry saw bodies.

"They were bad, right?"

"I…" Cole reached up and touched the scarred side of her face. It was the clearest he'd ever seen it. "I don't know, Jayney. We did what we had to do, okay?"

"Am I gonna get in trouble, now?" Her lower lip quivered.

"No, you're not going to get in trouble. Promise," Cole said. "Go, Jayney. Go see your friends. They always make you feel better, right?"

"Yeah," she said unconvincingly, then disappeared. Not in her usual black cloud of smoke. She left in ashes. It was the first time she'd really hurt anybody. She'd made the gun burn in Scott's hand, sure. But the guards she'd just burned for Cole weren't coming back. Cole could see them now, lying in the field out front of the clinic. Charred remains.

"Cole."

Cole turned around to see Lauren walking up to him from behind the clinic.

"You okay?" She holstered her gun.

Cole ripped the bottom of his shirt off and wrapped it around his hand.

"Yeah," he said. "You get them both?"

Lauren shook her head. "Other guy got away." She peered out over the field. Cole saw her do it, but couldn't bring himself to look at the burned bodies again. "What the hell?"

Cole stood up and looked at the field with Lauren. "Crazy, right?"

"Cole." He tried to ignore the fact that Lauren was staring at him, not at the bodies in the field now. "Hey." But he couldn't ignore her when she stepped right in front of his line of view. "I'm not an idiot, you know. You had something to do with that. Those guards didn't just spontaneously combust."

There was no way to explain it other than to tell Lauren exactly what had happened. But now wasn't the time, so he told her the same line he'd repeated over and over since returning to Wounded Sky. Pretended like there was still a deal, when there wasn't.

When there never had been.

"I can't tell you, Lauren."

"Yeah? Well, you're going to tell me, Cole. If not now, then later. Got it?"

"Yeah," Cole said. "I got it."

"Right," she said. "Now, let's get our people out of here."

19

EXODUS

TRISTAN, BRADY, AND MICHAEL MET Lauren and Cole at the front doors to the clinic. They had seen the guards burning; and they saw them now, lying in the field, lifeless. Cole told them what he'd told Lauren. Brady gave him a very familiar look in response to a very familiar refrain. But there were more pressing matters.

Inside the clinic, the lobby was quiet. Cole could hear the beeping of the heart monitors, muffled through closed doors.

"We need to split up," Cole said. "There are people upstairs and downstairs. We need to get them all out and fast. There'll be more guards coming."

"Yeah, probably because you had a bonfire with them," Tristan said.

Cole assigned each person several rooms and reserved himself for Eva's dad, intending to guard Wayne's life as though it were his own.

"We've got twenty minutes to get to Silk River," Cole said.

Upstairs and down the hall moments later, Cole pushed open the door to Wayne's room. It was dark and so quiet that it made the sounds in the room more pronounced. The ominous beep of the heart monitor. The drip of the solution feeding through the IV tube. Wayne's shallow breath. Cole walked across the room and nudged Wayne's arm. No response. He was middle-aged, a relatively young father, but his black hair had greyed, and he was pale and thin. Cole squeezed his hand to try again to wake him up. His skin was burning up.

"Hey, Mr. Kirkness, wake up."

The fluorescent lights coughed to life. Cole pulled his neck warmer back up and turned to find Dr. Ament standing by the light switch, just inside the door.

"If you think you're saving these patients, you're not," she said.

She was clutching a radio in one hand.

"That's exactly what I'm doing," Cole said.

"If you take them away from here, they'll die. That medicine," Dr. Ament pointed to the IV drip feeding liquid into Wayne, "that medicine is keeping them alive."

"Are you insane?" Cole asked. "You've injected them all with a virus, and you're probably trying to figure out a cure, but you obviously haven't yet. *You're* killing them."

"The closer we get, the better the chance they'll make it."

"Well, you're not getting any closer with the people here. We're saving all of them," Cole said. "And you're not taking anybody else, either. It's over."

"This is in the national interest," Dr. Ament said. "It's bigger than Wounded Sky. It'll protect this country and protect other countries, too."

"Are you serious? The national interest is creating a biological weapon to kill a shitload of people? The national interest is deliberately taking Wounded Sky residents and making them sick, killing *them*?"

"I've radioed Mihko to send more guards. You and your friends better run."

"We'll leave," Cole moved to take the line out of Wayne's arm and carry him out if he had to, "but we're bringing everybody with us."

Dr. Ament stepped in front of the door, like she could keep him from leaving. "They'll kill you."

Cole shook his head and lowered his neck warmer. He gave Dr. Ament a half-smile. "They're not too good at killing me."

Dr. Ament fell backwards and hit the wall. She tried to collect herself, but failed. Her entire body was shaking, and she was ghost white. "Cole Harper?"

"Now." Cole walked towards her. She recoiled, tried to dig her heels into the floor, but they slipped, making black streaks on the white tiles. He crouched in front of her. "I'm leaving and don't try to stop me."

"We killed you," she said weakly. "I saw your body. I…you'd almost no blood left."

"What? Blood? What are you talking about? You killed me to cover up what you were doing, same reason you killed Ashley and Alex."

Dr. Ament looked away, like she couldn't stand to look at him, like if she didn't look, he'd go away. That it would mean this wasn't real. "We only ever wanted your blood. Dead or alive."

"So you could use it to make a new cure?"

She nodded. "We're modifying the virus, testing out its efficacy, for what we need it to do. And—"

"This time, you'll have it. It won't be only in my body."

Cole's mind felt like it was about to burst, but he didn't have time to mull it over. Guards could come rushing into the clinic at any moment. He got Dr. Ament on her feet and led her over to a chair. Sat her down.

"What are you doing?"

"Just stay there." He looked around the room. Settled on the metal bar at the side of the hospital bed. He ripped it off and returned to Dr. Ament. "Keep still."

"What are you going to do, beat me with that?"

Cole put the bar behind the chair and positioned it properly. "You know everything about me. When I take the bus, when I practice basketball, who my friends are. All the things you know about me, and you think I'd beat a woman to death with a metal rod?"

She looked at him like he was still just a walking corpse. "Clearly, we don't know what you're capable of."

"You're right, you don't." Cole bent the metal rod into a circle around Dr. Ament. He grabbed her radio, dropped it on the ground, and crushed it with his foot.

"It's too late."

"It's never too late."

Cole turned around and picked up Wayne. He carried Wayne out of the room, and only then did Wayne's eyes flutter open. He squinted, trying to focus, and looked around, realizing that he was being carried.

"Who are you?" His voice was faint.

"I'm here to get you out," Cole said.

"Out where?"

"To see your daughter."

Brady was in the lobby with the three patients he had gathered, two of them able to walk under their own power, and one leaning on him heavily. There was a guard on the floor, dead to the world. Maybe the same guard Cole had encountered earlier, when he'd gone to find Pam.

Cole nodded at the guard. "What happened there?"

"Tristan took care of that one," Brady said. "No roasting sticks required."

"Well, I'm glad I almost died in his arms then," Cole said. "Where's everybody now?"

"Already on their way to the boats."

"One of the doctors called for backup. We have to get out of here."

No new guards had arrived yet, but Cole could hear them coming from the research facility. He couldn't tell how many, and he didn't want to wait to find out. They left the clinic for Silk River as fast as the patients could go, following the edge of Blackwood Forest from behind the clinic through some thick grass and brush and down an embankment. Michael, Lauren, and Tristan were there, already helping people onto the boats. The guards were closer. Maybe at the clinic, Cole figured. Finding their colleagues knocked out, burned. They would check inside the clinic and find Dr. Ament strapped to the chair with a bent metal rod and all the patients missing.

"Is that it?" Lauren asked, when she saw Brady and Cole.

"Yeah." Cole put Wayne down and helped him into Eva's boat. Both she and Dr. Captain had looked anxious to get going, but when Eva saw her dad, she ran to him.

"Dad!" she said through tears. "What did they do to you?"

"Too many…romance novels…" He tried to laugh, but coughed violently instead. "Took the wind…out of me."

"You idiot." She hugged him carefully. "Let's sit you down, okay?"

"Where…we going?" he asked.

"Elder Mariah's."

Cole watched Eva with her dad. He smiled in spite of the night they'd had, the night they still had ahead of them. She and her father were together again, after over a month of being kept apart. First, he'd been in the clinic for the gunshot wound to the stomach. The bullet that had been meant for Eva. Then, after Mihko had taken over the clinic, he, like the others, had become part of the new experiment.

Lauren offered to drive their boat, so Eva could sit with her father. Cole, Brady, Michael, and Tristan helped get everybody else on board. They got into the packed boats after Tristan helped the last person on. Cole could hear the guards coming their way. He did a quick headcount, and satisfied, called out to the drivers. "Let's get out of here!"

The engines roared to life. There was a loud *pop* over the motors. Tristan, who'd been sitting next to Cole, hit the ground.

Standing on the embankment, his gun raised, was Mark.

"No!" Cole shouted.

Another *pop*, and Cole felt a bullet hit his shoulder.

He looked at Mark, looked at Tristan, who was bleeding out on the floor of the boat. He leaped out of the boat and charged Mark. Another shot missed. Cole laid his shoulder into Mark's stomach and drove him into the ground.

"What did you do? Why?"

He straddled Mark and pummeled his face. Mark was out after one punch, but Cole kept going. He wouldn't have stopped, would've beaten Mark into the ground, if it weren't for Michael, who grabbed Cole's arm while it was raised in mid-air ready for another strike.

"Cole, stop! You'll kill him!"

"I *want* to kill him!"

"No, you don't!"

Cole jerked his arm away from Michael, knocking him over, and raised his arm again. He clenched his fist. It was shaking. His entire body was shaking. Heart racing. Chest heaving.

"This isn't you!"

"It is tonight," Cole said.

"Please!"

A bullet whipped past Cole's face. They were coming.

Cole stared at Mark. Bloodied. Beaten.

"We have to go, Cole."

He lowered his fist, stood up as another bullet narrowly missed his body, and ran with Michael back to the boats. As soon as they were in, they took off, speeding away from Wounded Sky and into Blackwood Forest.

Eva was cradling Tristan in her arms. Blood dripped from his mouth. His hand was on his chest, painted red. Reluctantly, Cole moved Tristan's hand away to reveal the wound. It was right over his heart.

"Don't think…I'm gonna…heal…like you…Harper."

"You're okay."

"You…you're a…shitty liar."

"I know."

Tristan grabbed Cole's hoodie. "You finish…it…promise me."

"I will." Cole took Tristan's hand. He bent over until his lips were right by Tristan's ear, so only Tristan could hear him. "I know where you're going, Tristan. Don't be scared. Do you see the northern lights? Remember those stories?"

Cole looked up, to see Tristan staring at the sky. "Yeah, I… rem—remember."

"They're true, man."

Tristan laughed, then coughed, and blood misted into the air. "Bull…sh—shit." Tristan's head fell to the side, and his eyes, still open, tore into Cole's.

20

ESCAPE PLAN

COLE COULDN'T TAKE HIS EYES OFF SILK RIVER, watching the churning water directly behind the boat and the ribbon-like trails left in their wake. He watched those trails dance their way to the shorelines, like the northern lights. This helped dampen his shakiness. The weight of the day pressing down on him and what had just happened.

Back in the city, at one of his sessions, his therapist had written down *anxiety* on a sticky note and stuck it to her palm.

"Now," she said, *"put your palm against mine."*

Cole didn't at first. Whatever she was doing felt weird, and he didn't like showing his palms to anybody. He used to walk around school with his hands in his pockets. He used to sit on the bench during basketball games, palms down. He used to like how much he played in games because there was always a basketball covering the scars.

"Just for a second," she encouraged.

She jerked her hand slightly, in a way that Cole thought was meant to be encouraging. Finally, he raised his hand and kept it closed into a fist until the last moment, before he had to put his palm against hers. His scars must have felt disgusting to her, against her skin. He thought they were disgusting, too.

"Okay, so first, push against my palm," she said.

He pushed and felt the resistance. After a few seconds, she stopped pressing, and Cole did as well.

"Put your palm face up now," she said.

Cole looked at her curiously, but now they were into it, and that curiosity emboldened him to move his palm away from hers and point it to the ceiling. She placed the sticky note, the paper with anxiety *written on it, onto his palm.*

"Easier, right?"

He nodded.

"Accepting you have anxiety, rather than fighting so hard against it, is one of the most important steps you can take," she said. "Not to judge yourself for feeling the way you do, thinking the way you do, but just to acknowledge how you feel and keep living. Keep breathing."

Cole took a deep breath, and then expelled it. Five seconds in, seven seconds out. There was only now. Only their boat cutting through the river water, only the churning water expelled by the engine, only the trails left behind them, dancing at their freedom. And they were free, now. Cole's body was shaking. It was okay. His anxiety hadn't been left dead when his body had been resurrected. His body *should* be shaking. He might've killed people and had seen others die. Saw another one of his friends, one who had originally hated him, die while saving others. Then there was Lucy. Choch. Reynold being alive. He put all of this in his opened palm and accepted it.

And there was Pam. Cole turned away from Silk River and scanned the boats until he saw her, curled up onto a seat, a blanket over her body, her head propped up on a rolled-up jacket. He stepped around two other patients and sat down in front of her. Her eyes were closed. She looked peaceful. He put the outside of his hand under her nose to feel her breath. Warm, but short. He looked up at Dr. Captain's boat ahead of them. He wanted her to come treat Pam, now. Make her better. Save her. He looked around the boat again, at the people they'd saved, each in their own stage of the illness, and wondered how many of them would be around tonight, tomorrow, the next day. How many had they *actually* saved? Cole shook his head. He returned his attention to Pam.

"Hey, you're okay," he said.

Her eyelids fluttered, but stayed closed.

"Pretty soon you'll be teaching me how to play *Fortnite*, you know?"

He wanted an IV and a needle, so he could give her some of his blood and make her well, like he'd done before in the clinic. His blood wouldn't do anything now though, not with what they had given her. He caught Eva's eye; she was sitting with her dad, Wayne leaning his head against her shoulder, sleeping. She smiled at him, nodded. A thank you for saving her dad. He smiled, nodded back.

Cole leaned back against the seat, took a deep breath, and only then looked behind the boat again, down the river, at the trails they'd left behind. He closed his eyes and felt the shakiness, felt the unsteadiness in his limbs, in his joints, within his body, and accepted those feelings for what they were. That despite everything they'd gone through, over the last month and a half, over the last few hours, they were here now, and on their way to someplace better. And that all the people they'd brought with them, they'd be better, too.

Time passed slowly. It was always this way during the most urgent moments. They had saved everybody, but they needed to get to the cabin and into the care of Elder Mariah and Dr. Captain. He hadn't been wrong to bring them away from there, Cole knew that. It wasn't like Dr. Ament had said. But Cole began to wonder if it had made what they'd done right.

"You're thinking." Eva had left her dad sleeping on the seat, and had come over to sit beside Cole without him noticing. "Again."

"I've been trying to do things differently," Cole said. "But I'm not sure I'm doing any better."

"And there's Cole being hard on himself again," Eva said. "It's like we've gone back in time."

"People are dying again. Lucy. Tristan." Cole looked at Tristan's body, right near his feet. Covered up with blankets they'd found under the seats.

"Cole."

"I keep thinking how if I'd just stayed in the ground, Lucy would still be here, because I wouldn't have gone to Reynold's house."

"Stop."

"Tristan wouldn't have had to…"

Eva took his hand.

"I'm supposed to be saving people."

Cole wiped a tear away from his cheek. There was only this moment. Right now. He felt the wet spot on the outside of his hand. How the wind made it feel cool, even as the spot dried. Here, then gone.

"What about these people?" Eva asked. "You saved them, didn't you?"

"I don't…" Cole looked up at the northern lights, the ribbons swirling in their dance to music he could no longer hear. "I don't know."

"You're the math whiz, right?"

"That doesn't make it better."

"It makes it…I don't know." She sighed. Getting frustrated at Cole, like she used to as well. "It makes it what it is, Cole. It makes it what had to happen. Tristan knew what he was doing, coming with us. We all knew it would be dangerous."

"I just wanted it to happen differently."

"We all did," Eva said. "I wanted to be there tonight with you guys. Remember that? How do you think I feel, knowing that maybe *I* could've done something? But I've got to let that go and so do you."

"And Lucy?"

"Do you think you started all of this?"

Cole looked down. River water pooled together in the cracks between the floorboards of the boat. She put her hand on his chin, and made him look at her.

"Do you think you started all of this? Why are you here, Cole?" "To save the community?" he said.

She leaned back against the seat. "You didn't start this. You're here to finish it."

Cole let her words percolate. He shook his head. "When you think you've got it all figured out…"

"Is that the start of a meme?"

Cole smirked. "No, it's just. I was ready to go all hard core, like Rambo Cole or something. Thought I was over this kind of stuff, then I just slip back into it."

"You thought you were reborn as somebody else?"

"Something like that."

"You left as Cole, and you came back as Cole. You're just learning and accepting why you're here. That doesn't mean you're a different person, or that you still don't have things to learn."

Cole had been looking off into the woods, where his thoughts had enough room to breathe. Now, he looked at Eva until, maybe, she felt his eyes on her. She turned to him, smiled, and looked away shyly. "What?"

"I love you," he said. "I mean…"

She reached over and put two fingers against his lips. "You can stop, now. That was enough."

They looked at each other. He was waiting for her to say it, too. He wanted her to say it. But she just took her fingers from his lips, put her hand back on his, and turned away.

"Brady, come drive this thing for a minute," Lauren said.

By Cole's estimation, they had to be close to Elder Mariah's cabin. Eva had gone back to sit with her dad, his head resting on her lap, her arm protectively draped over his shoulder. Cole sat sideways on the bench, watching the water. Brady stood up and walked to the front of the boat. Cole listened as Lauren moved from the steering wheel, and Brady took her place. He felt a tap on his shoulder.

"How's she doing?" Lauren asked.

"Same," Cole said.

"We'll be there soon."

"Yeah, I know."

"And they'll be here soon, too."

"So what do we do? We can't move the cabin, and they…" Cole lowered his voice. "…they can't last much longer in this boat. They need Dr. Captain, and they need Elder Mariah."

"Brady told me we were close, but he didn't tell me where the cabin actually was. Is it near the river?"

"A few hundred yards maybe."

"Two football fields," Lauren said thoughtfully. "That might be far enough."

"If they see the boats, they'll come looking. If they come looking, they'll find us. Everybody gets taken back, we probably get taken, too."

"What if they saw the boats in a different place? Far enough away that no matter where they looked in the forest—"

"They wouldn't find us."

"We drop everybody off and keep driving the boats farther down the river, deeper into the woods," Lauren said.

"*We* means us," Cole said. "Dr. Captain and Brady, they need to be with the people. Eva needs to be with her dad."

Lauren looked up, looked all around, at the sky visible through the forest's towering trees, then looked at Cole. "On the plus side, it's a nice night for a walk."

Soon, the boats pulled up along the shore, where, a relatively short distance into the woods, was the cabin. Eva, Michael, Dr. Captain, and Brady were briefed on the plan.

They helped the patients off the boat and removed Tristan's body as quickly as possible. Cole and Lauren helped get their people away from the shore and into Blackwood, so that when the boats chasing them passed by, everybody would be safely out of sight. By the time they were ready, there were lights in the distance.

Mihko's security force were coming.

"Let's go!" Lauren jumped into one of the boats and took off down the river. "Follow me!"

Cole got into the other boat and pushed the throttle.

21

WALK IT BACK

LAUREN CUT THROUGH SILK RIVER like a race car driver. Cole just tried to keep up, keep her in sight. She navigated the bends in the river with expert precision while Cole did his best not to crash the boat, at least not until they'd gone far enough that the others were safe. Cole had never been this deep into the woods before. He wondered how long they could go before finding the end of Blackwood. It made him realize just how remote Wounded Sky was. It wasn't just Blackwood that kept the community separated from what felt like the rest of the world, either. Soon after Silk River finished its journey through Blackwood, it fed into Little Playgreen Lake. At the southern end of the lake rested Wounded Sky's closest neighbour, Norway House Cree Nation.

Cole took inventory of all the sensations coursing through his body—the fight-or-flight sensations so familiar to him, although right now, the adrenaline was warranted; they were engaged in an actual chase. He hoped the guards had taken the bait, and that Brady, Eva, and the others were, by now, at the cabin.

They'd gone about five kilometres before Lauren pulled up to the shore ahead. He slowed to a stop behind her. They both jumped out and crouched by the boats for a minute, hidden from the view of anybody approaching. Listening, waiting. If the guards had stopped, if they weren't following anymore, they'd have to drive the boats back. If the guards were still coming, they had to hightail it, lead the guards on what Cole hoped would be a long and futile search.

"Hear anything?" Lauren asked.

Cole closed his eyes and listened carefully. He heard engines in the distance. "Yeah, it worked. They're following us."

Lauren let out a sigh of relief. Even if the two of them weren't safe, the others were. "How close, you think?"

"Too close." Cole started to climb up the embankment, on the side of the river the cabin was on.

Lauren yanked at his hoodie.

"What?" he asked.

"We should go a bit farther out, on the other side of the river, throw them off."

Cole looked to the other side of the river, where the thick woods offered plenty of cover. "Good plan," Cole said, "*if* they have somebody with them who can track."

Lauren shrugged. "We'll make it obvious. Pull the boats over to the other shore and break a bunch of twigs and branches, press down the long grass."

"Yeah, even I could follow that trail."

Lauren jumped back into the boat, pushed off from the shore, and let the weak current bring her to the other side. Cole did the same, and when they'd both got out, he pulled the boats onto the shore, so they wouldn't drift off. They stomped the grass down from the shore, up the embankment, and into the forest for several yards. They broke some branches that had fallen across their makeshift path, made sure to kick at the ground to leave obvious prints, and tore leaves off the underbrush.

"I think that's good," Lauren said after they'd spent an efficient minute or so doing the work. "We don't want to make it *too* obvious."

Cole looked over their path, from where they'd ended it, to where it sloped down to Silk River. "It'll get them started anyway."

"And by the time they realize they're idiots…"

"We'll be long gone."

"Let's get the hell out of here."

"Double back on the other side here, cross far up ahead, make our way to the cabin."

"Probably an hour on foot."

They (Cole in particular, who still felt like a rookie in the bush) were careful not to leave a path for the guards to follow from there on. They made their way out, directly away from Silk River for about a kilometre, then turned back in the direction they'd come from with the boats. They'd been running the whole time and continued to run for an acceptable distance before Lauren slowed to a walk. Cole did the same. She was in amazing shape, but was huffing, struggling for air. She needed a break.

"We're…" she looked back, at the thick black of the forest, "…good now. We'll be…good."

"Good." Cole could've run all the way back. But maybe, like Lauren had said earlier, it was a nice night for a walk. To just be in the quiet, to come down from the stress and excitement. The forest offered quiet and peace. The only sounds were their footsteps and Lauren's heavy breathing, which, after a few minutes, evened out.

"Can I ask you something?"

"Sure."

"Call it the cop side of me, I guess." As if to display her cop side, she zipped up her RCMP jacket, now that her body heat was lowering. Her badge was on full display.

"It's fine."

"Did you…" she paused, like she wanted to ask something else, but didn't. She continued. "…was it easier, being away for all those years?"

"Yes and no," he said. "I mean, on the one hand, I had no idea how much people hated me up here, so…"

"Some people."

"Some people," he corrected himself. "So, because I didn't know, that probably made things a bit easier. You know, ignorance is bliss sort of thing. If I did, I'm not sure if it would've been harder, or easier to be away from that."

"But you didn't know, so…ignorance…was it easier?"

"I think I thought it was easier. I mean, I convinced myself it was easier. I convinced myself that I could just, I don't know, run away from the pain. That if I was far enough away, I'd be okay."

"But it wasn't."

"No," Cole said. "I was on anti-anxiety meds, having panic attacks, seeing a therapist, all of that. All of that because you can't run from those things. I couldn't run from what happened. The more I thought I could, the more all that shit found me and burrowed inside my mind. And then, you know, it would explode. My whole body would explode."

"And that's why you needed the pills."

Cole took a deep breath. In for five, out for seven. "She, my therapist, wanted me to try different things. Exercise, mindfulness. I tried all that. I really did. Sometimes, it even worked. But yeah, I took the pills."

"That's okay," she said, "that you needed that. It doesn't make you weak or anything."

"Yeah, I know."

That moment hung in the air.

Pills. Cole could see them smashing against the wall in the basement of the research facility, right before he'd been shot. He could hear them scattering across the floor, sounding like distant rainfall. He didn't know why he'd thrown the bottle even now. Frustration. Anger. Exhaustion. He might've thrown anything he had on him, but he was glad it had been the pills. Even if he wanted one now, he couldn't have one. It forced him to do the things his therapist had tried to get him to do, like the mindfulness he'd practised on the boat. Dealing with his anxiety in those quiet moments was important, when his body wasn't being quiet at all.

"Cole?"

"Yeah?"

"You lied to me, back at the cabin, didn't you? When you said Jayne's name."

"I…" If he lied again, told her another lie, she'd be able to tell. Maybe it wasn't just Eva and Brady who could sniff him out, maybe it was anybody. Maybe he was just bad at it. He supposed lying wasn't a bad thing to be bad at. But, the question came again, of how much to tell her? He looked at her, and saw the desperation and longing in her face. The deal was off, but still, some secrets needed to be kept. If he were going to be a hero, however shitty he'd been at it so far, one thing he needed to do was figure out who could know what he really was and what he could really do. Since coming back to Wounded Sky, she was somebody he'd been able to trust. Batman had Commissioner Gordon. Didn't every superhero need somebody like Lauren? Or was that just making excuses for why he should tell her about Jayne, something he'd always wanted to do?

"You…" Lauren said.

"I was lying that I dreamt about Jayne."

Cole instinctively looked up at the northern lights, but he couldn't see them right now. The trees were too lush overhead. He allowed the memories of that time to come to him. Jayne wasn't there right now. She was still stuck on Earth because of Choch. Cole was sure, right now, she'd be in the cemetery with her friends, trying to heal from the trauma at the clinic. And often, Cole knew, she was with Lauren, watching over her since being pulled down from the waiting room. Why *was* she still here? Was she still captive until Cole saved the community, even if the deal with Choch was never really a deal? Even if Choch was dead? He looked away from the sky, back at Lauren.

"Do you know those wounds I had and how they healed like that?"

"Cauterized," Lauren said. "Yeah, why?"

"I don't know how to say this."

"Then just say it however it comes out."

"Okay," Cole took a deep breath, "I can heal faster than normal people." He unwrapped the hand that had been shot while breaking into the clinic and showed Lauren. He pulled his hoodie up for a moment and showed her the shot he'd taken while they were on the boat, too. They were starting to mend. They looked like bullet wounds that he'd got a week ago, not hours earlier.

"Oh, my God."

Cole re-wrapped his hand. "But I don't heal like those bullet holes healed tonight. Somebody did that for me."

"Cole, I was there the whole time, nobody—"

"Lauren." Cole stopped walking, put his hand on her shoulder, and she stopped as well. They stood there in the middle of the forest, in the black of night, in the dead quiet. "Jayne did it."

"What?" she whispered. "Screw off. Screw you for saying that."

"Jayney." Cole pictured her back at the quarry, dancing around the teenagers full of joy, pretending that they were watching her, that she had made them feel her joy. Dancing like an ember from the bonfire. "She's been with me since I came back home."

"*With* you? With you how? Stop messing with me, Cole. With you how?"

Cole kept picturing Jayne, dancing around the fire, dancing around the kids, dancing and smiling and getting brighter and brighter just from thinking she might make somebody smile. "I know this is going to sound strange, but since I've come back home, Jayne's been with me. Really with me. She was with me tonight. She cauterized my wounds. She helps me when I need her. She came down from the northern lights…that's what she told me."

"No…"

"I wouldn't mess with you, Lauren. I wouldn't do that."

"She was up there?" Lauren's voice was steadying, but tears were streaming out of her eyes. "Jayney? And now she's…" Lauren started to lose her breath, like Cole did when he was having a panic attack. "…she's here? In Wounded Sky?"

"Yes," Cole said, "and she's just like she used to be, when she was alive. She's okay, Lauren."

"How did she burn your wounds? Do…is she a ghost? Do ghosts do that?"

"She's…" There was no way to sugar coat this. "…half burning and half not. From the fire at the school. How she died."

"Half burning?"

"She's always half on fire, half of her body. The other half, it's normal. She can make people feel her heat. She can…"

"That was her at the clinic. The guards."

Cole nodded. "Yeah, and that's why she's not here right now. It made her sad. When she gets sad, her flames get dim."

"Do you know how this all sounds?"

"Yeah, I know how it sounds."

"But I know it," Lauren touched her chest. "Somehow, I know it. I…" she wiped at her cheeks. "…I can feel her sometimes."

"Because she's with you sometimes. She's told me that."

Lauren hugged Cole and held him so tight he could hardly breathe and kept him like that until she was able to speak, to breathe, normally.

"Does it hurt? Because she's burning?"

"It doesn't hurt her. She just…she's the same. She's happy, like, all the time. She dances all the time, too. She looks like a little flame, you know? She looks…beautiful."

Lauren pressed her face into Cole's chest, clutched his hoodie, and he could feel her sobbing, trying to be quiet. He put his arms around her and just hugged her again, letting her cry. Finally, Lauren moved back, and Cole let her go. She laughed when she saw the imprint of her tear-soaked face on his hoodie. Patted at his chest.

"Sorry."

"That's okay," he said. "You're not…this isn't going to make you sadder, is it? Like, it won't make you miss her more or anything."

"No." Lauren shook her head. "No, of course not. If I know she's okay, that's all I ever wanted."

"You can tell when I'm lying, right?"

"Yeah." Lauren wiped at her eyes with her sleeve. "Yeah, I think I can. It's just…this is a lot."

"I know. And I know she wouldn't want you to miss her so much that you forgot to be happy."

"I haven't been happy," she said. "Not since Jáyne died. Not really. I've lived. I've gone through the motions. Became a cop because I had this stupid thought that I could figure out what happened to the kids. To Jayney."

"That's not stupid. We're doing that, right now. We'll do it."

"I like what I do. It's not that. But…we were so close, and she was so…she was just *so.*"

"Yeah," Cole smiled. "She still is."

"I mean, have you ever been happy, since that night?"

Cole thought about that. Went over every second of his life since that night ten years ago and considered whether he'd been happy at any one moment. Really happy. "I've been distracted enough to feel happy, but it always went away so fast, when the distraction wasn't there anymore."

Lauren took a deep breath, trying to manage her still-quivering voice. "Maybe I can be happy again. Knowing she's somewhere good. That I'll see her again one day."

"You will," Cole said. "But let's make sure it's not too soon, okay?" Cole took a step forward, inviting Lauren to keep walking with him, and she did. "For you or anybody else."

They walked on the other side of the river until they were parallel to where they'd dropped everybody off. By now, the night was breaking, and shadows were stretching across the ground like beams of light.

"Hang on." Cole walked out of the woods, took the embankment down to the water's edge. Looked and listened in the direction where they'd left the boats. He couldn't hear anything, which meant that the guards were still out in the forest searching.

"Clear," he said. When Lauren met him at the water's edge, he asked, "That's what they say, right? Cops. When there are no bad guys."

"I mean, I've never really had to say it before, but if you go off movies or TV, sure," she said.

"That's exactly what I do."

"Then that's what they say."

They waded across the river. The freezing water reached up to Cole's chest and Lauren's neck. Cole held Lauren's arm under the water to keep her from losing her balance. On the other side, they ran. Cole would've liked to sprint again, but ran beside Lauren rather than ahead, to make sure she was okay. Being wet from the river, in this cold, was taking its toll on her. Cole was relieved when they entered the clearing where Elder Mariah's cabin sat. They saw a few modest fires burning, and a collection of tents had been erected around the cabin, smoke rising from within them. That's what Lauren needed, Cole thought, seeing how she could hardly walk anymore. She was shaking uncontrollably. She needed heat.

"Here." He picked her up. She didn't protest. He carried her through the field and into the little tent city. He looked in each tent until he found one with just one of the patients sleeping inside. He helped Lauren lie down on a blanket and tucked it around her body.

"You'd better take those wet clothes off," Cole said.

She tried to say something, but couldn't get any words out. Just stuttered breaths. He heard rustling under the blanket, and then, one by one, she tossed clothing onto the ground from under the blanket.

"Is she okay, Coley?" Jayne asked.

Lauren's suffering had been enough to summon Jayne. Lauren had the blanket covering her head. Her body was trembling within her self-made cocoon. Cole nodded at Jayne, who was still dimmer than he was used to.

"She's shivering so bad," Jayne said.

"She's really cold."

"Wh-wh-what?" Lauren said from underneath the blanket.

Cole put a hand on her shoulder. "Nothing. Try and get yourself warm."

He added a log to the fire, but the fire could only get so big inside the tent. She was going to get hypothermia. And could Dr. Captain or Elder Mariah do something about that? Was she too cold? Cole shook his head. He'd get under the blanket with her and give her all his heat, any heat that he had left. He started to take off his hoodie, soaked and icy itself from the waters and the late-autumn air.

Jayne put a hand on his forearm before he could.

He looked up at her, and she shook her head slowly. Once to the left, once to the right.

What? Cole thought. *I have to.*

But Jayne just shook her head again.

She's going to get sicker.

Jayne looked at Cole intensely, determined. She got brighter, and her flames climbed higher. The temperature within the tent rose quickly.

Cole picked up Lauren's clothing, pulled the string out of his hoodie, and tied it to the poles inside the tent to create a makeshift clothesline. He hung her clothes from it, which caused the tent to sag a bit, but it stayed in place. Jayne lifted her burning arm and directed heat at Lauren's clothing.

You're amazing.

"I know that, silly."

Cole zipped the tent open and looked back before he left. Jayne was where she loved to be, where she was most nights. Sitting with her sister, just being with her. Only now, she was doing more than that. She was keeping Lauren warm and alive. Cole used to wonder if Lauren could feel Jayne with her, if a part of Lauren knew that Jayne was there, and that Jayne was okay, whether Cole had told her or not. Now, Lauren really could feel Jayne, and maybe Lauren knew that Jayne was there beside her.

Cole felt like a zombie all over again. He wandered through the tents, trying not to fall into any of them, until he found the one he'd stayed in while he was healing. He fumbled with the flap, but managed to get it open, and collapsed inside as though he'd been pushed.

He didn't move, after he'd fallen onto the ground. He stayed where he was, on his side, facing a dwindling fire that had been started sometime during the night. He had one roommate in the small canvas dwelling, huddled under a blanket on the other side of the dying flames. Eva. She was asleep. He studied her face, every detail of it, so carefully that he could count her eyelashes. He studied her face until his eyelids grew heavy, until he lost the fight to keep them open.

22

BY THE FIRE

COLE WOKE UP GASPING FOR BREATH. He'd been having a nightmare. Dead again. Waking up from an eternal sleep. Emerging from eternity confused and broken and lost. Trying to suck air into decayed lungs. Clawing at the coffin to get out, to get here. He opened his eyes, and patted the ground around his body to reacquaint himself with reality. He felt his body, from his legs to his face, to make sure that he was alive and still healed. He looked at his scars. He looked to the side, where the fire was burning confidently, and where Eva was sitting cross-legged, watching him. A blanket draped over her shoulders and a cup of tea in her hands.

"Morning," she said.

Cole tried to gauge the time by the light coming in through the cracks in the tent.

"Or should I say afternoon," she added.

"Care to be more specific?"

"Just about two."

"Two?" Cole sat up, rubbed his face. "Why'd you let me sleep that long?"

"Because you needed it."

"I can't sleep when people are sick. Dr. Captain and Elder Mariah were probably up all night. Brady, too."

Eva sipped her tea. "You needed rest. You were out all night protecting us, weren't you?"

"*Everybody* here did something to protect Wounded Sky last night. Lauren and I pretty much just walked through the woods."

"You got shot before that. Like, a million times."

Cole shrugged.

"I rest my case."

Eva reached across the fire and handed Cole the tea. He accepted it and took a long sip. The moment the liquid slid down his throat, his stomach growled embarrassingly loud.

"Sorry." Cole blushed.

"When's the last time you ate?"

Cole thought about this, but couldn't recall. "I don't know."

"Okay, so…" She stood up, as much as the tent allowed. "…you need to eat. We need you strong. I mean, that's relative. Strong for you. Like, Superman strong."

"I'm not Superman strong."

"Superman needs some fish."

Eva ducked out of the tent and came back a few minutes later with a plate of fish, bannock, and berries. Cole inhaled it. By the time Eva sat down, this time at his side, he was already finished. He wiped at his mouth with the bottom of his hoodie, which made Eva wince.

"What?" he said.

"Nothing, it's just…imagine Superman wiping his mouth with his cape," she said.

"Enough with the Superman analogies please," he said. "Plus you don't know that. He puts his tights on one leg at a time, just like everybody else."

"Oh, but clichés are okay?"

They laughed. Cole finished his plate, set it to the side. His smile faded, and was replaced with concern. "How is everybody?"

Eva looked away from him, into the fire. Everything always came back to fire. She shook her head, while staring, unblinking, into the flames. "We lost one."

"Not…"

"No, not Pam. A guy. Eric. People called him Sauce. He worked at the grocery store."

"I remember him."

"Worked until there was no reason to work there anymore, right until the rationing started."

Cole sighed. "Mihko's keeping food from coming in, cutting off cell service, shutting down the ferry. This has to stop."

"I don't want to take *all* the credit, but now that you're on a full stomach you're way more likely to stop them," Eva said. "Just remember the little people when you're a big-time hero."

"Nobody knows about what's happening up here, remember?" Cole picked at some crumbs of bannock.

"Oh yeah I forgot."

He tossed the crumbs, one by one, into the fire.

"How's Brady?"

"Doing his best, as always. They all are. Elder Mariah, Dr. Captain. They don't want to lose anybody else."

"How's Michael? He didn't look so good."

"Who does?"

"Yeah, I guess you're right."

"I mean, he lost his sister, and then he lost me…"

"But you guys are still friends, right?"

"We're trying to be." Eva ran her hands through her hair. "But it's hard. When this is over, we'll all be okay. Whatever okay looks like."

"I didn't…" Cole maintained eye contact. "…come in here because you were here. I wasn't trying to do anything. It's just, that's where I ended up. I was pretty much sleepwalking."

"Well, I might not have kicked you out, you know."

Eva played with the sweetgrass ring hanging around her neck. The air was thick suddenly, and Cole felt flushed.

Eva cleared her throat.

"So, what's the plan?"

"I don't know," he said. "I want to make sure everything here is under control before I head back. Make sure the guards don't find the cabin."

"Do you think they're still out there looking?"

"I wanted to stay up and listen, but that didn't quite happen."

"You were out cold."

"I think it's a bit creepy that you were watching me sleep," he teased.

"Well," she said, "you were watching *me* sleep first, so…"

"Oh, I…"

"Relax, Cole. It was cute."

"Cute," he repeated, nodding his head. "Well, to answer your question, I don't know. I'll head back whenever it's safe to leave."

"Safe for us, not for you."

"I'll be okay."

"I know you will." She reached over and squeezed his hand.

"How do you know that?" He kept her hand there, holding it before she could take it back, if she was thinking about taking it back.

"Because you have to be."

23

SPOILER ALERT

COLE FOUND BRADY, DR. CAPTAIN, and Elder Mariah in a huddle outside the cabin. Eva had gone to visit the patients and check on how everybody was doing. "Sometimes just letting somebody know they're not alone helps, you know?" she'd said. Cole poked his head into the huddle. Whatever they had been discussing, they stopped.

"How's Lauren?" he asked.

"Sleeping," Dr. Captain said, "but she'll be okay."

"Good. And everybody else?"

"Some were farther along in the illness than others," Dr. Captain said quietly.

"We lost—" Brady started to say.

"Eric," Cole said.

"Yeah."

"Anybody else?"

"Not so far," Dr. Captain said. "We might get lucky."

"It's luck and the medicines nókom's providing," Brady said.

"Mostly that," Dr. Captain agreed. "All I can really do is give them fluids, keep their fever down, monitor them. I feel kind of…"

"You're not useless, Kate," Elder Mariah said. "Traditional medicine is important, and western approaches can be too."

"Nókom's answer is always balance," Brady said.

"That's right," she said.

"Uhhh…" Cole looked around Tent City.

"Pam?" Brady said.

Cole nodded.

"She'll be okay," Dr. Captain assured.

"She was awake this morning," Elder Mariah said.

"Could I…" Cole started.

"Come on," Brady put his hand on Cole's forearm, "I'll take you to her tent."

"Thank you," Cole said to the group, before following Brady between two tents to one that lay on the outskirts of the makeshift village they'd created. They stopped at the front flap. Cole went to raise his neck warmer over his mouth, the front skull's perfect teeth and hollow nose about to replace his features. But Brady stopped him.

"She doesn't need The Reckoner," Brady said. "She'll want to see Cole."

Cole lowered his hands, stuck them into his hoodie pocket as though restraining them there. "You're right."

"I usually am," Brady said with an exaggerated sigh.

"With you and Eva always right, how can anything ever be wrong?"

"Shut up and get inside." Brady patted Cole's back reassuringly, then left to continue his work.

Cole paused for a moment with his hand on the flap, ready and not ready to pull it to the side and walk in. Thinking about what Pam would say if she saw him do this exact thing—something like, "Come on, Harper, grow a pair and get inside,"—forced him into action.

Pam was sharing space with two others, and all three occupants were sleeping. They had IV lines going into their forearms. The IV bags hung from the poles within the tent. Each patient had a little notepad at their feet. Dr. Captain's charts, Cole figured.

If he hadn't known any better, he'd have thought Pam was just sleeping and not all that sick. Maybe suffering from a cold or flu or something, not some biological weapon. Whatever they were trying to accomplish at the clinic, Cole felt thankful that the virus they'd made didn't seem to be as potent as the previous one. Not yet. But if Eric had been infected after Pam, it meant Mikho was getting closer. How long before they gave up searching and experimented on other community members? Cole shook off the thought and drew in a slow breath. He repeated the mantra he'd been trying to adopt. *There is only now.* There was only him, sitting on the dirt beside Pam, and Pam was alive.

"Hey," he whispered.

She flinched.

"Pam," he said a bit louder.

She squinted, and her eyes opened. She stared at the ceiling, not at Cole. Cole wasn't sure if she was just disoriented from having woken up, or if she'd heard his voice and was deciding whether she was dreaming or not.

"You're okay," he said.

Now, she turned her head and met his gaze.

"Cole?"

Pam tried to sit up, but Cole eased her back down again and repositioned the pillow under her head.

"Easy, tiger," he said with a smile.

"Joking does not make this more believable," she said roughly. It must've hurt her throat to talk. "You're supposed to be dead."

Cole explained to her, what he'd explained to everybody else, and if she had any questions about his story, she didn't ask. Maybe she was just too tired. Either way, Cole was relieved.

"But speaking of dead," Cole said, "you came pretty damn close yourself."

"So I've heard," Pam said. "But here I am, still awesome."

Cole laughed. "Yeah, you are."

He looked at her carefully. Her hands folded over the top of her blanket, her chest rising and falling as though she'd just finished a race. She would be okay, but wasn't there yet. Dry lips, clammy skin, a bit of sweat on her brow that shimmered in the low light of the fire, and her black hair speckled with the odd strand of grey.

"How'd it happen?" he asked.

"How'd I get so awesome?"

Cole stifled another laugh, not wanting to wake up the other people in the tent. "No," he said, "how did you get taken? How did they—"

She turned away, to the side of the tent.

"Sorry," he said. "You don't have to tell me that…"

"I was coming home from school," she said. He could tell that each syllable required a monumental effort. "I was there late. Fixing up a connection thing. When I left, it was past curfew."

"They stopped you because of that."

"Said they were taking me to the detachment. Get a slap on the wrist, something. Then they just…took me."

"To the clinic."

"I was there a few days, and then everything blends together. Like it wasn't real. I wish it wasn't real."

"I'm sorry. I should've been there. I shouldn't have been so—"

"You know what's clear in my mind?"

"What?"

"Me telling you to stop apologizing for things."

She repositioned her head against the pillow, so she faced the tiny opening at the top of the tent. She stared out of that hole at the sky. It was a perfect blue.

"You should rest," Cole said.

She nodded.

He opened his mouth to say something, but he didn't know what, so he patted her shoulder, got up, and went to the flap. "If there's anything I can do…"

"Do you know what I really need you to do right now?" Her face was uncharacteristically devoid of any sarcasm, humour. Her eyes were digging into him, telling him about all the fear she'd gone through, and the pain in the illness, without uttering a single word.

"What's that?"

"Go get 'em, tiger."

They buried Eric and Tristan in the field by the edge of the forest. Cole had to dig the graves. Nobody else was strong enough to break ground, the soil stubbornly firm in the autumn. Once he'd filled earth in over their bodies, Cole placed a large rock at the head of each grave. There was a small gathering. Lauren, Eva, Brady, Cole, Elder Mariah, Dr. Captain, Brady's parents.

"Where's Mike?" Cole asked Eva.

Eva just shrugged. Dr. Captain looked annoyed at her son's absence.

Brady laid tobacco over the graves and said a prayer in Cree for Tristan and Eric. Cole kept going over the confusing relationship he'd had with Tristan while Brady said his prayer. Tristan, trying to beat the shit out of him. Tristan, saving people with him from the clinic. Tristan, taking a bullet that was probably meant for Cole. Tristan had just wanted to do what he felt was right. When he thought Cole was responsible, he was ready to do something about it. When he knew Cole wasn't involved, he was ready to work with him so that, as a team, they could take action. Cole followed those thoughts with his own prayer. Words in his mind only for Tristan. *I won't let you down.* He said, "Ekosani," at the same time as everybody else.

Elder Mariah had brought a drum to the ceremony. When the tobacco had been laid, when the prayers had been said, she sang the honour song, then the travelling song. Cole closed his eyes for both and tried to feel each beat of the drum vibrate through his body, into his chest. He tried to recall the feeling he'd had when he was in the place that Tristan and Eric were in now. He tried to imagine them as ribbons of light, dancing to the songs the Elder was singing. Cole remembered dancing to the beat of the drum. Maybe the songs they danced to there were songs being played here. Carrying through the wind, over Mother Earth.

They talked about moving Eric and Tristan to the cemetery in Wounded Sky after the winter, after this ordeal was over, if it ended in a good way.

"I think they should stay here," Brady said.

"Why?" Eva asked.

"It's where I want to be buried," he said. "It's where we all belong."

Eva looked around, turning her body three hundred and sixty degrees, and took in everything. She nodded. "Okay. Yeah."

"They can stay here," Elder Mariah said. "I'll care for them."

"I just hope we don't have to bury anybody else," Lauren said.

Dr. Captain looked out over Tent City. "They're doing well. They should pull through."

"And when they take more?" Lauren asked. "We can't just keep rescuing people, over and over."

"I won't let that happen," Cole said.

"Have you thought about how you're going to shut that place down?" Eva asked.

"Blow it up?" Cole said.

"With what?" Brady asked.

"We don't just have explosives lying around," Lauren said.

"Well, that's the only way to make sure they leave," Cole said. "Make sure they've got nothing to come back to."

"Burn it," Brady said.

"I don't..." Cole couldn't formulate a response. Brady was right, but it's not something Cole wanted to think about, and by the reaction of the others, it wasn't something they wanted to think about either. For a moment, he was a boy again, standing in front of the elementary school as it went up in flames, burning so hot and bright the sky was on fire.

Fire. The word kept echoing in Cole's mind. Night had fallen. He'd kept to himself most of the day, and after eating, left Tent City and found his way back to a small clearing in Blackwood Forest. Death to life. He watched the tiny ripples of water in the brook, but saw only flames. The kind of rolling flames he used to see when he was out camping with his mom and dad. He'd sit by the fire and look into the heart of it, where the flames looked like bright orange water. Fluid. Like it was dancing. Like ribbons. Cole stared wide-eyed at the water. He could hear the drums again, beating in the distance. A mist hung over the water like smoke. Cole shook his head.

"I can't do it," he whispered to nobody but himself. "I don't think I can do it."

"But there was all that tough talk at the beginning."

Cole turned around to see Choch strolling out of the forest, dressed in a bathrobe, his body surrounded by a blue haze. Translucent. He sat down beside Cole and joined him in staring at the water.

"Choch?" Cole couldn't believe his eyes. He moved his hand through Choch's body. "You're a—"

"Appropriate, given the title of this story, no?"

"—ghost."

"Close enough."

"Why are you back?" Cole asked.

"I feel conflict in your heart," Choch said.

"Okay." Cole shook his head, trying not to smile despite himself. "I get it, the whole Jedi thing. Choch as force ghost. But can you talk like Choch, please?"

"Pretty cool though, right?"

Cole took a deep breath, then let it go. In the brief moment of annoyance, he realized how much he'd missed Choch.

"Awwwww. Oh and feel free to get annoyed even though you missed me, like, soooo much," Choch said. "After all, what would there be to miss, if our relationship suddenly changed?"

"I'm still mad at you though," Cole said.

"As you should be."

"Do you have to be…" Cole moved both his hands through Choch's body now. "…you know. I mean, you're not really…"

"First off, that tickles," Choch said. "Second off, my heart was literally ripped out of my chest. You get this last visit, and then I've got to head back."

"You're not…what do you mean? You're not coming back?"

"It's not exactly my choice," Choch grumbled, "but it is what it is. Such is the cycle of life."

"But you're not human."

"Pffft. Details." Choch waved the notion away. "Now, where were we?"

"I was saying, *to myself,* how I didn't think I could do this," Cole said. "I mean, I want to end it, I want to do this because they're right; the facility has to go, but I don't know if I can do what needs to be done, if I have to do it this way."

"Okay wait," Choch said, "let me try to make sense of your very long sentence." He held up a finger and appeared thoughtful. "You know, long sentences in YA fiction are just…"

"Can you not do the whole book stuff?" Cole asked. "Please?"

"But don't you think that it's really quite poetic…" *I mean, sorry to point this out, because I'm sure Robertson had this grand plan all along, to end things how they began, and also that I'm ruining the whole "show don't tell thing," but it fits for the scene, so sue me.* "…that this all started with a fire, and now it has to end with fire."

"Not from my point of view," Cole said. "All I can see now is fire, everywhere I look."

"Cole, you're going to find that many of the truths that we cling to depend greatly on our own point of view," Choch said.

"Choch, I've seen *Jedi* like a million times, so could you please not quote it?" Cole said. "Just talk to me."

Choch put a hand on each knee and leaned forward. "Whether it's poetic or not, or frightening or not, if that's the way it has to end, then that's what you need to do."

Cole leaned forward too, elbows to knees. Stared at the ground between his feet. "You're right. It's not about me. I know that. I came back to finish this, and now I'm being a—"

"Whoa, even though I'm a ghost, it doesn't mean the whole swearing thing can start up again," Choch said. "I know you snuck one in while I was dying, but nobody swore when I was away, did they? Tell me the truth."

"You'll be amazed to know that I didn't take inventory of everybody's dialogue since your heart was ripped out."

"Awww! You talked like this is a story. You're so sweet."

Cole tried to get the conversation back on track. "I thought I was over...I just thought I was different. And since we've left the clinic, I feel like the same old Cole. I wanted to be, I don't know, *more*."

Choch laughed, put a hand on Cole's back, and Cole felt it, like a little breath of cold air against his skin. "Cole, do you know why I chose you to do this?"

"Why you tricked me?" Cole said, still staring at the ground.

"I could've tricked anybody," Choch said. "That's my whole thing."

Cole sat up straight, turned to the spirit being. "Okay, I'll bite. Why?"

"Because you're Cole Harper," Choch said. "Think about it."

"I don't have to be badass," Cole said.

"I mean, you *are* badass," Choch said. "But in your own anxiety-riddled, overthinking, caring, passionate, self-doubting way."

"I..."

"And don't you ever change," Choch said as though Cole were two years old, and even reached forward and pretended to pinch his cheek.

"Thanks," Cole said.

"Now," Choch said, "I'd love to stay and chat, but I'm actually really enjoying the whole dancing thing up there. There's this one ribbon, and they're *totally* into me, and..."

"Okay, Choch." Cole smiled. "I didn't miss you that much. You can go now."

"Kick ass," Choch said, and faded away, leaving a glowing blue translucent robe behind.

After several moments, it remained, and Cole just kept staring at it.

I know what you're thinking, and I'm not naked. I'm a ribbon, *remember? Pull your head out of the gutter.*

24

HOW IT'S GOING TO BE

"WHO'RE YOU TALKING TO?" Michael asked, walking into the clearing from Blackwood Forest.

Cole went to shove the ghost-robe off the rock, but it was already gone. "Nobody, just myself. Thinking out loud."

Michael sat on the rock, right where Choch had been. He surveyed the clearing. "It's getting late."

"Yeah," Cole said. "Think it's a great idea to be walking around in Blackwood? There could be guards in the area. They'll eventually find this place if they don't give up."

"You probably bought us a couple days. You and Lauren."

"There'd be nothing to protect, if you and the others hadn't got everybody to the cabin."

"I always wanted to be a part of the team," Michael said. "With you and Brady and Eva."

"You are now," Cole said. "That's all that counts."

They didn't talk for a long while. They sat together on the rock, cloaked in the mist and the calm of the clearing. The brook sounded like whispers.

"I was just walking around, trying to get some fresh air," Michael said, "thinking about, I don't know. Thinking how much everything's changed, so fast. You think your life's going to turn out one way, and then…"

"Yeah." Cole picked up a tiny stone and threw it at the brook. It hit the surface and disappeared. Life was going one way for Michael, then he lost Alex, and like Eva had said, then he lost her. Cole still had everybody close to him. At least, everybody he'd had for the last ten years, he'd still had for the last month and a half. "We're okay, right?"

"We're okay," Michael said. "Of course, we're okay." He looked at Cole. "I'm just glad you're back, so that we *can* be."

"Me too. Whatever happens, we're family. All of us."

Michael picked up a rock and threw it at the brook. "No matter what happens."

Eva was sleeping. She was on her side, facing the fire, curled up into a ball, knees to chest. Her hands were clasped together under her cheek. Cole didn't try to wake her. He just lay down on his side and faced the fire. He curled up into a ball, knees to chest. He got close enough to Eva that the top of his head touched hers. He measured his own breathing, as he listened to her breaths. He counted the seconds as he drew a breath in, and he counted the seconds as he let a breath out.

He did this until he fell asleep.

"Cole!"

Elder Mariah's voice startled Cole awake. Both he and Eva sat up quickly and looked at each other, confused. The Elder's voice was desperate.

"Somebody die?" Cole asked Eva.

"I don't know." Eva sounded desperate, too, as though the feeling had been carried through the air, caught like a virus. She stood up and tossed a sweater over her t-shirt.

Elder Mariah, and somebody else, started slapping on the exterior of the tent.

"Cole! Get out here, now!" Dr. Captain said.

"Coming!"

Cole and Eva ran out of the tent.

"What's going on?" Eva asked.

Cole examined their faces. They looked how they sounded, but with a side of tired. Somebody had to have died. He would've known if the guards had found their hiding spot. It wouldn't have been rustling his tent, it would've been gunshots and screaming.

"Brady," Elder Mariah said. "He's…"

"He's what?" Cole asked.

"And Michael," Dr. Captain said.

"What the hell's going on?" Eva asked.

"They're gone," Elder Mariah said.

"They're what?" Cole asked. "What do you mean they're gone?"

"I woke up early to check on the patients," Elder Mariah said, "and he wasn't there. He sleeps in the same spot every night, on the floor beside my cot."

"And Michael has been staying with me," Dr. Captain said. "He's missing too."

"Have you looked in the forest?" Cole asked. "Last night, Mike was out for a walk."

"Of course we did," she said.

"We've been looking all morning," Elder Mariah said.

"Why didn't you wake us earlier?" Eva asked.

"We weren't worried earlier," Dr. Captain said.

"I thought Brady might've gone to check the tents without me, to let me rest," Elder Mariah said.

"That sounds like Brady," Cole said. "But you've been through all the tents?"

"If we've checked the forest…" Dr. Captain started.

"We've looked everywhere," Elder Mariah said.

"So where else could they be?" Eva asked. "Did Mihko find us? Did they take them?"

Cole shook his head. "They would've taken everybody."

Nobody said anything. Each one of them was trying to think about where Michael and Brady could've gone to, but the silence spread thick.

"Cole. You there? Cole?" Michael called out. His words were followed by static and a click.

"Michael?" Dr. Captain called out.

"He's not here," Cole said. "That's…" he was already gone before he could finish the sentence, following the sound to where Michael and Dr. Captain had been sleeping while the others followed him. He went into the tent and searched through Michael's belongings until he found a long-range radio.

"Michael?" Cole said into the receiver.

He took it outside. By then, Eva, Dr. Captain, and Elder Mariah had followed him.

"Cole," Michael said. "You there?"

"Where are you?" he asked.

"I have Brady," Michael said.

Cole breathed a sigh of relief. "Thank God. What happened?"

"He's okay," Michael said.

"Where are they?" Dr. Captain whispered to Cole.

"Where are you guys?" Cole relayed to Michael.

"Wounded Sky."

"Wounded Sky? Are you crazy? Why'd you guys go back there?"

"I brought Brady here."

"You took Brady to…Mike, what are you doing? Why would you do that?"

"I brought him to the facility. I'm sorry. They—"

"No matter what happens." Cole breathed out the words Michael had said to him last night. "Mike, you have to bring him back. You have to come back here."

There was a long pause. Finally, the radio clicked back to life.

Michael's voice was shaky.

"They…they want you to come get him."

The radio fell the ground, and Cole dropped to his knees. He cupped his hands behind his head and tried to breathe. Five seconds in and seven seconds out. He couldn't. He punched the ground as hard as he could and just stared at the imprint of his knuckles in the dirt.

"He couldn't do something like that," Dr. Captain said. "I know my son."

"He wouldn't," Elder Mariah said. "Not if he had a choice."

"*They* want Cole to come get him," Eva said. "Mihko. They're doing this. Somehow, they got Michael to take Brady."

"That's what's been wrong with him." Cole stood. "That's why he's looked so off. They're making him do this. Kidnap Brady or else…" "Or else what?" Eva said.

"Does it matter?" Cole asked. "Brady's gone, and it's as much my fault as it is his."

"Don't talk like that," Elder Mariah said.

"They only took Brady to get to me," Cole protested. "Is there another way to see it? They need me for something, or they want me dead."

"There has to be another way," Dr. Captain said. "You can't just go back to Wounded Sky. They'll be waiting for you."

"No, there isn't another way," Cole said. "They took Brady because they know I'm going to get him. I'm going to get both of them."

"And if we lose all three of you?" Elder Mariah asked.

"I was always going to go back," Cole said.

Dr. Captain picked up the radio and spoke into it. "Michael. Michael. Pick up. Michael!" She waited, but there was no response. She tossed the radio back to the ground. Stood there, hands on her hips, staring at it. "I can't lose both my kids."

"Nobody's losing anybody," Cole said. "As soon as it's dark, I'll leave. It won't take me long to run there."

"You better leave sooner than that," Eva said.

"Why?" Cole asked. "They'll see me if I do. They're not Stormtroopers, you know. They can actually hit targets."

"You're an idiot," she said.

"An idiot? Why? Do you think I should stay here and hope Mike just decides to bring Brady back in a crisis of conscience?"

"You need to leave soon," she said calmly, and slowly, like he wouldn't understand her otherwise, "because I'm not as fast as you are."

"Eva, no, you're not coming," he said. "It's too dangerous. What if something happens to Brady and you? Then what will I do?"

"After all the shit we've been through, you still don't know that you need me?" she asked. "You still don't know that we're in this together?" Her eyes narrowed. "Tell me that I can't come. Just try it. This is how it's going to be."

It was in her posture, it was in her face, but more than that, she was just right. Cole knew it. And there was no talking her out of it. Maybe he didn't want to. He did need her. So did Brady.

"Alright," he said, "*we* better leave earlier."

Eva and Cole took time to smudge with Elder Mariah. Cole smudged last, and when he took the smoke, he showered his body with it. Cupped it in his hands, and ran it through his hair, over his face, against his chest, into his heart. Elder Mariah prayed in Cree, and Cole understood some of it. She asked Creator to watch over them, to give them strength and resolve for the task that lay ahead.

"Ekosani," Cole and Eva said in unison, after the prayer was finished.

Then, they set off to save their friend. But Cole knew it was more than that. It wasn't just to save Brady, it was to save them all.

He knew, with each step closer to their home community, that this was why he'd come home.

25

FIGHT OR FLIGHT

COLE AND EVA MADE THEIR WAY THROUGH BLACKWOOD FOREST. Eva's face became stuck in a scowl, her eyebrows collapsed inward, her eyes narrowed, her jaw clenched. Thinking, worrying, calculating, all at once. But she didn't talk. Not until Cole asked, "What's up?"

"Have you thought about the fact that we saved twelve people, and there were about twenty missing?"

"I haven't really had the chance."

"I have. Like, if Pam was getting transferred to the facility, why? Were the others already taken there?"

"Maybe," Cole said. "We'll find out soon enough."

"And if they're there, how are we going to get them out? There's just two of us."

"Brady makes three. We handled about that many, three each, moving people out of the clinic."

"If the building's destroyed, and Mihko's gone, we won't have to bring them to the cabin at least. Elder Mariah and Dr. Captain could treat them in Wounded Sky."

"Yeah," Cole said, "I guess."

"You guess," Eva said. "What's that all about?"

"What's what all about?"

They separated to pass around a large tree and came back together on the other side. The sun was beginning to set. They'd been walking for hours.

"Don't keep anything from me, okay?"

"It's just," Cole said, "Pam was already so sick, and by the time they were going to transfer her, she would've been even sicker. Maybe dead."

"So there might not be anybody to get out."

"Maybe, I don't know." Cole pinched the bridge of his nose. "Maybe they're doing something with their bodies."

"Cole…" Eva said in disbelief.

"Like they haven't done worse?"

"I wish I could say that you're wrong."

"It's a…pretty shitty thought. Sorry."

"I told you to tell me," she said. "And I don't know where else they could be."

Cole took Eva's hand, held it tight, and they walked together like that, closer to Wounded Sky with each step. Eva wondering where the others could be, that missing eight, got Cole thinking. If not at the facility, then where? What if they had never been at the clinic at all? What if their absence wasn't related to the other twelve? Cole shuddered.

"What's wrong?" Eva asked. She traced his palm with her fingers. "You're sweating."

There was no point keeping it from her. "I didn't tell you much about Reynold's place. About Reynold. When I fought him, before I got shot, it hardly looked like him anymore. He was changing, just like the stories."

"I know," she said. "I never believed them before, until all of this."

"There wasn't anything human left. He was like this…like an ice giant or something. He couldn't even stand straight in his house. Like a giant, but just skin and bones. I know…" Cole did one set of his breathing as his body rebelled. "…I know when it gets that far, Upayokwitigo, they aren't eating animals anymore. They need something bigger."

Eva covered her mouth with her free hand. "Some people were missing before you died, before Mihko had more people in the community."

"He was feeding then," Cole said. "He must be feeding now."

"Don't say it," she said.

Cole didn't. But he knew that taking down the facility wasn't the last thing that he needed to do, not if Wounded Sky was really going to be safe. "People must've gone missing because of him, and people are going to keep going missing, whether Mihko is here or not."

"Cole…" Eva pleaded. "…this can't all fall on just your shoulders."

"Who else can stop him?"

"I…"

"Medicine men, or a volunteer, in our communities, used to dream of how to defeat these things."

"Dream?" Eva asked. "Have *you* dreamt of it? How are you going to kill him?"

"I'm going to rip his heart out." Cole thought of Choch, and how he just stood there while Upayokwitigo mortally wounded him. "Maybe I *was* shown how…"

"And if he kills you? Then what?"

"Is it better not to do anything? If you see something that's wrong, and you just watch, what does that make you?"

"You've already given this community everything."

"Not everything," Cole said, "not—"

"Wait." Eva stopped Cole.

He tried to keep walking, but she pulled him back.

"I said wait," she whispered and crouched down to hide herself in the underbrush.

When Cole didn't crouch, she yanked him down.

"Holy shit, Eva, what's gotten into you?"

"Shhh!" She put her index finger against her lips, and nodded forward, to the place where they were about to walk.

Cole saw a guard standing there, looking in their direction, one hand on his rifle, the other at his side. Cole and Eva sat on the ground, out of view.

"We're near the perimeter," Cole whispered.

"Got a plan?" Eva asked.

"What's worked for me lately is I've run really fast at guards and knocked them out."

"Wow," she said, "intricate."

"Last time, when I was coming through with Brady, he walked up to the guy, and I climbed up a tree, got past them, and dropped behind the guy. It worked, so…"

"And that seems overthought."

"I'm not sure that'd work now," he said. "They're probably on high alert since the clinic breakout."

"Okay, so run at the guy really fast then, I guess," she said.

"Right."

Cole took off from behind the bush, but as soon as he was in view of the guard he saw a spark, and there was a *pop*. He felt a burning sensation in his stomach just before he fell backwards. He scrambled over to Eva, holding the wound. She helped him to safety.

"Let me see." She moved his hand away.

He'd taken a bullet. His stomach was gushing blood. She replaced his hand, added another for good measure, and applied pressure.

"I think I'm going to pass out," he said.

"Hey you! Stand and come out with your hands up!" the guard called out.

"He can't get up you asshole! You shot him!" Eva called back.

Jayney, Cole thought. *Jayney.*

"Who are you?" the guard asked.

Eva didn't respond, she had her hands over Cole's hands, trying to stop the bleeding with him. "Can you…die from this?" she asked.

"Kinda feels like it," he said. *Jayney!* "Maybe, if I…don't get this…" Black spots filled his vision.

"Cole!" She slapped his cheek. "Stay awake!"

"Get out here, now!" the guard demanded.

Cole's eyes began to close, but then he saw a bright light standing over him. He knew better than to think it was the light at the end of the tunnel, although he felt pretty close to that moment. He struggled to open his eyes again, and saw Jayne.

"You're bleedin', Coley!"

"Remember…what you did…at the…trailer?"

"Is Jayney here?" Eva asked.

Cole nodded.

"Yeah, I remember!"

Cole looked down at his wound. Moved his hands away. Eva tried to stop him, but then didn't. He lifted his sweatshirt up to reveal the bullet wound.

Eva gasped and covered her mouth with her bloodied hands.

"Oh no!" Jayne cried.

"Burn…it…" Cole saw spots again. More. He could almost only see black.

"But…" Jayne protested.

"Now!"

"Okay, okay, you don't have to yell you know that!" Jayne bent down and placed her hand over the wound. Cole smelled his flesh burning first, then felt the scalding flames as the wound cauterized. He cried out from the pain.

Eva held his hand tight.

Footsteps approached. The guard was coming towards them.

Jayne removed her hand. The bleeding had stopped.

"Are you okay now?" Eva whispered.

"Need…a bit," Cole said.

"How long?"

"I can…"

"Hands up!" The guard's rifle lowered slightly when he saw Cole's wound. Blood was smeared over his skin, all over the ground, but the bullet hole had been closed. "What the hell? I shot you. I know I shot you."

Cole lowered his sweatshirt over the wound. "I got…better…"

"No," the guard shook his head. "That's not possible."

Jayney, stop him. I'm too weak right now. He'll shoot us.

Jayne's fire got dim. She crossed her arms. "I can't do that again, Coley. I can't burn nobody anymore."

"Jayney, please…"

"Are you Jayney?" the guard asked Eva.

Cole hadn't intended to say Jayne's name out loud. He still felt faint. He urged his body to heal faster.

"Yeah, I'm Jayney." Eva put her hands up.

Jayney, you have to.

"I want to Coley, but it made me so sad before."

Just…

"I'm sorry." Jayne left in a cloud of black smoke. Left him and Eva behind, with a guard standing over them, rifle moving back and forth between Eva and Cole.

"Wait a minute." The guard's head tilted as he looked Cole over carefully. "You're Cole Harper."

"Are you…the guy who…shot me in the…head?" Cole asked, trying to keep the guard talking while his strength built up.

"No," the guard said, "but I'm going to make sure you're dead this time." The guard's pale face belied his bravado, but there was nothing Cole could do right now to take advantage of that.

"And you think a bullet is going to finish me off?" He tried to sound stronger than he felt. If anything, maybe the guard would scare, run off, and leave him and Eva to continue on to Wounded Sky.

"S-stay down!" the guard shouted. He reached for the two-way radio on his belt.

"Hey." Eva stood up slowly.

Cole knew what she was doing. Stalling him, keeping him from calling more of Mihko's security force, giving Cole more time to heal. But he didn't want her to.

"Eva…"

She ignored him.

"You know what he can do," she said to the guard.

The guard loosened, then re-gripped his rifle. Aimed it at Eva, from Cole. Blinked out some sweat.

"D-Don't move…don't take another step," the guard said.

"We'll let you go." She looked back at Cole. "He'll let you live."

"I'm the one w-with the rifle," the guard said.

"And that was so effective at McCabe's place, right?" She took a step forward.

"I said not to take another step!"

Cole got ready to move, strong or not. If he thought for one second the guard would shoot Eva, he was ready to do whatever he could, with all that he had in him.

She slid her foot along the ground. "We just want our friend back, alright? Is that worth dying for?

"They'll kill me anyway if I let you go," the guard said.

"So you can die now or die later." Eva took another step.

"Enough!" The guard moved too fast for Cole. He needed more time. Another minute. He didn't have it. The guard grabbed Eva, spun her around. He dropped his rifle, took out his pistol, and pushed the muzzle into Eva's temple.

"No!" Cole shouted.

"Now," the guard said, his voice and hand shaking, which seemed more dangerous to Cole, "run the other way, and I won't shoot Jayne here in the head."

"Don't," Eva said to Cole. "Let me go. They'll kill me anyway. What you have to do is bigger."

"No," Cole said weakly, demanding his body to fill with strength, every ounce he needed. Right now. There was only right now. There was only this moment that mattered.

"I'm going to count to three," the guard said, "and by the time I get to three, I want you to be walking the other way."

"I know where I'm going," Eva tried to keep her voice steady, but it was shaking like the guard's. "You showed me where I was going."

"No, Eva, I can't," Cole said.

"You have to."

"One," the guard said.

Eva tried to move the guard's arm away. She gripped both her hands around the forearm wrapped around her body. Cole saw her muscles tense. But he jerked her into submission and pushed the muzzle into her temple harder.

"Don't you hurt her!" Cole shouted.

"Two," the guard said. "Get moving, Harper."

Cole got to his feet. Still dizzy. Still struggling to move. There was nothing he could do. He felt weaker doing what he knew he had to do, now. He stared at her face. Tried to memorize every single detail. Watched the sweetgrass ring swing back and forth like a pendulum.

"Cole," Eva said. "You know what to do when…when this is over…"

He looked away from the ring, met eyes with her.

"Don't." A tear fell, as though shaken loose by the word. He was in a dream. In a nightmare. He pictured Eva dancing in the northern lights. A ribbon of light away from pain, a ribbon he would dance with one day. He knew it. She did, too.

"I love you." She closed her eyes.

"I love you, too." He got ready to move.

"Three." The guard cocked the hammer on his gun.

Eva screamed. Cole felt like his eardrums burst. The guard staggered, dropped his gun, but grabbed onto her tighter. Wind rushed in like floodwater from all directions. So strong, so quick, it knocked Cole to his knees. The wind crashed together where Eva and the guard stood. Cole looked up in time to see Eva and the guard lifted into the air as though shot from a cannon. They rose above the trees and stopped twenty stories above the ground. Cole could see them struggle, helpless, from the ground. A speck broke loose and hurtled to the ground. The guard connected with the earth at Cole's feet, and an explosion of blood splashed across his body. Cole stepped away, kept moving away until he backed into a tree. He looked up, wiped blood away from his face, terrified Eva would fall to the ground next.

But when he saw her, she was floating down to Earth, towards him, slow and graceful. She landed without a sound right in front of him. When she did, she looked as stunned as he was. She looked at her legs, her arms, her hands, like her body was foreign to her.

"Eva...what just happened?" Cole felt weird and weak for another reason entirely now.

"I don't know," she said, her hands outstretched, her eyes fixed on them. There were tiny little tornados dying out over her palms. She closed her hands into fists and held them behind her back.

Cole looked at the sky, then at Eva, then at what remained of the guard, then back at Eva. She was looking at him, too.

"Did you just fly?" he asked.

"I think I just flew," she said.

"You flew. Holy shit!"

"I was just in the air. I didn't even think. I was just...*there*."

"You didn't think," he said, "but did you feel? Did you...what... something must've happened." "I just..." Eva looked around, then at the sky, as though she could still see herself there. She lowered her gaze, slow and graceful, to Cole. She looked at him, eyes wide, mouth slightly open. Finally, she gasped, in almost a whisper. Quick and quiet. "Oh, my God."

"What?" He asked.

"Oh, my God," she repeated.

"Eva, what?" He reached behind her back and took her hands. They were cold.

"I know why," she said. "I know what happened."

She took one of her hands away from Cole's grip and placed her fingers against his cheek. The cool touch of her skin sent shivers across his body.

"How did you do that?" he asked.

"I can't..." she shook her head. "I can't tell you."

26

AMBUSH

"YOU KNOW, I *ALWAYS* HAD POWERS, RIGHT? I mean, I didn't know it, but I did." Cole had been trying to get something out of Eva since they'd left the remains of the guard. Eva hadn't budged, and still wouldn't. "Maybe you've always been able to, like, fly, and you just found out? What do you think?"

Now, she was just annoyed.

"Yeah, I don't know, maybe."

"What does 'Yeah, I don't know, maybe' mean? You just gave me three answers at once."

"I told you; I can't say," Eva said.

"Can you do other stuff? What other stuff can you do?" Cole asked. "Shoot tornados out of your hands? Because that would be—"

"I don't know, Cole," Eva said. "Drop it, okay? Brady and I weren't this annoying, were we?"

"Probably not," Cole said. "It's just, when you have powers, and then you find somebody who has powers? Totally different thing."

They were coming to Wounded Sky now, slowly making their way to the research facility. Cole's wound felt much better now, but he caught himself grimacing from pain every few moments. Stabs of pain inside his stomach, a low burn across the cauterized skin. Eva caught it too.

"Does Jayne come whenever you call her?" Eva asked.

"I mean, usually," Cole said. "But she's kind of been, I don't know, off and on for a bit. Even before I got shot in the head. Like, seven gunshot wounds ago."

"How so?"

"Like, before," he said, "she was afraid of the boogeyman, which was Reynold. So she was hiding during the day."

"But she helped today, so how is that *usually*?"

"I wanted her to do something about the guard, but she wouldn't, she…"

"She what?"

"It was setting those guards on fire, when we broke out of the clinic. She'd never really done something like that before. She doesn't want to hurt anybody again."

"I can't imagine doing something like that when I was seven."

"She's been around just as long as us, though," he said. "It's just, she *looks* seven, that's all."

"I can't really remember what she looks like."

Cole didn't think of the fire that enveloped half her body all the time. He just pictured her how he saw her. "She's beautiful," he said. "She just loves everything, and I've asked her to do too much."

"Sounds like she wants to help, though, right?"

"I don't think that's the kind of helping she had in mind."

They came to the edge of Blackwood, to a spot where they could see the research facility. Mihko's security force was patrolling the building and the exterior of the electric fence. Ants around an anthill. Cole and Eva sat behind a large tree.

"We should wait until it's dark," Cole said. "Any advantage we can get…"

He put his hand under his sweatshirt and felt around the healing wound.

"You okay?" Eva asked. "We should wait just so you can get all the way better."

"Yeah," he said, "I'll be okay, when it's time."

"What's going to happen?" she asked. "If everything goes how it should go?"

Cole shrugged. "I don't know. I'm not sure I thought I'd ever get here. I'm not sure I even knew this was what was supposed to happen."

"But you know it now?"

"I think so." A shooting pain from his stomach made Cole wince again.

"Let me see that." She lifted his sweatshirt and inspected the wound. Poked at it gently. "I still can't believe you can do that. Just heal from whatever."

"Being invulnerable to pain would be nice."

She lowered his sweatshirt.

"What happens after all of this is over?" Eva asked.

"We recover, I guess," he said. "Get Anna Crate into the position she should've been in, once Reynold and Mihko are gone. Rely on her to lead us out of this mess."

"And what about you? What's next for you?"

"If we do this," Cole said, "if we actually pull this off...I don't know...I'm kind of looking forward to just being a kid again."

"Do you really think you can do that?" she asked. "With what you can do, do you really think you should?"

"With great power comes great responsibility? That sort of thing?"

"Yeah, that sort of thing."

"So what does that mean for you then? You know, now that you can fly?" Cole asked, then added, "and no, I won't ask how you can fly again."

"I think things will be different for me, too."

"Maybe you can be my sidekick."

"Like hell, I'm your sidekick," she said. "Who saved your ass?"

Cole relived the moment. Every second of it. From when he'd got shot, to when the guard stood over them, to when Eva had a gun to her temple, to when the guard fell to the ground. Cole kept going back to one moment: As the guard had counted down, Eva told Cole that she loved him. He wanted her to say it again, and again, and never stop saying it.

"Did you mean it?" he asked, expecting her to have read her mind, like that was a power she had too, along with flying.

The pause after his question made him realize that she knew exactly what he'd asked about. Maybe she'd been thinking about it, too.

He waited, with bated breath.

"I mean, if you said it just because you thought you were dying, that's cool."

She just nodded.

"So...you said it because you were dying, or because..."

"Oh, my God, Cole. I meant it."

"I meant it, too."

"I know."

When the sun set, they crept out of Blackwood Forest. They waited for the right moment to go, but there wasn't one moment that was better than the last. There were always guards at every section of the fence. Cole figured they'd have to fight off at least six.

"I think we just have to do it," Cole said finally.

"Yeah," Eva agreed.

"Do you think you could, you know, fly over them?"

"I don't even know how I did it in the first place."

"Could you try?"

"You don't want me to fight the guards," Eva said, her voice dripping with accusation.

"I don't want you to get hurt," Cole said. "Plus, if you flew over them, you could get inside and look around, while I—"

"Do all the hard work? Get shot? Get killed again? I don't think I could..." But she stopped herself.

"You don't think you could what?" Cole looked away from the guards to focus solely on Eva.

"Nothing," Eva said. "I'm coming with you. That's it."

Cole stared at her. Tried to decipher her, like she could decipher him. But he just shook his head. "Stay behind me. You can fly, but you can't heal. I can."

"You sound like that old commercial. That War Amps commercial."

Cole went from shaking his head to trying not to laugh. "Astar?" He mimicked the voice. "I can put my arm back on; you can't."

"Yeah, that. That's exactly what you sounded like."

"I'm not sure about my arm," Cole said, "but you get my point, and you're not winning this argument."

"Fine," she said, "I'll stay behind you."

"Okay, let's go."

She leaned over and gave him a peck on the cheek. "Good luck."

In that moment, with Cole's muscles tensing for another sprint towards guards and bullets and fists, with the feeling, Cole swore, of wind rushing in at them from all directions again, like Eva was about to fly, he heard the sound of a click behind him. And that solitary click was followed by the sound of many more, like rain crashing against the ground.

"He'll need more than luck, girl," a voice said.

Cole relaxed his muscles, even as his nerves went into overdrive. Pounding heart. Shaking limbs. Cold sweat. Light-headedness. He knew what he'd see when he turned around, but did anyway. They were face to face with ten rifles.

"We've been expecting you," a man said.

Cole recognized him as Cameron Xavier, the man who had represented Mihko at the school assembly held to honour Cole.

"Michael?" was all that Cole could force out of his mouth.

"He's a good kid," Xavier said. "A good soldier." "Why not just take us at the cabin then? Why wait for us to get here?" Cole asked.

"That's a fair question, Cole," Xavier said. "Originally, Michael was told to slit your throat while you slept." He laughed. "And Captain would've done it, too."

"But…"

"The cure we're developing isn't working," Xavier said. "Those people you took are just going to die anyway."

Cole didn't tell him that they weren't dying. Had Michael kept some things from Mihko? Why? "We had to try," he said.

"Commendable," Xavier said. "At any rate, things changed."

"Then why'd you kill him before?" Eva asked.

"We got what we needed from him then," Xavier said. "His body was disposable."

"But you need me again," Cole said, "because your cure isn't working—"

"And we might just get that cure out of you," Xavier said. "So it's lucky for us that you rose from the dead, as it were."

"I'm going to fucking kill you," Cole said.

He got ready for a fight, pressed his palms against the earth to find some momentum to charge at them, but as soon as he shifted, the muzzles came closer to him, and to Eva. Eva would've been dead before he could do anything. He raised his hands in surrender.

"Good choice," Xavier said.

"Take me," Cole said. "Let Eva go."

Xavier *tsk*ed. "Sorry, we won't be able to do that. We need her, too."

"Why? You have me. You can get the cure from my blood."

"Yes," Xavier said, "but how will we know if it works?"

Xavier's smile grew wider. It looked as though the corners of his mouth might touch his ears. He nodded to one of the guards. The guard flipped his rifle around and butt-ended Cole in the head.

27

THREE LITTLE PIGS

COLE GROANED INTO CONSCIOUSNESS AND FELT PAIN surge through his body. He opened his eyes to a light glaring overhead, so he shut them again.

"Sorry about that," Dr. Ament said. "Thought we could keep you asleep."

He heard her walk up to him. He was in a rather uncomfortable bed. A hospital bed, he determined. Just like the one he'd been in, when he'd been stabbed by Scott. Scott, who was missing, too.

Dr. Ament shifted the light away, and Cole opened his eyes to find a second person standing over him. Cameron Xavier. He'd probably always been there. Cole had only heard one set of footsteps.

"It's incredible, really," Dr. Ament said. "I've given you enough sedative to put an elephant down, and it's still not enough."

Cole looked from Xavier, to Dr. Ament, who was ready to push more sedative into his IV line.

"Wait a second," Xavier said. "I'd like to talk to the boy."

"What…what are you doing to me?" Cole tried to move, but he was strapped down. He craned his neck to look at his body. The IV line was sticking through the black straps. The straps covered his body, from his feet up to his chest. He tried to move again, to break out of them, but it was no use.

"Easy, now," Xavier said. "There's no breaking out, son."

"Don't call me that."

Cole took inventory of the room. Cameron Xavier and Dr. Ament were standing by his bed. Michael Captain, in full guard uniform, a sight that made Cole feel sick, was stationed at the door. He had a standard-issue rifle and handgun. One of the flock. Michael looked straight ahead, deliberately, but his face couldn't lie about the conflict he must have been feeling. Why Michael couldn't look at him. Not after what he had done. Eva and Brady were in beds, too. They looked as sick as the patients had been in the clinic. When Cole saw them, he tried to break through the straps once more. He felt some fibres burst. But that was all. "What did you do to them?!"

"Dr. Ament, do you want to explain what's happening to Cole?" Xavier asked.

"You're probably feeling pretty awful," Dr. Ament said. "We've dosed you with a high concentration of God Flare 2.0."

"That's a super clever name," Cole said.

"It's a new strain. If we'd given a normal human what we've administered to you…"

"It's the whole elephant thing again," Xavier chimed in.

"Yes," Dr. Ament said. "So you're quite sick, but your body is working to heal from the virus, you see. It's creating antibodies. We've been taking your blood and trying to create a cure for this new strain." She looked at Brady and Eva. "Your friends here are going to show us if the cure works. They're heroes, really."

"Screw you," Cole said, and turned to Eva and Brady. "Guys, guys wake up! Wake up! Please!"

"They can't hear you," Xavier said.

"They're sedated," Dr. Ament explained. "We're watching how the virus progresses. If my theory is correct, the sickness will slow, then abate."

"Then what's going to happen?" Cole looked around the room again, and it was so familiar to him. The sterile environment. The white walls. The fluorescent lighting. The sliding metal doors, shutting them off from the rest of the building. The doors. Cole jerked up, then collapsed. This was where he'd found his dad.

"I know," Xavier whispered. "I know what you're thinking. You died here. Is that it? Your dad was over there," Xavier pointed right to where Cole had been shot while sitting beside his dad's decayed body, "and you were so distraught. You didn't even notice the boy approach with the gun. Not until it was too late."

"Boy?"

"I'm getting wordy, aren't I?" Xavier leaned in closer, so close Cole could feel his breath against his ear. "To answer your question: you are all going to die." He stood up and spoke at a normal volume. "But not from the virus, hopefully."

"Reynold."

"That's right," Xavier said. "Very good. He's right here, in this basement. Have you ever seen that movie, *Return of the Jedi*? That part where Luke Skywalker is dropped into the cavernous pit? That creature was being held behind huge metal bars, and then it was released?"

"It was a rancour."

"Right," Xavier said. "Well, you get the picture."

"Luke killed it."

"Oh, but you see, Luke wasn't strapped down."

"He *was* in a cage."

"The point being—"

"Reynold McCabe, Upayokwitigo, is just standing around in the basement, waiting, reading a magazine." Cole shook his head. "You're full of shit."

"We have an…" Xavier thought for a second. "…agreement."

"An agreement."

"Yes," Xavier said, "we keep him fed, and he stays docile. Relatively speaking."

Fed. The word shouted on repeat in Cole's mind, until it hit him.

"You're catching on," Xavier said. "See, this place is like a manufacturing business. In a business like it, there are processes. An assembly line, if you will. The people get sick, they don't get well, which admittedly is our fault, we do an autopsy over here, and then, well…all that *waste* has to go somewhere."

"You bastards!" Cole's body jerked violently from side to side. He tried to push his arms free. His legs. Tried everything. It was no use. Cole locked eyes with Xavier, but didn't say anything. Couldn't think of what he could say.

"Can I tell you why Chief McCabe is so excited?" Xavier asked. "If I don't tell you, you'll never know, because he'll just want to kill you. You are the curious type, aren't you Cole?"

"You're going to tell me anyway," Cole said. "Just get it over with."

"That's true," Xavier shrugged. "Cole, the truth is, you're the only one left."

"Only one left of what? What are you talking about?"

"Of the Harpers," Xavier said, as though it had been obvious. "I mean, in the end, when it's all said and done, it's your father's fault, isn't it?"

"I know he killed my dad," Cole said.

"Your father was trying to help Reynold's girlfriend, Vikki I believe her name was, escape. To take her away from him."

"Escape? Not…"

"Reynold, naturally, wanted revenge. It's a human response."

Escape. Cole tried to remember the emails between his dad and Vikki. They'd never talked about an affair; Cole had just read into their exchanges. In the end, was his dad trying to save Vikki from Reynold? From Mihko? From both? He thought of his dad's headstone, of the chiselled-off word: *Father.*

"But that wasn't enough," Xavier said. "You can't really blame him, though, can you? I mean, look at what he's become. He's always wanted more. He's insatiable."

"He's a monster."

"So, he decided that he was going to kill two birds with one stone," Xavier said. He paced around the room. Each time he passed Michael, Cole noticed Michael's jaws clench harder. He was getting angry.

"Just say it," Cole tried to sound defiant, but instead, his voice was broken. He didn't need to hear it. He knew what Xavier had meant.

"Of course, he didn't expect that you'd go off and make your little girlfriend a ring," Xavier said. "He thought you were both in the school when he burned it down."

Hearing it made it real, though. And Cole screamed. He arched his back, and pushed upward with every ounce of strength he had. His muscles burned. His heart threatened to burst out of his chest. He felt the straps begin to tear. Xavier nodded at Dr. Ament, who pushed half the clear liquid from her syringe into Cole's IV line. Cole felt the liquid course through his veins. He started to feel drowsy and weak. But she hadn't given him enough to knock him out.

Michael looked like he was about ready to bend his rifle in half. His father had died in that fire, too. Michael, Cole was certain, had never heard this before. He prayed that Michael would act on the rage he felt. But he didn't. It looked as though he was physically being held back.

"So," Xavier clapped once dramatically, "that leaves us where we are now. And, like I said, Reynold's dying to finish his work. He's waited a decade. Can you blame him?"

"Michael…Michael…you can still…make up for what…you did. It's never too late…you can…"

"Michael Captain?" Xavier walked over to Michael. Put his hand on Michael's shoulder. "You're right that he probably wants to shoot my head off, and Dr. Ament's, and certainly Reynold's, but he won't. Do you want to tell him why, Mr. Captain?"

Michael shook his head, short and sharp.

"He's only got his mother left, poor kid," Xavier said. "If something were to happen to her, well, you can only imagine. He'd have nobody left."

"You'd have…us…Michael."

"I think mother trumps estranged friend," Xavier said. "I mean, after all, the only person he actually did shoot in the head… was you."

"Michael?" Cole looked at his old friend for any sign that what Xavier had said was a lie.

Michael was shaking. Cole could see it all through his body. His lips were quivering. He looked like he could drop his rifle at any moment. Rage to regret.

He'd done it.

"Michael, no," Cole said, like he wasn't already certain that it was the truth. That Michael had followed him down into the basement, into this very room, and killed him.

"I'm sorry, I—"

"Ah, no talking, Mr. Captain. You know the rules." Xavier looked at the watch on his wrist. "Look at the time. Dr. Ament, would you mind putting Cole down again? I think we've said all there is to say."

Dr. Ament injected the rest of the syringe into Cole's IV line, and Cole started to feel his consciousness slip away.

"I'm going...to...kill..."

"Better pump some more while you're at it," Xavier said to Dr. Ament.

"Way ahead of you." Dr. Ament was already pulling out another syringe.

"Don't worry," Xavier said as Dr. Ament emptied the syringe into the IV. "You can try. To kill Reynold, to kill me, whoever. When we are sure your blood works to cure God Flare 2.0, we'll wake you up. Reynold will want you to watch him kill Eva and Brady."

"Let them go...let them go..." Cole was desperately trying to stay awake.

"And then he'll want to look you in the eyes before he kills you."

Those were the last words Cole heard, before he lost consciousness.

28

WOUNDED SKY

"DONALD, KNOCK IT OFF," COLE'S MOM SAID, *but though the words were stern, the delivery was not. She was trying not to laugh and had barely managed to admonish Cole's dad at all. They were in the living room of their house, and it was morning. A beautiful part of the day where they were all together and could spend time in each other's company. Before Cole's dad went to work and after breakfast.*

That was the sweet spot.

Cole's mom was on the couch watching Cole and his dad wrestle on the living room floor. They'd been going at it for several minutes now, playing the game they always played at this time of day: Unbreakable Hold. Cole's dad would put Cole into a hold that was "unbreakable," and Cole would try to get out of the hold, proving it to be, in fact, breakable.

He'd never broken a hold, however.

"One more!" Donald pleaded, sweat dripping down his face. He didn't even check the clock. He didn't worry if he might be late for work.

"Would you let him win one time, Donald?" his mom whispered, as though Cole couldn't hear her.

"What'll he learn, then? Hey?" Donald asked.

"I want to do it on my own!" Cole shouted, and then he made himself a rag doll on the ground, waiting for his dad to put him into a new hold. The catch of the game was that it had to be a different hold each time.

"Alright," she said, "one more."

"Ready kiddo?" Cole's dad asked him.

Cole nodded, and his dad went to work. He wrapped his arms around Cole's arms and chest, securing his upper body, and curled his legs around Cole's. The simplest hold his dad had ever attempted, and the one that made Cole feel the most claustrophobic.

"Okay, go," his dad said.

Cole struggled, tried to break out. He snaked his body left and right, arched his back and tried to push his dad's arms away, but nothing worked.

"Give up?"

Cole shook his head, but he started to feel panicked. Started to feel his heart race, his body get hot and shaky. He couldn't breathe. The hold was too tight. He needed to get out.

"Donald, he's scared," his mom said. "Let him go."

"No!" Cole shouted.

He pushed his arms out, strained to spread his legs to the side. He screamed from the effort, and then his dad's arms and legs were off, and Cole was free. He rolled across the living room floor, triumphant. Stood up with his arms raised. But both his parents had looks of shock on their faces, and Cole's dad was rubbing his arms as though they were in pain.

"How did you do that?" his dad asked.

"I dunno," Cole said. "I just felt lots of energy."

"Cole."

That was the first time he had used his powers. There, in his living room, in his dad's strong embrace. Maybe his dad knew then, even if Cole didn't. Maybe that was why he'd done his own experiments on Cole, because of what had happened, because he thought that Cole had to be the answer to finding the cure.

"Cole!" a sharp whisper.

Eva. Cole's eyes blinked open. Dr. Ament and Cameron Xavier were gone. He looked to his right to see Eva staring at him intensely. Brady was awake, too. The cure had worked. And that meant they didn't have much time. He looked at the door, where Michael had been standing guard, and then down the hall, as far as he could see.

Nobody was there.

"They could be back any second," Eva said.

"Do you think you can get out of those straps?" Brady asked.

"Come get me…" Cole started, but for the first time he noticed that Brady and Eva were tied down as well. Handcuffs locked around the bed rails.

"Yeah," Eva said, "can't fly out of these."

"Fly?" Brady repeated.

"I'll tell you after, B."

"I can't get out of these straps," Cole said. "I've tried. There's too many of them."

"You've got to try harder," Eva said.

"You can do it, Cole," Brady said. "I know you can."

Cole closed his eyes and went back to that moment, with his dad on the carpet in the middle of the living room. He imagined his dad's arms and legs wrapped around his body. An unbreakable hold. Then, he pushed his body to the limit. Strained harder than he ever had before. It was why he was here. This was the moment. There was only now. Just now. Muscles ripped. Veins popped. Sweat dripped from every pore. And he pushed himself more. Harder. A buckle popped. He could hear it under his bed.

"You're doing it," Eva said.

His body shook from the effort. He opened his eyes and saw red littered with black spots. Harder. More. He knew he could give more. He pictured Eva. Brady. They'd die if he couldn't do this. Another buckle popped. He grunted through clenched teeth. Arched his back. Everything was on fire. Every inch of his body.

Then, his body gave out.

The sweat on his face was joined by tears. He was breathing heavily and too fast. His heart wouldn't slow down. He could feel his hands, arms, legs, trembling. He turned to Eva and Brady.

"I'm sorry. I'm so sorry."

"It's okay," Eva assured, her face resolute. "It's okay."

"You did your best," Brady said.

"I just can't…" Cole closed his eyes again, cursing himself for another failure, the one time he couldn't afford it. He didn't care about the panic attack. In fact, he begged for more.

He deserved more.

"Cole!" Eva whispered.

"Keep your eyes shut!" Brady added.

Cole heard footsteps down the hallway, approaching the room. They stopped.

"What's going on in here?"

It was Michael's voice. Eva and Brady didn't respond. They must have closed their eyes too. Playing dead. Hoping, Cole figured, that Michael would leave, and he could try again. But there was no point. He couldn't do it. Even if they had more time, which Cole was sure they didn't. If Michael was back from wherever he'd been, that meant Xavier and Dr. Ament would be coming. They'd see Eva and Brady were better—you couldn't hide the fact that they weren't sick anymore, no matter how tight they shut their eyes—and, soon enough, Reynold would be let loose on them.

Cole heard Michael cross the room and stop at his bedside, and then felt his old friend inspect the straps underneath the bed.

"You're trying to break out?"

Cole opened his eyes. "I'm not just going to lie down and let everybody die."

"You wouldn't, would you?" Michael stood up.

"You shot me, kidnapped Brady…" Cole shook his head, not able to hide his disgust. "Should I go on?"

"You forgot about the fires," Michael said, but his lip was quivering. He was fighting back tears, just like earlier, when he was fighting back rage.

"Michael," Eva said, "you don't want to do this. You can't do this."

"They'll kill my mom," Michael said.

"Oh Michael," Cole said. "They're going to kill her anyway if we don't stop them. They're going to kill everybody."

"Let us go," Eva said.

Michael turned to her.

"We've already lost so much," Brady said.

"She's all I've got left," Michael pleaded. "I have to do this, I can't…"

"Mike," Cole said, grabbing Michael's attention. "Do you remember what I said, back in the clearing?"

"We're family…"

"All of us," Cole nodded. "Nobody's going to hurt your mom. Not if you let me go."

Michael looked them all over, one by one. He looked them over, and then looked down the hall, as though Xavier would have something to say about it, or that he might appear at any moment.

He knelt beside Cole. "I'm sorry. Everything I did…"

"You didn't have a choice," Cole said. "I know."

"Promise me you'll protect her."

"I will."

Cole felt Michael start to unbuckle the straps underneath the bed. One by one, they slid off his body. Michael worked quickly, and soon Cole was free.

"You have to get them out of here," Michael said. "Now."

"What about you?" Cole asked. "I'm not leaving without you. I told your mom—"

"No," Michael said. "I'll hold them off as long as I can."

He loaded his rifle.

"Michael…"

"Go!"

Cole could see that he wasn't going to change Michael's mind. He nodded at Michael, and they shared a look for a split second that said more than they could with words. Fear had led Michael to do awful things. Fear had done horrible things to Cole, too.

He freed Brady and Eva and helped them to their feet.

"You guys okay to walk?" Cole asked.

They both said they could.

"Let's get out of here."

The sliding doors had been left open, waiting for Xavier and Dr. Ament's return. They went to the doorway, and stopped there. Michael was standing in the middle of the room, watching them.

"Thank you," Eva said.

"Tell my mom I love her," Michael said.

"We'll tell her you saved us," Brady said.

Cole heard voices. They ran across the hall, to the doors that led to the first floor. Raced upstairs. Cole quickly took out the guard in the hallway on the first floor. Eva picked up the guard's rifle, and they continued on. They ran by a few stunned Mihko employees in lab coats to the back door.

There were two guards stationed at the gate. Cole, Brady, and Eva didn't break stride. They ran to the electric fence, and at the same time, Cole jumped and Eva flew, leaving Brady behind on the other side of the fence momentarily. They landed in front of the guards. Cole punched one out, while Eva shot the other. Cole tore the gate off, and let Brady out.

"Ummm, holy shit," Brady said. "You really can fly."

Eva shrugged.

"We've got to keep going," Cole said.

"But how—"

"Don't worry," Cole said. "She won't tell me either."

They rushed through Blackwood Forest until Wounded Sky and the facility were a few hundred yards behind them. They stopped there. Brady and Eva were gasping for air, looking pale and clammy. They weren't going to make it far like this. They'd been cured, but they hadn't recovered.

"Wait here," Cole said. "Stay out of sight."

"What about you?" Brady asked.

"No," Eva said. "Don't do it."

"I have to get Michael out of there," Cole said.

"They'll kill you," she said.

"If I go now, they won't be ready. I'll get him out, and I'll bring him home. He's family, too."

"But Reynold," Brady said.

"I'm going to kill him." Cole pictured his dad, his mom, and everybody else who had died by Reynold's hands. He pictured the white headstones in Wounded Sky Cemetery. Maggie. Ashley. Alex. The chains Reynold had strung through the school's door handles. "It's the only way Wounded Sky will be safe again."

"Be careful," Brady said, relenting.

Eva threw her arms around Cole's neck, pressed her lips against his, and in the desperation of the moment, he didn't want her to move. But she did. She got down from her tiptoes and looked up at him in his breathlessness. In hers.

"You know what I'm going to say," she said.

"But I want to hear it," he whispered.

"Then you'll have to come back to me."

Cole ran back to the facility. He didn't stop running. Inside the building, down the hall, around the corner, down the stairs. The place was deserted. It wasn't right. Nobody had been on the first floor, and nobody was in the basement. Nobody except Michael, standing in the middle of the room like he hadn't moved since Cole had left with Eva and Brady. Frozen in place. Rifle at his side. Cole walked slowly, from the stairs to the doorway.

He stopped there.

"Mike?" he said tentatively. "What're you doing?"

"You shouldn't have come back, Cole."

"I wasn't going to leave you here. You had to know that."

"After everything I did? Yeah, I thought you'd leave me. I wanted you to leave me. I deserve to—"

"No, you don't."

"I didn't think you'd come back," Michael said, sounding more and more like he was in trance, "but they did."

Michael was looking past Cole now, down the hallway. Cole turned, but not in time. Reynold was charging at him. Cole barely had time to brace himself. He flew across the room and crashed into the wall. He scrambled to his feet, but Reynold was already on him. Raining punches down on Cole. Cole covered his head with his arms and waited for a moment when he could strike back.

"You!" Reynold kept shrieking. *"You! You!"*

Cole couldn't wait any longer. He'd get beaten to death if he didn't act. He crouched low and then exploded with a right uppercut. It connected with Reynold's head, and the monster fell backwards. Cole pounced. He straddled Reynold's waist and punched Reynold with both fists over and over again.

A shot rang out, and blue blood erupted from Reynold's chest. It just made the creature angrier. Reynold stood up with Cole in his arms and rammed him into the wall. They punched each other at the same time, and Cole slid across the floor, through the doorway. Michael backed away from Reynold and shot him again, this time in the stomach.

Reynold let out a horrifying shriek.

Cole stood up to go back into the room, but Michael stepped in his way.

"What are you doing?" Cole asked.

"You've done enough," Michael said. "It's my turn, now."

"You can't beat him."

Reynold was getting to his feet. His head just below the ceiling. His skeleton pushing through his pale skin. Blood dripping from his wounds and out of his mouth.

He shrieked again.

"Yes, I can." Michael drew his handgun. He aimed it at the keypad Cole had used to open the doors the night Michael had shot him. The code word flashed in his mind. He heard his dad's voice. *Sorry, kiddo.* Michael shot the keypad, and the doors slammed shot, blocking Cole from the room.

"No! Michael!" Cole shouted, banging on the glass.

Michael detached two grenades from his belt. "You have go now, Cole."

"Open the doors, Michael! Now!"

Michael pulled the pins from the grenades. "I can't."

"Please!"

"Get out of here."

Cole stopped banging. Stopped shouting. He put his hand on the door. Reynold lunged at Michael.

Michael dropped the grenades.

Cole gave Michael one last look, then ran to the door, up the stairs, around the corner, down the hall. He heard the grenades go off and ran faster. The explosion caught up with him at the back door; the force of it threw him into the air. He landed hard against the ground and rolled to a stop just before the electric fence.

Cole turned over onto his back and watched the building go up in flames. The fire reached up over the trees, into the sky to touch the northern lights. The spirits danced to the beat of the drum, dancing around the flames as though they were a sacred fire. He could hear Elder Mariah's voice, telling him the story of how this place had got its name.

A long time ago, an Elder named this place. He looked up at the sky one night and thought the northern lights looked like ribbons of scars. The Elder thought, before we were here, something must have happened. The sky had been cut and out of that wound came the heavens. The wound healed, but that past was still there, in the scars that were left behind. It helped shape the beauty that we see now.

The day Cole arrived in Wounded Sky, it seemed as though that wound had opened. Tonight, it looked like those ribbons of scars were bleeding red, all the way down to Mother Earth, but for the first time since coming home, Cole felt like those wounds could heal again. And he knew that it had never been just his deal. It had never been just his mission.

It had been Eva's. Brady's. Michael's. Dr. Captain's. Elder Mariah's. All of theirs.

29

BEGINNING

COLE STOOD IN THE ORANGE GLOW OF THE FIRE, feeling the heat from the burning facility. He stared at the sky where the flames mingled with the northern lights. He shifted his gaze to the building, the back door. Watching, waiting, for Reynold to come charging through the fire.

That's how these stories go, isn't it? Cole thought. Something Choch would say. But in reality, something that might happen. Charging out the back door, or maybe, out the front door. That's where Cole had encountered Upayokwitigo the first time, why not the last time? And what if he missed the creature, and it got away?

Wounded Sky would continue to be haunted by its presence.

Cole got to his feet. His body ached. He was probably covered in bruises; bruises that would be gone by morning, but hurt like hell now. But just like when Elder Mariah had applied the paste to Cole's zombie-like body, this was a good pain. He was alive. So were Eva and Brady.

"Michael."

Michael was why they were alive. Everything he'd thought he knew wasn't true. Michael was a hero. Cole's dad hadn't cheated on his mom. He'd tried to save Vikki from Reynold. His dad was a hero as well. It seemed that everybody was a hero but Cole. And he was okay with that. It was like Choch had said. He was Cole Harper. It may not be what the story should've been, but it's what the story was.

Cole staggered along the perimeter of the burning research facility.

He used the fence for support; the fire had kicked out the electricity. The old picnic bench, the one he'd sat on with his mom and dad, was intact. Old, dried wood somehow not burned by the flames raging just feet away. Cole let go of the fence and stumbled to the bench, but fell onto his stomach. He tried to push himself up, but collapsed again.

He felt hands around his shoulders, and he was lifted to his feet. Eva was on one side of him, Brady on the other. Eva wrapped his arm around her shoulders. They helped him over to the bench and sat him down.

"What happened?" Eva asked.

Cole just shook his head and watched the front door.

Nothing came out.

"Michael?" Brady said.

"No," Cole said in a whisper. "He, uhhh…he sacrificed himself for me." A crowd was gathering. Cole could hear rustling, murmuring, people running up to the fence. He didn't turn around. He didn't want anybody to know he was alive yet. "He sacrificed himself for everybody."

"Let's get you out of here," Eva said.

Cole ran his hands across the surface of the bench. He imagined his dad, and his mom, sitting there with him. He stared at the ground, where he'd thrown an apple seed long ago. Where, he'd thought, a tree might grow, and keep his dad away from work and home with him. *Sorry, kiddo.*

"Yeah," Cole said, "let's go."

Brady and Eva helped him to his feet. They ignored calls from the crowd about what had happened and about who was with them.

Behind the building, away from the crowd, they stood together, Cole's arms draped across his friends' shoulders. They stood there long enough that the fire began to die down and all the warm colours bled into the sky, dancing with the ribbons overhead.

"I need to go in," Cole said. "I need to make sure it's really over."

"We'll go with you," Brady said.

"Yeah," Eva said. "You're not allowed to go off on your own, like *ever* again. Got it?"

"I'm okay with—"

"Wait!"

Cole felt Brady pull back, just as they started moving.

"What is it, B?"

"Look." Brady pointed to the doors, where a large flame was moving within the building.

"What the—"

They froze. Cole's heart raced. Reynold. He'd survived. Once outside, he'd come after them again. Cole pushed Eva and Brady to the side and tried to keep his feet firm on the ground.

Finish this.

The flames moved closer, out of the building towards them.

Cole clenched his fists and summoned whatever strength he had left.

"Come on," he said.

As the flames approached, floating through the air, they unfolded gracefully to reveal two figures: Jayne and Michael. The flames receded, until they disappeared into Jayne.

"Michael," Cole said. "You…"

"You said he was…" Eva started.

"He *was…*" Cole shook his head and looked Michael over, from head to toe. His face was covered in soot, his clothes were burned, he had cuts on his arms, but he was alive. "How's this possible?"

"Now I'm the one who was supposed to be dead, hey?" Michael said.

"I saved him!" Jayne exclaimed.

Eva got on her knees, so she was eye level with Jayne, and took her non-burning hand. "Jayney."

"I did good, right Eva!"

"You did *so* good."

"I didn't even have ta hurt nobody again," Jayne said to Cole.

"What happened?" Cole asked.

"The grenades were about to go off," Michael recalled, "and then Jayne was there, between me and the grenades. She wrapped these, like, wings of fire around me. I heard the grenades explode, but I didn't feel anything. She led me out, she…"

"I made sure he couldn't get too hot, that's all," Jayne said.

"Reynold?" Cole asked.

"Dead." Michael took something out from his cargo pants and handed it to Cole.

Cole inspected it thoroughly. An icicle. But it had thin, blue veins covering it like a spider web.

"Nókom will know what to do with it," Brady said, gently taking it from him. "But if he's dead, I know that this place," Brady motioned to the facility, "this place needs to be protected for now. Nothing can happen here, not for a long time."

"I don't want to come back here again, ever," Eva said.

"There *is* somewhere I need to go," Cole said.

"The school," Brady said.

"Yeah," Cole said. "I mean, since we're not supposed to be apart from each other…"

"We're in," Eva said.

"Me, too," Brady said.

"Mike?" Cole asked. "You're part of the group, right? Family?"

"I know," Michael said. "But there's family I really want to see right now, if that's okay."

Cole, Eva and Brady, with Jayne skipping alongside, made their way through Blackwood Forest, avoiding the large crowd gathered around the facility. Michael started walking back to Tent City, where Dr. Captain would be waiting for him. He would tell the others what had happened in Wounded Sky.

Before long, they were at the steps that led up to the doors of the ruined school. The others stayed behind Cole to give him space. He could see himself there, as a boy, standing at the doors, in front of the burning school. He could see himself wrapping his hands around the chains that Reynold had put there and pulling on them with all of his strength, until they shattered.

Cole knelt down, picked up one link in the chain and held it in his palm. The metal perfectly matched his scar. He closed his hand around it and held it firmly within his grip. Steam rose from his skin. He opened his hand, and let it go. The link rolled off his open palm, and landed against the ground. The scar on his palm had disappeared.

"Nice trick," he whispered, but decided, in that moment, to keep the other scar.

"You okay, my friend?" Brady asked.

Cole got to his feet. "Yeah, I think I will be."

"Can I ask you a question then?"

"Sure."

Brady turned Cole around, so they were both looking at Eva and Jayne. Eva was holding Jayne's hand.

"You can see her?" Cole asked.

Brady nodded. "Do you know how?"

"Yeah, why can everybody see me alla sudden, Coley?" Jayne asked, positively beaming.

"I don't know." But then he did. He could see it, now. Embers began to rise from the flames covering half her body.

"What's happening?" Jayne felt around the burning half of her body, sounding panicked.

"You're okay," Cole walked over to her. "Breathe. In five seconds, out for seven."

The flames broke off Jayne's body, until they were all gone, and all that remained was her glow. She was healed. For the first time, Cole saw Jayne the way she used to be, before the school fire.

A tiny, beautiful, seven-year old Cree girl.

"Oh, my God." Eva cupped her mouth, and in Jayne's generous glow, tears glistened on Eva's cheeks.

Jayne touched her face, and then she started to jump around. "I'm me again! I'm me again!"

Cole picked her up, and she wrapped her arms and legs around his body, buried her head into his shoulder.

"I'm me again," she whispered.

"You were always you," he said.

Jayne's glow became more of a shine. He put her down and she began to fade.

"Now what's happening?" Jayne asked.

"You're going home," Cole said.

"Like Choch promised!?"

"Yeah," Cole said, "like Choch promised."

Moments later, Jayne was gone, and the night was dark again. The three of them stared at the place where Jayne had stood. Cole could hear Eva breathe. And in the glow of the northern lights, he memorized every inch of her face all over again.

"So," she said.

"So," he said.

"You're back."

"I'm back."

She let go of his hands and put her arms around his neck. She leaned forward, and he did too, until his lips touched hers. He closed his eyes until she pulled her lips away.

"You're not going to forget about me are you?"

"How am I going to forget about you?"

"When you go back home."

"I am home." Cole brought her close, into his arms. "Besides, I need my sidekick, don't I? If I'm going to be a superhero?"

"Shut up," she said, and they kissed again.

"Ummm guys," Brady said. "I'm like, right here."

EPILOGUE

COLE AND EVA WERE SPEEDING DOWN THE HIGHWAY, away from Wounded Sky First Nation. They were in the Mustang. Cole had spent the last few weeks fixing it up, with help from Michael, Eva, and Brady. He'd started work on it right after Pam had gotten the cell towers working again, and all their phones had lit up with weeks' worth of messages. Most of Cole's texts had been from his one friend back in Winnipeg, Joe. Cole had left without saying goodbye, and now was, in Joe's words, "Ghosting him." Joe's last text had read: **Dude. Are you seriously ghosting me right now? WTF?**

"You can leave you know," Eva had said. "It's going to be okay here."

She'd been right. He could leave. It was his choice now.

"But I don't want to leave you," he'd said.

"Oh, I'm coming," she'd said. "I'm not letting you out of my sight."

So, they'd set to work fixing up the car, and as soon as it was ready, they drove it out of the community, over the winter road, and onto the highway. Speeding to Winnipeg, and then, wherever they wanted to go after that.

"Oh shit," Cole said.

"What?" Eva asked.

Cole looked in the rear-view mirror and saw an RCMP truck chasing after them, lights and sirens. They'd not gone more than fifty kilometres. Cole pulled over and put the car into park. The truck pulled up behind them. The officer stayed in the car for an uncomfortably long period of time, just staring at Cole as Cole stared back. The officer got out of the car and walked over to the driver side door. Cole rolled down the window.

"Can I help you, Officer?" Cole asked.

"Do you know how fast you were going?" the officer asked.

"Fast?"

Eva punched Cole in the arm.

"You going to get smart with me, kid?" the officer asked, and leaned over, pretty much sticking his head into the car.

Cole tried to move his seat back subtly.

"No, sir. Sorry."

The officer was wearing a motorcycle helmet, even though he had not been driving a motorcycle, and aviator sunglasses. He was dressed like a movie cop, not a real cop.

"Don't get smart with me again, meow," the officer said.

"I won't," Cole said.

"Meow, who's your friend?"

"Are you saying 'meow'?"

"I told you not to get smart with me, meow!"

"You're…" Cole sighed. "I've seen *Super Troopers*."

"Oh." The officer cleared his throat awkwardly. "Right. Sorry. You see, I don't usually do the pop culture references. That's the job of the author, historically speaking. Well, I guess I have done a few, come to think of it, but…"

"What's he talking about?" Eva whispered to Cole.

Cole couldn't help but smile. "This is not a book," he said to the officer with mock frustration.

"Well, I suppose this time I can let you off with a warning," the officer said.

"Thanks, Officer."

"But drive carefully, you hear? You've got precious cargo."

"Yeah, I know."

"I'll be following behind for a bit," the officer stood up, "just to keep an eye on you."

"I wouldn't expect anything different."

"Oh!" the officer stuck his head back into the car, and this time, looked directly at Eva. He paused for an extremely long time. "You."

"Yes?" Eva sounded more than a little confused.

"I do apologize for being rude," the officer said. "It's just that I haven't thought of a good nickname for you yet. EK? Even Steven? Captain Kirk because Kirkness? It's just, Eva doesn't lend itself well to…it's already short you know?"

"Okay…"

"Anyway, don't go too far, Captain Kirk." The officer winked. "You never know when I might need you."

The Reckoner will return.

ACKNOWLEDGMENTS

ALTHOUGH THE RECKONER TRILOGY has been my newest work, the story has been with me for well over a decade. Cole's story will continue, but this does feel like the end of a journey. There are many people to thank and acknowledge; too many, I'm afraid, to address in this small space. However, I don't think it's cheating to defer to the acknowledgments in the previous two instalments in the trilogy, *Strangers* and *Monsters*, in order to hit a few birds with one stone. To those people, I continue to be grateful.

Ghosts was the funnest, and most difficult book to write in the series. I'd say that it was bittersweet, and it was, but I'm glad to be continuing the story in a different literary form. Thanks to Jay Nickerson for giving an early draft of *Ghosts* a read. It helped shape what this story became. Thanks, as well, to Liz Culotti, for reading that same infant version. The one person I have mentioned previously, and will acknowledge here again, is my editor Desirae Warkentin. Dee, your keen eye for story and structure, passion for this story, and blunt, thoughtful feedback, helped make every instalment of this series what it was. Thanks, partner.

I'd like to thank my agent, Jackie Kaiser, and my publisher, HighWater Press, for helping to make this book, and series, a reality. Catherine Gerbasi, Annalee Greenberg, and the entire team have put their hearts into ensuring that HighWater Press provides opportunities to Indigenous writers to tell their stories. I am forever grateful for the platform and trust they have given me.

The Reckoner Trilogy has always been about one thing: representation. Accurate portrayals of Indigenous People and those living with mental health problems. It is empowering to see yourself reflected in literature. It is vitally important that others are exposed to stories of truth, through lived experiences.

Ekosani.

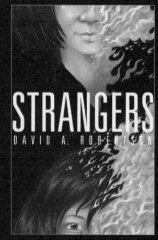 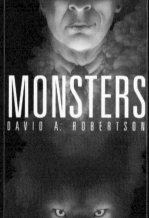